"Have I depressed you?" Rachael asked quietly.

Jason cupped Rachael's face and used his thumbs to brush away her tears. "I'm not depressed, and neither are you. You're sad, and I'm sad for you, but you're going to be okay. You proved that just by coming here today. You're a very strong lady, Rachael. I don't think you have any idea just how strong you really are."

She managed a smile. "Keep telling me that, and maybe I'll believe it."

Jason shook his head. "That's something you have to discover for yourself."

"I'm trying," she whispered.

"I know you are." Unable to resist her nearness, Jason bent his head to hers and touched her lips lightly.

And suddenly Rachael knew she could brave anything if Jason was at her side....

ABOUT THE AUTHOR

Talented Missouri-based author Connie Bennett loves a challenge, and writing an engrossing romance about two people coping with loss was almost as challenging as writing a "psychic" romance—a previous book—or a romantic murder mystery—an upcoming book. *Changes in the Wind* is Connie's fourth Superromance, which newfound fans have undoubtedly been awaiting!

Books by Connie Bennett

HARLEQUIN SUPERROMANCE

293–SHARE MY TOMORROW
327–THINKING OF YOU
364–WHEN I SEE YOUR FACE

Changes in the Wind

CONNIE BENNETT

Harlequin Books

TORONTO • NEW YORK • LONDON
AMSTERDAM • PARIS • SYDNEY • HAMBURG
STOCKHOLM • ATHENS • TOKYO • MILAN

Published September 1989

First printing July 1989

ISBN 0-373-70373-2

Printed in U.S.A.

To Forest
with all my love.

CHAPTER ONE

THE TOMB WAS even quieter than usual today. Jason Burgess paused at the door, amazed that twenty people working in one open, sunny room could be so silent. There was the occasional creak from an unoiled chair and some rustling of papers as drawings of animated characters were riffled on the lightboards to simulate movement, but other than that, the room was justly deserving of the nickname Jason had given it.

Many of these artists were the same fun-loving pranksters Jason had observed raising the roof at office parties and casual get-togethers, but once they entered this work space horseplay ceased. As founder, president and director of the production company, Jason knew he should be grateful that these employees took their jobs so seriously, but he couldn't help feeling there was something creepy about a roomful of animators who were so... inanimate. If things didn't liven up in here soon, he was going to have to rename the place The Morgue.

He moved into the room and walked past rows of slanted lightboards and the artists who were hunched over them. The thick carpet muffled his progress toward the glassed-in office of the chief animator, but the infinitesimal squeak of his shoes betrayed him and one of the artists glanced up. Upon recognizing the boss, he smiled around the pencil stuck between his teeth. Jason returned the smile and kept moving toward the front office.

"I want to know your secret," Jason demanded as he closed Robb Weston's door and perched his lanky six-foot frame on one of the stools beside Weston's cluttered lightboard.

The chief animator tossed his pencil into a trough on the bottom of the board and swiveled toward Jason. "And exactly what secret is that?" he drawled in an accent that placed him conspicuously south of the Mason-Dixon line. "I've told you over and over again, you cannot have my recipe for catfish gumbo. It's a closely guarded family secret handed down from generation to generation. My great-great-grandmother Kitworth would turn over in her grave if I gave away her secrets to a Yankee."

"Far be it from me to disturb Grandma Kitworth's repose," Jason said magnanimously, tugging absently at the close-clipped beard that adorned the lower half of his face. "And delightful though your gumbo is, the secret I was referring to is a little closer to home." He jerked a thumb toward the quiet room beyond Robb's office. "Do you threaten these people with whips and chains to keep them in line, or what? It gets quieter every time I come in here."

Robb looked affronted. "I take great offense, suh, at your unjustly accusin' me of premeditated vi'lence. Ah am a gentlemun."

Robb's accent had turned even thicker than his famous gumbo and Jason indulged in a much-needed laugh. The other man was old enough to be Jason's father, but a spark of youthful humor always burned brightly in his pale blue eyes.

"We'll debate your dubious aristocratic heritage later, Robb," Jason said, still smiling. "Right now I need your help."

"I am at your service."

"Good. I'm taking personnel recommendations from all the department heads and it's your turn."

"Looking for a new assistant?" Robb asked, quirking a shaggy eyebrow.

Jason looked at him in surprise. "News travels fast around here."

"We have a highly organized, efficient grapevine and this morning a hallelujah went up because Paul Harris is no longer among us."

Jason nodded, affirming the gossip. "We had an agreeable parting of the ways—he agreed to leave if I agreed not to fire him." The confrontation had not been particularly pleasant, and Jason's shoulders drooped slightly as he talked about it. Letting Harris go had been a tough but necessary decision. "Paul is a talented kid, but he was just too much of a hotshot. I need team players around me, not wet-behind-the-ears kids on ego trips. We're weeks behind on the storyboards because Paul liked tooting his own horn more than he liked an honest day's work."

"I saw this comin'," Robb said with a philosophical nod. "That boy just got too big for his britches. You put up with him a lot longer than I would have, that's for sure."

Jason sighed. "Well, it's over now. But that means I've got a big hole in my directorial staff that needs immediate filling. Any suggestions?"

"Hmm..." Robb looked out at the artists in the workroom. He didn't bother asking what qualifications were needed for the job because he already knew the answer. Jason Burgess was a tireless, exacting artistic genius who, in ten short years, had catapulted himself to legendary status in the genre of animated fantasy films. His name ranked a close second to the industry's revered pioneer, Walt Disney, and at the age of forty-one it looked as though Jason and his company, Animators Inc., had years of ground-breaking achievement ahead.

Though everyone knew that Animators' success was directly attributable to Jason's seemingly limitless talents, he maintained that he was only as good as the craftsmen he surrounded himself with. Jason was a patient, fair-minded boss, but since he demanded the best from himself he felt justified in demanding the best of his staff as well. Robb knew that whoever was chosen as Jason's new assistant would have to be just as much of a perfectionist. He needed someone who could take his verbally expressed ideas and put them on paper in Jason's distinctive style. He also needed someone who was fast, efficient, cooperative and creative. Paul Harris, who'd been hired straight out of college, had been creative, but had fallen severely short on the fast, efficient and cooperative end of the scale.

Keeping those qualifications in mind, Robb studied the various artists in his workroom and immediately discarded the five animators from consideration. They were all highly trained specialists whose talents would be sorely needed as production geared up over the next two years on *The Quest*, the film currently under production. He had one assistant animator who would very likely be promoted soon, and Robb wasn't willing to give him up, either. As for the rest, they were all talented, hard-working and eager to climb up from the lower rungs of the company ladder. All, that is, except Rachael Hubbard.

Robb glanced toward the back of the room at the dark-haired, fragile-looking woman who had recently refused, for the second time, a promotion from breakdown artist to assistant animator. She was a puzzle in contradictions, and though she'd been working for him for nearly two years, he was no closer to understanding her than when she'd started. Without question she was the hardest worker he'd ever seen. If needed, Rachael could do the work of two people. She never once refused to stay overtime when they were under deadline pressure, and best of all she had a swift, sure, artistic touch that was so adaptable he could put her on any animation team and be assured that her work would be flawless. She never complained or gossiped. She simply came to work every day, as regular as clockwork, did her job expertly and went home.

Rachael Hubbard was quiet, pretty, unassuming . . . and completely unknowable. She kept to herself and never fraternized with the other artists, yet somehow she managed not to be considered stuck-up or standoffish. Both the lady and her apparent need for privacy were respected by her coworkers because they knew that while she wasn't going to be their best pal, she could be counted on to lend a hand when anyone needed it.

Most unusual of all, she claimed to be perfectly content where she was, at the bottom of the Animators' artistic ladder. As far as Robb was concerned, it was a crime for someone that talented to be satisfied working so far below her potential.

Some of what he was thinking must have shown on his face, because Jason perked up and tried to guess which of the artists Robb was studying so intently. "You have a candidate in mind?"

"As a matter of fact..." Robb looked at him. "You ever met Rachael Hubbard?"

Jason searched his memory. "I don't think so. The name is familiar, but that's probably because I sign her paycheck every month. Which one is she?"

"Brown hair and big glasses, over in the corner. Looks like she might break if you dropped her."

Jason picked her out immediately and approved of Robb's assessment. Rachael Hubbard did indeed look as fragile as rare porcelain. Her short, dark hair was a rich sable color, and bangs skimmed the top of the enormous glasses that accented huge, dark eyes. Though her slanted lightboard hid most of her body, Jason could tell that she was a small woman, delicately built. A lightweight, black sweater hugged her square shoulders and arched, elegant neck. He also noted she had an endearing habit of catching her full, lower lip between white, even teeth while she concentrated on her work. She was pretty but not remarkable, and her concentration was no more or less intense than that of any of the other artists around her. Strangely, though, she seemed out of place.

"She's a breakdowner?" he asked, assessing her job by her position in the row.

"The best I've ever seen," Robb stated. "In fact she's far too good for the work she's doing."

"That's high praise coming from you. Why haven't you promoted her?"

Robb sighed heavily. "I've tried, believe me. She says she's happy where she is, but frankly, I think she could do any job in this company—except yours and mine, of course," he added with a quick grin. "She'd be perfect as your assistant."

"If she wants the job," Jason amended.

"Get real," Robb advised him sardonically. "There's a world of difference between bein' promoted to assistant animator and gettin' to be assistant to *the* animator himself. Not to mention a salary increase of...what? About fifty percent? Makes my mouth water just thinkin' about it."

"Sorry, Robb. I need you here cracking the whip in the animation department. And besides, you already earn more than my assistant will ever hope to."

"Yes, but I could always use another fifty percent."

Jason laughed. "Dream on."

"No harm tryin'. Anyway, nobody in their right mind would turn down a job opportunity like you're offerin'."

"True. Have you seen her portfolio?"

"No. Rachael's not the type to bring in her own drawings to show off the way most of us do. She's real shy, but sharp. When she says something in that sweet, soft voice of hers I've learned that it pays to listen 'cause she's usually right."

"But if you've never seen her do anything but copy someone else's work, how can you know she's got the creativity I need?"

"Oh, I didn't say I hadn't seen her work—I just said she's never shown off her portfolio. Every day she sits in the cafeteria at dinnertime and doodles in the little sketch pad she carries around all the time. I snuck a peek once, and I tell you, Jason, her 'doodles' put most finished artwork to shame. Now, I can give you a couple'a other possibilities for the job if you want to waste your time interviewing, and I imagine the other supervisors can, too, but Rachael's the one you'll want. After Motormouth Harris a dose of serenity is just what you need."

Jason grinned. "All right, all right, I'm convinced. Give me the names of all your potential candidates and I'll pull their personnel files. I'm going to start interviewing tomorrow morning, and as a special favour to you, I'll talk to Ms Hubbard first. Before she leaves today tell her to report to the Bull Pen with her portfolio at nine o'clock sharp. Set up your other candidates in thirty-minute intervals after that, and I'll have my secretary confirm the names and times with you later this afternoon."

"Will do." Robb cracked a toothy smile. "As long as I've got you here you wanna take a look at the new roughs?"

"Sure," Jason said. While Robb retrieved the sketches that had to be approved before they could be passed on to an animator, Jason looked at Rachael Hubbard again. She was completely focused on her work. At first glance she seemed like the shy, mousy type, not the sort who stood out in a crowd, yet there was something disturbing about her. And something familiar, too.

"Here you go." Rob put the sheath of drawings in front of him, and Jason pulled his rapt gaze away from Rachael to give his full attention to the roughs.

Tomorrow would be soon enough to figure out why shy, unassuming Rachael Hubbard looked like a fragile rose growing in a patch of daisies.

IF RACHAEL'S GRANDMOTHER could have seen her granddaughter's furnished, ground-floor apartment she'd have sworn that it was so small there wasn't room to cuss a cat. Rachael knew that wasn't true, though, because the cantankerous feline who'd wandered through the patio doors one balmy evening the previous summer and made himself at home had given her plenty of opportunities to prove the old saying didn't apply.

Cat seemed to take great delight in showing her who was master and who was slave in the Hubbard household. He demanded prompt feeding, left long yellow hairs on her furniture and in general made himself a nuisance in any way that suited his fancy. In return for putting up with him, Rachael received the supreme honor of having him ignore her assiduously. Because she hadn't expected him to hang around this long, and she certainly hadn't planned to become attached to the feline, Rachael hadn't even bothered to name him. He'd been called "Cat" the day he arrived, and he would be "Cat" until the day he disappeared. They tolerated each other with mutual suspicion and occasional hostility, but if Cat thought the apartment was too small, it was one opinion he kept to himself.

Rachael was a few minutes late getting home from work because her brief conference with Robb Weston at quitting time had caused her to miss her usual bus, and as she let herself into the apartment she could see Cat at the patio doors giving her his most accusatory glare. His topaz eyes told her he was far from amused by being kept waiting.

Knowing it would irritate him, Rachael took her time, sauntering leisurely into the bedroom to hang up her jacket in the minuscule closet. She hung her purse on a hook and stepped out of her loafers into a familiar pair of bedroom slippers. Returning to the living room, she switched on the local evening news and glanced again at the patio doors.

Cat had decided two could play this game and had turned his back to her. He was now staring with apparent absorption at the wrought-iron table and chair that took up most of the enclosed patio. Knowing she'd lost round one, Rachael gave in and unlocked the door.

"Won't you come in, Your Lordship?"

Cat threw her a droll look over his shoulder, decided he'd made her suffer long enough and swaggered past her feet. Just to make sure she knew who was boss, he applied one clean swat of his tail to her shins.

"Table for two?" she asked as he meandered into the kitchen.

"Meow."

"Ah, dining alone this evening. What a pity." She sighed regretfully as she followed him. At the entry to the long, narrow kitchen, Cat took a sharp left turn, deliberately bypassing the spot where his food and water normally sat. Instead, he headed straight for the refrigerator, plunked himself down and dared Rachael to defy him. She did anyway.

"And what will you be having this evening?" she asked softly as she opened a cabinet door and grabbed a can of tuna-and-cheese Kitty Kut-ups. "The cracked crab is especially nice today, and the chef is very proud of his duck à l'orange." She applied a can opener to the lid. "And you'll want to start with the shrimp cocktail, of course."

"Meow."

"Oh, how silly of me, sir. Naturally you'd prefer the *soupe du jour*—clam chowder." She dumped the tuna into a bowl and placed it on the floor. "And here you are, sir."

Cat looked at the concoction suspiciously, then pranced across the room and fell on it as though he was starving, which Rachael knew was not the case since she'd fed him generously in the morning, before they'd both left the apartment.

Even though the meal hadn't come from the coveted refrigerator, Cat seemed to enjoy it. When he tossed in a contented purr between bites, Rachael turned away and began preparing her own supper. "Why thank you, sir, we do try to please. Speedy service is our hallmark."

She put together a sliced turkey sandwich and poured a glass of iced tea, but before she could sit down with her supper, Cat was at her feet, waiting for his dessert. She poured him a small bowl of milk and a larger one of water, placed them on the floor and settled into a chair at the tiny dinette at the end of the kitchen.

Except for the muted babble of the TV in the living room the apartment was quiet. There was noise outside, of course—city noise: cars honking, pedestrians cursing at the cars, a police siren shrilling in counterpoint to that of an ambulance on a thoroughfare a little farther away than the police car.... Two years ago when she'd come here from the quiet of rural Vermont, the never-ending city noise had been a much-needed distraction. She could focus on the noises outside and let them drown out the voices and memories in her head. Now she hardly heard them at all. The memories weren't so persistent anymore, either. She'd buried them with the pain, so that she could live in harmony with the silence of her life. Simplicity, order... and silence. None had been easy to achieve.

Finished with her supper, she washed the few dishes she and Cat had dirtied, returned to the living room, settled onto the sofa and put her feet up. The ottoman, a plump, overstuffed confection that cradled her feet, was Rachael's only contribution to the apartment's furnishings. Everything else was clean but drab. Pictures on the walls might have given the place a personality, but Rachael had never bothered. She liked the simplicity of the barren room.

A stranger, wandering in, might readily assume that Rachael Hubbard was barely scraping by in a job that afforded necessities but no luxuries. That same stranger—if he was well off—might even feel sorry that the poor woman couldn't afford to add a little life to her home.

No one looking at the way Rachael lived would ever dream she had more money than most people see in a lifetime. They'd never guess she had an outside income that made it unnecessary for her to work another day in her life. Rachael Hubbard could afford cars, furs, multiple homes, maids, chauffeurs...anything she could possibly want. But all she really wanted was simplicity, order, and silence....

Obviously Robb Weston didn't understand that, but then there was no reason why he should. He was a nice man, very caring and concerned, but she'd never confided in him and he'd been gentleman enough not to pry into her life, so he couldn't really know just how much Rachael wanted to be left alone. When she'd refused his offer of a promotion to assistant animator not once, but twice, she thought perhaps he'd gotten the message. Obviously she'd been wrong. By putting her into contention for Jason Burgess's personal assistant, he'd created a problem for her. Rachael ignored the droning television in order to work out what she would do tomorrow.

A large sixteen-by-twenty sketch pad and a pencil lay on the table to her right and she picked them up out of habit. Cat had sprawled on the ottoman beside her feet, and she absently began to draw him while her mind worked calmly on the problem. In a way it surprised her that she wasn't more irritated by Robb Weston's actions. But then Rachael had finally achieved a much-sought-after, blessed state of numbness that rarely let any striking emotion surface, and that was the way she wanted to keep it. Which was why Jason Burgess had to be dealt with carefully. She didn't want to anger him or rouse his curiosity about her, but neither did she want the responsibility of being his assistant.

She thought back to the irony of her conversation with Robb this afternoon when she'd told him she wasn't interested in the job.

"You worked in comic book art before coming here, didn't you, Rachael?" he had asked, trying a new tactic.

"Yes," she'd replied softly, dropping her eyes. She didn't like to be reminded.

"Well, Rachael, you've worked on the animation end of this business long enough to know that Jason Burgess is to the animated film what the late Garrett Mallory was to comic books. Surely you wouldn't have turned down the opportunity to work with him! Just think what Jason could teach you."

He'd been so impassioned about making his point that he hadn't noticed how Rachael had winced at the mention of the legendary Garrett Mallory. The pain she'd worked so hard at submerging had almost come bubbling to the surface, and she'd had to clamp down on it hard. She had mumbled something about what a genius Jason Burgess was and how she wasn't qualified to be his assistant, but Robb had refused to listen. In the end, he'd told her that if she didn't want the job she'd have to tell Jason herself, and that had been the end of their conversation. Now she was going to have to deal with Jason Burgess personally, something she'd known she could avoid as long as she stayed far down the chain of command in the animation department.

She flipped to a fresh page in her sketch book. Would Burgess remember her, she wondered, her pencil flying absently across the paper. It had been years since they'd met, and he'd only seen her that one time at the awards banquet.... Surely he wouldn't remember. Her hair had been longer then, and she'd been happy, clinging proudly to Sander's arm. Jason wouldn't remember her tomorrow because her hair was short and she would wear the glasses she only needed for close-up work. He wouldn't remember her because the woman she was now was as cold and dead as her husband.

The drawing on her pad came into focus, registering in her mind, and she closed the notebook quickly and returned it to the table. It was an ordinary sketch, nothing remarkable...but without thinking she'd signed it "Garrett Mallory."

"Damn," she muttered, focusing all her attention on the television. Maybe if she could fill in the missing letters of a puzzle on the popular game show, she wouldn't remember that too many pieces of herself were missing....

CHAPTER TWO

PROMPTLY AT 9:00 a.m. Rachael was ushered into the Bull Pen by Jason's secretary and told that he'd be with her in just a few minutes. The door clicked softly as the secretary departed, leaving Rachael alone to take stock of the infamous Bull Pen. This was where the great Jason Burgess met with his directorial staff and worked out the plots of his fabulous animated feature films. Sessions were known to run long into the night, and even though Rachael rarely listened to office gossip, she couldn't avoid having learned that this inner sanctum was revered as a monument to the great man's talent.

She'd also heard that Burgess had a nickname for nearly every room in the entire six-acre complex, but why he'd named this the Bull Pen she had no idea. Maybe he was a baseball fan as Sander had been. Rachael brushed the thought aside and concentrated on the room.

It wasn't quite as large as she'd envisioned it, but it was still a big room, nonetheless, with a huge oval table in the center and an enormous coffee urn near the wall by the door. To her left was a second door, which led, presumably, to Burgess's private office. The remaining wall space was totally devoted to large panels of cork board. These were the storyboards that outlined the movie in detail. When completed, each storyboard would contain sixty drawings, with each panel devoted to a specific segment of the film. By starting with the first board it was theoretically possible to follow the plot from beginning to end.

As Rachael glanced around she capitalized *theoretically* in her mind because the storyboards for *The Quest* were pitifully bare. Except for the first three, which seemed to have been completed, the remainder of the boards contained only fragments of action. Applicable pages of dialogue were tacked to each board, but the vital drawings used as the foundation of everything else that went on at Animators were few and far between. Though the movie was still in its early stages—at least two years from completion—Rachael could see that Burgess did, indeed, need an assistant... desperately.

The challenge represented by those empty storyboards caused Rachael's heart to beat a little faster, like that of a marathon runner whose adrenaline shot up before a race. The feeling startled her and she tamped it down. She wasn't ready to be creative again. She didn't want to have to deal with people, because people demanded that you give something of yourself, and Rachael had nothing left to give. The job she had now was rote and routine. Doing it, she could let her mind go blank and retain her blessed state of numbness. Jason Burgess was a powerful, dynamic man; he wouldn't settle for an assistant who had nothing to give him, nothing worth contributing.

Containing her unwanted feeling of excitement, Rachael stepped to the first storyboard. She recognized segments of the story she'd been working on lately, and followed the progress of the plot as far as she could. It would be a good movie—another triumph for its creator. *The Quest* was the story of a handsome, muscular warrior named Phoenix who inhabited a mythical fantasy world filled with wizards and sorceresses, monsters and magic.

It was the stuff cartoons could be made of, but no one would ever have dared put that label on it. Burgess's work bore about as much resemblance to flat, loosely animated Saturday-morning cartoons as a Rembrandt painting bore to a stick figure. His films were universal, equally appealing to adults and children, and his characters appeared as full, three-dimensional figures. In fact, one of the few criticisms Rachael had ever heard of Jason's work was that if he was going to make his characters so lifelike, why not just use real people in an ordinary movie? Rachael had forgotten where she'd read that criticism, but she remembered that Burgess had answered, "Because what I do isn't ordinary and it never will be."

Looking at the sketches in front of her and remembering the work she and others did to bring his fantasy worlds to life, Rachael knew he'd spoken out of honesty, not ego. Jason Burgess was an extraordinarily talented man.

One particular drawing several boards down caught Rachael's eye, and she moved to it, instantly captivated. It was a large sketch, much larger than a four-by-six-inch storyboard drawing. Rachael assumed that it was a rough sketch Jason had done for the background artists. Phoenix's quest took him to an evil netherworld, and Jason's drawing had captured the gates of Hades magnificently. Featuring his characteristic bold, sure outer strokes, offset by intricate detail, the drawing depicted Phoenix standing before the gates that towered over him like a thousand serpents forming an impassable barrier. Beyond the writhing wall, flames and ethereal smoke formed patterns of hideous monsters in the thick air.

It was only a pencil sketch, devoid of color or movement, yet Rachael could almost see the monstrous patterns dissolving and shifting to form more hideous figures. She could almost smell the acrid scent of sulfur and taste it on her tongue. It was an incredible drawing, terrifying, and at the same time compelling. It touched something deep inside her, and the moment she recognized what it was, she stepped back, but could not look away. Those particular gates of hell existed only in Jason Burgess's mind, and yet

Rachael had seen them before. Like Phoenix, she had stood at that portal, dwarfed by the power of the horrible unknown beyond.

In *The Quest*, Phoenix would traverse the netherworld and emerge unscathed into the light. Rachael knew that she was still stumbling around inside the gates and for her there would be no safe exit.

"Do you like it?"

Startled, Rachael whirled toward the voice and found Jason standing at his office door, studying her with the same intensity she'd been studying his drawing. She found his close scrutiny unnerving and moved quickly away from the sketch.

Wanting to look anywhere but at his startling blue eyes, Rachael placed her purse on the table and fussed with the strap. "I'm sure you don't need me to tell you how good your work is, Mr. Burgess," she finally answered softly.

Jason grinned and stepped farther into the room. "True. My ego is not in such sad shape that I need constant reinforcement," he told her. "But I didn't ask if it was good, I asked if you like it."

Rachael managed to look at him. "A picture like that is hard to like, but impossible to ignore."

Her answer must have pleased him tremendously because he smiled broadly, and Rachael noticed what a nice smile it was. In fact, his entire face was nice, and she studied it with an artist's detachment. The angular lines of his forehead, cheekbones and jaw were softened by a wavy mop of tawny hair and a beard that was slightly darker. There was a little silver at his temples—more in his mustache and beard—but the youthful twinkle in his engaging eyes belied any hint of age. His was a friendly face, open and honest, and like his drawing, completely impossible to ignore. He had a tall, lanky build, but beneath his comfortable-looking blue work shirt and denim jeans, Rachael could tell there lurked a body that was as lean and hard as an athlete's. Jason Burgess was a handsome man—so handsome that Rachael found herself responding to his good looks and compassionate, winning smile. She looked away and quickly brought the uncomfortable, unfamiliar feelings under control.

"Why don't you have a seat, Ms Hubbard, and we'll get down to business," Jason suggested. He pulled out a chair to sit, but when Rachael didn't follow suit he stopped.

She cleared her throat tentatively. "Actually, Mr. Burgess, I don't think I'll be here long enough to warrant getting comfortable." She fidgeted with her purse strap. "When Robb Weston told me to report here this morning, naturally he explained the purpose of this interview."

"Then you know I'm taking recommendations from my department heads on the hiring of a new assistant."

"Yes, sir."

"Robb wanted me to interview you first because he was sure that once I did I wouldn't have to look any further. He has a great deal of faith in your ability."

"I...appreciate his confidence...but he submitted my name without consulting me." She looked at him, her voice quiet and faintly apologetic. "I'm flattered that you would consider me for the position, Mr. Burgess, but I'm afraid I'm not qualified to handle the job, nor am I interested in leaving the animation department. I explained my feelings to Mr. Weston, but he felt I should tell you in person." Rachael picked up her oversized purse and adjusted the long strap to her shoulder. "I don't want to take up any more of your time than I already have, so if it's all right with you, I'll just go back to work now."

She started for the door and had made it halfway there before the stunned Jason finally found his voice. "Wait a minute!" This wasn't going at all the way it should. Jason liked things to be logical and orderly, and Rachael Hubbard had just turned his first interview of the day upside-down.

Obviously she didn't really understand what the job entailed—and what an opportunity she was about to pass up. Jason valued Robb Weston's opinion more than almost any other person's in the company, and if Robb thought she was perfect, Jason felt sure she was qualified. He didn't want to make the mistake of letting a potentially good assistant get away just because of a misunderstanding.

"Would you please come back, Ms Hubbard?" He smiled to make the words sound less like a command. "I appreciate your desire not to waste my time, but it *is* my time, and I don't feel it would be wasted by a few minutes with you. Please—" he held out a chair for her "—have a seat."

Rachael stood uncertainly for a moment, then decided it would be best if she complied. Burgess was, after all, her boss. She sat as he directed, placed her bag on the table to her right and clasped her hands loosely together on the table in front of her.

"Thank you." Jason moved to the opposite side of the table, opened the personnel file he'd brought in with him, but didn't look at it. "Ms Hubbard, I don't know what your concept of the job as my assistant is, but before you make a decision you might later regret, I think we should discuss the qualifications I'm looking for—and also the benefits that go with the job itself. I'm looking for someone who can translate my ideas into the sketches necessary to complete this storyboard." He gestured toward the nearly blank cork wall behind him.

"As you can see, I need someone fast and efficient, which Robb assures me you are. But the work will be far from drudgery. I think you'll find the variety involved is far more challenging than what you're doing now as a breakdown artist. I don't want an automaton who works by rote. I need someone creative enough to flesh out my ideas or present new ones if there's a better way of doing a scene."

He smiled encouragingly but doubted that she noticed, since she seemed to be looking at one of his shirt buttons instead of his face. Her reticence, rather than irritating him, for some reason fascinated him. Looking at Rachael, he was reminded of the old adage "Still waters run deep," and he had a gut feeling there was a deep, sweet underground well beneath her shy exterior. He was talking to her about challenge, yet somehow it was she who was challenging him to tap that wellspring, not the other way around.

He opened her personnel file, glanced at her salary, then back at her. "Are you aware that the job as my assistant pays a great deal more than you're making now?" He smiled. "Naturally I'd like to believe that everyone who works at Animators is here for no other reason than love of their art or craft, but I'm not that naive. If this job goes to you, you'll be doubling your salary."

Rachael moistened her lips, and Jason followed the gesture closely, unable to imagine why he found himself so drawn to this woman. She wore no makeup at all, but then, she really didn't need any. Her features were delicate and her skin pale, but she was much prettier than he'd thought yesterday, seeing her only from a distance.

"Mr. Burgess, money isn't really a factor in my job consideration," Rachael told him, wishing she could escape. He was looking at her so intently that she felt exposed and vulnerable. "As I said before, I'm very content with my present job."

"I see." Jason fell silent for a moment. He wasn't about to badger her into taking a job she didn't want, but his curiosity had been aroused and he figured at least he was entitled to satisfy it. "Since you'd obviously made up your mind about this today before you came in, I assume you didn't bring your portfolio."

"No, I didn't."

"Robb tells me you always carry a small sketch pad around with you. Is it in your purse there?"

That brought her eyes to his, finally, and Jason felt triumphant, as though he'd scored a major victory.

Rachael placed her hand on the purse in a gesture that was almost protective, and Jason knew he'd been right. She did have the sketch pad with her. "Well?" he prompted.

"Yes," she confirmed. "But it contains nothing but a few idle doodles. I like to keep my hands busy—it's just a habit." She smiled a little then, a small, self-effacing expression that tugged at Jason's heart. He had the feeling she wasn't accustomed to smiling. It was such an embarrassed little grin that he wondered if perhaps she'd forgotten how to do it right.

"Would you mind if I looked at your...doodles? I promise not to make any snap judgments or offer my unsolicited criticism."

Rachael hesitated for a moment, more than a little tempted to refuse. She'd already told him she didn't want the job. Why was he being so persistent? Her hopes for a speedy escape had gone down the drain, and rather than make a scene she decided the best course was simply to agree to his little whim. She reached into the voluminous bag, produced a five-by-seven-inch sketch pad and pushed it across the table toward him.

Keeping his curiosity in check, Jason opened the pad and flipped slowly through the drawings. Robb had told him that her doodles were better than most people's finished pieces, but as much as he respected Robb, Jason hadn't expected to agree so wholeheartedly. A few of the drawings were ordinary, but very few. The rest were magnificent. Even the simplest subjects were portrayed with a distinctive style and remarkable attention to detail.

There were gremlins and gnomes, delicate fairies playing in beautiful patches of flowers that had never seen the light of day on this planet or any other. One after the other, Jason took in the sketches, each one compounding his admiration for the creative imagination of the artist who'd done this extraordinary work. The thought had occurred to him that Rachael might not be right for the job because she was too shy. Now he was positive she wasn't right because she was simply too talented. No one who could do this kind of work should be anyone's assistant.

Was it possible that no one had ever encouraged her to explore her talent before? She was over thirty years old, Jason judged. Hadn't someone along the way seen what she was capable of and tried to foster her ability? It was hard to imagine, but if it was true that no one had, Jason wasn't going to be one more person who allowed this artistic gem to remain hidden.

Enthused, feeling as though he'd just discovered the Hope diamond, Jason grabbed a sheet of blank paper off the stack that always stayed on the table. "Here," he said, excitement coloring his voice. He came around the table and handed her the paper and a sharpened pencil. "I want you to draw something for me," he insisted, forgetting that she didn't want the job he was about to offer her. "I want you to visualize the scene I'm going to describe to you, then put it on paper, all right?"

Rachael looked up at him, confused. This was getting completely out of hand. "Mr. Burgess, I—"

"Just do it, Rachael," he commanded. His voice was much harsher than he had intended or realized, but it worked. Rachael, who had always been intimidated by authority, found it easy to slip into that old habit of compliance. She picked up a pencil and waited for Jason to tell her what to do.

"I want you to draw a ruined fortress sitting atop a cliff with a forest encroaching on it from the left."

"Do you want me to approximate your style?" she asked quietly without looking up.

"Yes. As closely as you can," he replied, though he would rather have seen it in Rachael's own distinctive style. But he was on the verge of choosing an assistant here, and he had to be practical.

Already Rachael's hand was flying across the page, and she seemed oblivious to him. Jason moved away. He wanted to see the drawing finished, not in its progressive stages, and he didn't want to make her nervous by looking over her shoulder.

Just to have something to do while he waited, he picked up her personnel file and leaned casually against an empty storyboard. Rather than study her resume, though, he covertly watched Rachael Hubbard. As she had yesterday, she captured her lower lip gently between her teeth and focused all her concentration on the paper, giving Jason the opportunity to observe her unnoticed.

Close up she was as delicate as she'd seemed yesterday. She had a quality that he recognized and had responded to instantly—it was a fragility that made a man want to enfold and protect her, keep her safe and shielded from the world. There was also a deep sadness etched around her eyes, and Jason had responded to that, too, without even realizing it.

She was as shy as Robb had said, yet she hadn't been reticent to tell him straight out that she didn't want a promotion. And she hadn't minced words on the subject of his netherworld sketch, either. In fact, despite her soft-spoken manner she'd been quite blunt, informing him that he didn't need anyone to tell him he was good. She was innately honest, and Jason respected that. But she also seemed tentative, unsure of herself and almost... afraid. But of what?

Of him? His reputation? The authority figure he represented?

And what was it she'd said earlier? "I'm not qualified for this job." That was a laugh! Rachael was vastly overqualified, at least, artistically speaking. If she would consent to apprentice with him for a few months so that he could teach her the various facets of his operation, he could then put her in a job that would utilize her talents to their fullest extent. If she could handle color, she'd make a wonderful background artist, or possibly a character stylist. Robb was right—there probably wasn't a job in the entire complex she couldn't do.

So what was the problem? Nothing other than the fact that Ms Hubbard was determined to downplay her talent and hide her light under the proverbial bushel. It would be a crime to allow that to happen, but what could Jason do if she wasn't prepared to do something about it, herself?

Without really seeing what she was drawing, Jason watched the swift, sure strokes being made by Rachael's delicate hands, then returned his scrutiny to her face. Once again he was struck by the feeling that he'd seen her before, and not just somewhere within the Animators' complex or at a general staff meeting, but face-to-face. Sometime...years ago. But where? In order to create realistic characters, Jason studied people constantly—their mannerisms, their bone structure, their expressions. He'd studied this woman once.... But where? When? Why did she seem so familiar?

As though sensing his intense gaze, Rachael finally lifted her head and placed her pencil on the table. As she had with the sketch pad, she pushed the drawing toward him and folded her hands, waiting.

"You're finished already?" Jason asked, astonished. He hadn't thought of glancing at his watch when she'd begun because this wasn't a timed test, but he knew she couldn't have been working more than ten minutes. Obviously she hadn't realized he wanted a drawing of some intricacy. Holding back his reservations, he stepped forward to retrieve the sketch, prepared to hand it back and ask for more detail.

The request was unnecessary. What Rachael had given him was so amazing he could hardly believe his eyes. His heart pounding with barely restrained excitement, he took her sketch, tacked it next to the netherworld sketch and stepped back. The drawings were so close stylistically that even Jason could barely tell them apart.

He stared in astonishment for nearly a minute, taking in the general feel of the picture, then removed it from the board and sat at the table for a close-up study. It was exactly what he'd asked for, and yet it was so much more, too. The decrepit castle fortress looked deserted and forlorn, its battlements crumbling, its turrets twisted with vines. And the forest that enveloped it was as menacing as the living being Jason had intended it to be—would have made it had he drawn it himself.

Ghostly, windswept trees reached out in an evil embrace, and he looked closer to see how she'd accomplished the effect. He saw it immediately: branches twisted into sinister faces that projected their evil intent subliminally rather than overtly. The sad castle was full of subtle, subliminal messages as well. Looking closely, he could see that one wall had actually crumbled away, leaving its rock formation in the vague, but softly effective profile of a woman's face. The cliffs, too, held hidden menaces of their own. The decrepit fortress was besieged from all sides, vulnerable and compelling.

The bold lines, the subtle detail, the vivid imagery... they were all there, perfect and stunning.

Jason had lost track of the number of times he'd been called an artistic genius because the label didn't feel right to him. He knew his own strengths and weaknesses and worked within the bounds of both. Looking at Rachael's drawing, he was suddenly swept by the feeling that now he finally knew just what that lofty phrase meant. If anyone in this room was a genius, artistic or otherwise, it was Rachael Hubbard.

"This is brilliant," he said quietly, almost reverently. He looked at her directly, willing her to meet his eyes so that he could find some clue about what made this fragile woman so special.

She did look at him, her dark eyes clouded, but Jason found no answers, only more questions. "Thank you," she replied softly.

"The job is yours, Rachael. It's so far beneath your talent I'm almost embarrassed to offer it to you, but I'd be a fool to let you get away. And once we get this storyboard in line, we can talk about another promotion. I'd like to see you try your hand at being a background artist eventually."

Upset, losing her grip on the calm she'd worked so hard to maintain, Rachael closed her eyes for a moment. Her brows came together in a delicate frown. "Mr. Burgess..." She forced herself to look at him. "Please don't think I'm ungrateful, but I told you before, I'm not looking for a promotion. I'm very happy doing breakdown work. I mean no offense, but—" she shrugged her shoulders helplessly "—I wouldn't be comfortable here."

She stood up, trying hard to ignore the look on his face that told her he wasn't just disappointed that she'd rejected his job offer, but he was disappointed in her, personally. For some inexplicable reason she wanted very much not to disappoint him, and that made what she was doing that much harder.

"May I go back to work now?"

Jason leaned back in his chair and studied her closely. He was intrigued, puzzled, fascinated and confused.... How could anyone so talented be content to do nothing but doodle in a sketch pad no one was meant to see? Something was wrong, and Jason was determined to find out what it was. Rachael Hubbard wasn't going to be the one to help him figure it out. She was standing there, looking for all the world like Bambi's mother had in the moments before the hunter's rifle had brought down the gentle doe. And what was worse, she was making Jason feel as though *he* was the heartless hunter who had her in his sights.

In that protracted moment as they looked at each other, something about Rachael reached deep inside Jason, and he felt his heart twist. Unbidden, the sweet-sad memory of Molly came back to him, though nothing about Rachael was even vaguely similar to the impish, vivacious young girl Jason had married and then lost so many years ago. No, what Jason saw when he looked at Rachael was not his late wife, but himself as he'd been in those first empty years after Molly's death.

He glanced at Rachael's personnel file, quickly finding the line that read: "Marital status: widow." His instinct had been correct. The sadness etched in her dark eyes had been put there by devastating loss—the kind of loss Jason understood only too well.

He looked at her, wishing he could do something to ease the pain that now seemed so obvious. At the moment, though, nothing came to mind. The best he could do was relieve the anxiety he was creating. "Yes, Rachael, you may go."

"Thank you." She turned and departed swiftly, leaving Jason wondering what he was going to do about the fragile beauty who so obviously needed someone's help.

Her personnel file in hand, Jason returned quickly to his office and buzzed his secretary on the intercom. "Gretchen,

CHAPTER THREE

"LAMPLIGHT COMICS. May I help you, please?" The receptionist's voice was friendly, and Jason responded in kind.

"Yes. Would you please tell Roger Lampasat that Jason Burgess is calling?"

"Of course, Mr. Burgess. Right away!"

Jason smothered a chuckle as his call was transferred. It never ceased to amaze him that just the mention of his name could garner such an enthusiastic reaction. He glanced down at Rachael Hubbard's personnel file, and the receptionist was immediately forgotten as the reason for his call came back into focus. When Rachael had filled out the Animators' standard employment application, she'd listed Roger Lampasat as her only reference. Jason hoped the referral was a valid one. Otherwise he would reach a dead end in his search for information almost before he started looking. The only other name on the application was a sister in Connecticut who was listed as next of kin, and Jason knew he wouldn't feel comfortable about calling a member of Rachael's family for information. It was Roger or nothing.

Rachael's delicate, somehow-familiar face floated in front of his mind's eye, and he wondered what Roger would be able to tell him about her. Obviously she'd worked for Lamplight at one time, but she was so talented that Jason found it hard to believe that Roger would have let her go. Lampasat published a dozen of the most popular comic books on the market, and his need for good artists was as pressing as Jason's.

Jason cringed at the thought of Rachael working as a fill-in artist—someone who merely colored in the backgrounds drawn by a comic book's primary creator. She was capable of so much more than that. And yet, he reminded himself, she was doing similar work at Animators as a break-downer. In Robb Weston's department, the major components of a particular character's movements—say, Phoenix leaping across a ravine—were done by an animator who executed rough sketches that might depict Phoenix taking off and landing, with three or four frames in between to show his position in flight. Those drawings then went to the assistant animator who cleaned up the rough sketches and added detail.

In order to simulate realistic movement it might take twenty to thirty individual drawings between the takeoff and landing, and Rachael's current job was to do about half of those. She drew the same character over and over, making minute adjustments in body position. From there the drawings went to the inbetweener, who completed the sequence. The jobs of assistant animator, breakdowner and inbetweener were demanding ones that required talent, patience and meticulous attention to detail, but they allowed the artist little room for creative growth or expression. Rachael was capable of more—much more—than was currently being asked of her.

Why had she left Lamplight? he wondered. Had her husband's death somehow precipitated the career move? Why was she so reluctant to use her God-given talent?

Those questions and others plagued Jason, but in order to answer them he needed more information, and he fervently hoped he was coming to the right place.

"Jason! How are you? This is an unexpected pleasure!" Roger Lampasat's bombastic voice made Jason pull the receiver away from his ear in self-defense.

"Hello, Roger." He brought the phone back to his ear tentatively. He could almost visualize Lampasat's cherubic smile. A small man with a big voice that belied his size, Roger was a human dynamo—a pleasant combination of enthusiasm, intelligence and ambition. It was no fluke that his company was one of the most successful, well-organized, pleasant workplaces in the business.

"So, Jason, to what do I owe this honor?" the editor asked. "Have you changed your mind about producing a feature based on *Ravenmede*? I keep telling you, it would make a hell of a movie!"

Jason chuckled, knowing he should have realized Roger would jump to this conclusion. A few years ago the editor had approached Jason about doing a movie based on Lamplight's most popular comic, *Ravenmede*, but Jason hadn't wanted to tackle that project. He had his own visions to bring to life, but more than that, he wasn't sure that anyone—including himself—could successfully pull off such an ambitious project. The style of the fantasy art comic was remarkably similar to Jason's—so much so, in fact, that Jason had refused to ever do more than glance with admiration at the monthly periodical.

As was most of Jason's work, *Ravenmede* was set in a mythical medieval kingdom, and Jason had resisted becoming a fan of the comic because he wanted to avoid the possibility that he might subconsciously imitate or be influenced by any of *Ravenmede*'s story lines.

Just as Jason had set new heights of excellence in the world of fantasy filmmaking, *Ravenmede* had done the same for art comics. It was respected, even revered in many circles. Until the death of one of its creators several years ago, the comic had been, quite simply, the best there ever was. Even now, it was still relatively popular, but Jason knew from gossip on the industry's grapevine that the comic was slipping into mediocrity. Roger Lampasat would be only too happy to endorse Jason if he decided to make *Ravenmede* into a feature film, since such a move might catapult the comic back to its former popularity.

Jason was sorry to have to disappoint him. "No, Rog, I'm sorry. I still can't see myself taking on *Ravenmede*. I'm not sure I could live up to the standards Garrett Mallory set for it, but I appreciate your faith that I could."

Jason's refusal was no surprise to Roger, but the mention of Garrett Mallory took the wind out of his sails. More subdued but still friendly, he said, "If anyone could do it, kid, you could. But enough of that. If I can't sell you the film rights, what can I do for you?"

Leaning back in his chair, Jason tapped Rachael's employment application against the edge of his desk. "I need some information on one of your former employees who's now working here and used you as a reference."

"You think the reference is phony?"

"No, it's not that—"

"Then what's the problem?"

"There's no problem," Jason corrected hastily. "At least she's not a problem in any normal sense of the word."

Roger chuckled. "You'll have to forgive me, Jason, but you're not making a whole lot of sense. What's her name?"

"Rachael Hubbard. Do you remember her?" Static crackled on the long-distance line between L.A. and New York, but other than that, no sound at all greeted Jason. "Roger? You still there?"

It was another moment before he replied. "Yeah, I'm still here."

"Do you know Rachael Hubbard?" Jason asked again, though he sensed that Roger's hesitancy had nothing to do with a faulty memory or lack of recognition. Roger Lampasat knew something about Rachael Hubbard and he was simply trying to decide whether or not he was going to pass the information along.

"Yes, Jason, I know Mrs. Hubbard. She worked for Lamplight . . . a while back."

"And . . ." Jason prompted.

"And . . . nothing." Jason could almost visualize Roger shrugging his narrow shoulders. "She was a good employee."

"Then why did she leave Lamplight?" Jason felt as though he was pulling teeth. Roger wasn't what Jason could consider a good friend—too many miles and a lack of opportunity to develop a friendship stood between them—but he liked the editor and felt he knew him well enough to know when Roger was behaving strangely. This was definitely one of those times.

"Jason...look..." Roger paused as though torn by some momentous decision. "I don't know what to tell you."

"Tell me about Rachael Hubbard."

"She's not in some kind of trouble, is she?"

There was genuine concern in the older man's voice and Jason hastened to reassure him. "No, of course not. At least none that I'm aware of. She's a breakdowner in the animation department here, and I happen to believe she's working way below her potential. This morning I tried to promote her to my personal assistant and she turned me down flat. And, too, there's something that seems familiar about her. I just thought maybe you could clue me in on her personality a little so I can figure out why she's content to waste her talent. Do you have any ideas on the subject?"

There was another pause, but this time when Roger spoke he had obviously resolved the conflict he'd been wrestling with.

His voice sounded resigned and somewhat weary when he answered, "Yeah, Jason, I have some very definite ideas. Frankly, it's always bothered me that Rachael is hiding out like this. I had hoped that after she had a chance to recover from Sander's death she'd come back to Lamplight where she belongs."

"Sander was her husband?" Jason asked, then hastened to explain, "I learned that she's a widow from her personnel file."

"But you really don't know who she is?"

"No, but I have a feeling I should. You want to tell me why?"

Roger sighed audibly. "I really shouldn't, Jason. When Rachael left Lamplight she made me swear that if anyone ever called for a reference I wouldn't tell who she was. I agreed, first of all, because she's a friend, and secondly, because I desperately needed permission to continue using her and Sander's pseudonym on the comic they'd created."

All the pieces suddenly fell into place and Jason muttered, "Oh, my God," as the realization hit home. A husband-and-wife team working at Lamplight under a pseudonym. A husband who died in a violent car crash, leaving behind a grieving wife—and a failing comic book. *Ravenmede*. "Rachael Hubbard is the surviving half of the Garrett Mallory team." He didn't bother phrasing it as a question.

"You didn't hear that from me," Roger reminded him humorlessly.

"Oh, brother." Jason was in a state of shock. Not thirty minutes ago he'd been testing one of the most talented artists in the country, and had counted himself magnanimous for wanting to help further her career! "Why didn't I figure it out for myself? All the clues were there—a widow who'd worked for Lamplight, a—"

"Don't be so hard on yourself," Roger said, glad that Jason knew the truth. Someone needed to do something about bringing Rachael back to the land of the living, and it was just possible Jason could succeed where everyone else had failed. For two years now, Rachael had cut herself off from her family, her friends, even her real work, and no one had been able to reach her. Oh, everyone who loved her knew where she lived, and some—like her sister—even talked to her regularly, but no one had yet been able to draw her out of that horribly dark, lonely place within herself that she'd retreated to when her world had collapsed. Roger hoped that after all this time she'd made some progress toward the light, but if Rachael was still refusing to use her talent, obviously Roger's hopes had been in vain. She was still alone and in hiding.

"Why should you have figured it out?" he asked. "Rachael and Sander made the name Garrett Mallory famous, but there probably aren't a handful of people outside the comic book industry who know their real names. In fact, that's why there was so little publicity about the accident."

"I'm ashamed to say I don't even remember who told me about it," Jason admitted. "I was in the final production stages of *Chariot* when I heard about the wreck, and I remember thinking what a tragic waste it was. I met them six or seven years ago at an awards banquet—that's why Rachael seemed so familiar to me," he added. "I didn't have a chance to talk to either of them, but they were introduced to me as Mr. and Mrs. Garrett Mallory. It wasn't until a couple of years later that I learned that was just their pseudonym. If anyone ever told me their real name was Hubbard, it went in one ear and out the other." There was a slight pause as Jason tried to figure out what to say next. "Roger... why did she abandon *Ravenmede*?"

The older man sighed again. "She said it was Sander's baby and she wasn't skilled enough to make it work without him."

Jason knew the answer to his next question before he asked it. "Is she right?"

"Hell, no!" Roger snapped. "Sander wasn't half the artist Rachael is. They created *Ravenmede* together while they were still in college. Apparently Sander came up with the original concept and Rachael did most of the designs. To tell the truth, Jason, if Sander hadn't connected with Rachael, his idea never would have sold, much less become the hottest art comic on the market. Sander did the story lines and a few of the first draft renderings on each issue, but Rachael's talent is what made *Ravenmede* so extraordinary. I just haven't been able to make her see that. I love Rachael, but I don't think I've ever met anyone with so little confidence in herself."

That observation fit perfectly with the conclusion Jason had come to during his brief interview with her. Rachael Hubbard obviously needed a strong dose of self-confidence and an even stronger sense of self-worth. Given time and the opportunity, Jason was certain he could help instill both in her. But she also needed time to recover from the devastating loss of her husband and partner, and Jason knew only too well what a long and lonely road that was. Losing his sweet Molly to cancer fourteen years ago had devastated Jason. For a time he'd wanted to curl up and die. But he hadn't. He'd had an eight-year-old daughter depending on him, and he'd had his work, as well. Both had saved him.

Rachael, on the other hand, had no one, and she didn't feel worthy of continuing the work she considered as her husband's. An ache of sorrow for Rachael and everything she'd lost settled around Jason's heart.

"So, what are you going to do now?" Roger asked, drawing Jason away from his thoughts.

"Do?" Jason said the word as though he'd never heard it before. "I don't know what I can do, Roger."

"I'll tell you what you can do," he answered with conviction. "You can find a way to get Rachael to accept that job as your assistant! Challenge her! Force her to think, to create... to feel again, for crying out loud!"

"Roger, the woman's trying to cope with having lost—"

"That's just the point, Jason, she's not coping, she's running away! I've talked to her a number of times over these past two years, so I know that what I'm telling you is true. She's cut herself off from her family and friends—she's alone there in L.A., not living, just existing! Somebody's got to reach her, make her live again, work again!" Roger forced himself to calm down and continue more sedately, but no less sincerely. "I need her back, Jason, and it just could be that working as your assistant would be an important first step in that direction. *Ravenmede* is going down the tubes without her.

"I've got a team of the best fantasy artists money can buy working under the Garrett Mallory pseudonym, but without Rachael's special touch, *Ravenmede* is just any other comic book. Lamplight needs Rachael Hubbard, so I admit I do have an ulterior motive, but I also care deeply about that girl, and I can't stand the thought of her throwing away her life. And that's exactly what she's doing."

Jason recognized Roger's genuine concern and was surprised to realize how deeply he himself shared it. Something about Rachael had touched him profoundly. Maybe it was his empathy with the grief he'd sensed in her, or maybe it was just the feeling that she'd forgotten how to smile that had gotten to him. Whatever it was, Rachael Hubbard wasn't just an employee to him any longer. "I agree with you, Roger, but I can't force her to do something she doesn't want to do."

"You can try," Roger replied shrewdly.

Jason sighed deeply. "Maybe."

"Come on, Jason," Roger cajoled. "Put on your Good Samaritan cap and help her out. Rachael needs it, and heaven knows she'd make one hell of an assistant."

CHAPTER FOUR

"NOW, MISS EMILY, what would you like for supper?" The moment the words were out of his mouth, Jason knew he'd made a big mistake. Given an option, what three-year-old would ask for broccoli and carrots? He looked down at his granddaughter toddling along beside him and his fears were confirmed. Her bright smile had junk food written all over it.

"Hot dogs."

Squirm your way out of this one, Grandpa. "Hot dogs are not very nutritious, Emily," he told her with a reasonable smile.

"Don't want 'tritious," Emily replied just as equitably. "Want hot dogs."

"Wellll..." Jason opened the refrigerator, hoping that his housekeeper had left it stocked with something tempting yet healthy. "Oh boy, Emmy, look at this. Beef stew! You like Mrs. Ramos's stew, don't you?"

Emily's look turned mutinous. "Hot dogs, Grandpa."

Jason knelt, bringing himself level with the little girl's elfin face. "How about if we compromise? Let's eat stew for supper and have hot dogs for dessert! Whadda ya think?"

Emily's heart-shaped mouth puckered adorably as she sucked in her cheeks. Her look of fierce concentration always tugged at Jason's heart. It had been passed down from Molly to her daughter, Lorna, and now to little Emily in the same way the child's shock of bright red hair, freckles, and misty blue eyes had passed through three generations of

Burgess women. Molly was no longer with him, but Jason considered himself fortunate that he had his daughter and granddaughter to keep the memory of his late wife alive.

Emily finally decided that beef stew would be acceptable if it was followed by the more appealing hot dog, and Jason was delighted that he wouldn't have to explain to Emily's health-food-conscious mother that a three-year-old had gotten the drop on Grandpa. After the disturbing day he'd had, plagued by thoughts of Rachael Hubbard, the last thing Jason needed was a petty dispute with his headstrong daughter about Emily's supper. Lorna was so unhappy these days that she tended to take her anxieties out on her father, and Jason believed in avoiding conflict wherever possible.

That was probably the reason he hadn't confronted Rachael today, either. It was an extraordinarily delicate situation, and he'd needed time to think about a course of action. Unfortunately for his state of mind, he'd been able to think about little else. He'd completed all the other interviews he'd had scheduled for the day, and had found two likely candidates, but Rachael was the one he wanted as his assistant—for her sake as much as his own.

Whistling merrily for Emily's benefit, Jason popped two servings of stew—one large, one small—into the microwave, put the water for a hot dog on to boil, then turned to the task of preparing a small fruit salad he knew his granddaughter was particularly fond of. With any luck at all, he'd be able to make her forget about the preservative-filled hot dog.

Emily picked up the melody of the tune Jason was whistling and began humming along as she did her share of the work. Without being asked, she went to one of the lower cabinets, extracted two colorful plastic picnic plates, then put them on the table that sat at the end of the large kitchen. She moved back and forth from the cabinet to the table, retrieving a pair of unbreakable glasses, place mats, napkins and cutlery, methodically piling each set of items on the edge of the table before climbing into a chair to distribute them.

Jason hid a smile as he watched the little girl work. She was so meticulous that she moved everything at least twice before it suited her, and while the final arrangement of the place settings probably wouldn't have pleased Emily Post, Jason would never have considered correcting the little girl's errors. As far as he was concerned, it was more important for a child of three to accept small responsibilities and take pride in her accomplishments than to perform with adult perfection. That was why he'd arranged a special cupboard filled with unbreakable dinnerware just for Emily. When his schedule permitted, he encouraged Lorna and her husband Cole to bring Emily over to stay with him if they went out for an evening or just wanted an intimate night at home alone. Given the state of the couple's troubled marriage, Jason was glad he could do them this small favor.

Jason's work kept him busy, but he always made time for Lorna and Emily. Losing his beloved Molly had taught him early that nothing was more important than family. That fact had been driven home again during these past few years since Lorna had married and moved out. As he rattled around in his big, empty house Jason was finding that there were too many lonely corners in his life. Keeping Emily one or two evenings a week filled some of them, but he was getting tired of pretending the others didn't exist. He filled up the spaces with his work, but the emptiness he felt when he was alone at home was getting harder to ignore.

"Did I do good, Grandpa?" Emily asked, dragging Jason toward the table to inspect her handiwork.

Jason looked the table over carefully, taking in everything from the jumbled place settings to the brass candle holder that held a large plastic carrot instead of a candle. The carrot, part of a Holly Homemaker set Jason had given her for Christmas last year, swayed drunkenly in its makeshift socket. "You did great, sweetheart."

Emily beamed and took her seat while Jason put their supper on the table. He sat across from her and waited while she said grace, but when he started dishing up their meal, Emily stopped him.

"Light the candle, Grandpa," she instructed seriously, as though he'd almost committed a serious breach of etiquette.

"Of course! How silly of me to forget." He smiled sheepishly, digging into the pocket of his jeans for an imaginary book of matches. With great ceremony, he pantomimed striking the match and lighting the wobbly carrot. Emily giggled when he moved his hand closer to her so that she could blow out the "match."

Supper proceeded smoothly. Throughout the first course of beef stew, Emily kept a watchful eye on the hot dog smothered in mustard, which sat in lonely splendor on an otherwise empty serving dish, but course number two—the fruit salad—almost overshadowed the coveted hot dog. By the time Jason announced it was time for dessert and placed the hot dog on her plate, cutting it into bite-sized chunks, Emily barely nibbled at one piece, and then only for show; she'd insisted on having a hot dog and her three-year-old ego demanded that she at least put up a good front.

Together they loaded the dishwasher and when all their chores had been completed, they adjourned to the huge family room that overlooked Jason's cypress deck, Olympic-size swimming pool and the vast, haphazardly landscaped lawn beyond. The old Spanish-style ranch house that sat on a thirty-acre estate was lovely, but Jason had occasionally reflected that given the state of its interior decor he'd never be featured on *Lifestyles of the Rich and Famous*.

His furnishings were all solidly built and the best money could buy, but everything in the house was put there with an eye for comfort and convenience. The enormous family room was plastered with movie and fantasy art posters, and one huge corner of it had been given over to Emily. A pint-size table-and-chair set, Lorna's old dollhouse, doll-lined bookcases, and every convenience necessary for the pleasure of a three-year-old occupied the corner. Across the room, at the end of a huge, overstuffed sofa sat a lovely wooden toy chest, and the entertainment center opposite the sofa had one full shelf devoted to videotapes of Disney movies and Sesame Street. It was an eclectic, homey room, not at all the sort of place one would expect of a man who'd been a bachelor for more than a decade. Somehow, though, it suited its owner perfectly.

Jason plucked a sketch pad off the slanted drawing board that occupied one corner of the huge room, and when Emily saw that Grandpa intended to draw, she decided that pastime was good enough for her, too. She found her crayons and coloring book in the toy chest she kept neatly organized, and snuggled up beside Jason on the sofa.

While Emily concentrated fiercely on choosing just the right colors for an elegant butterfly, Jason began working on sketches for Adana, the beautiful princess Phoenix would love and lose during the course of his quest. Over the past few weeks, Jason's wastebasket had been littered with dozens of sketches of the mysterious princess, but so far he hadn't found the essence of the elusive heroine. He'd experimented with exotic hairstyles, and had varied the shape of her face and eyes dozens of times, but nothing pleased him. This latest sketch was no different. The woman he'd drawn with a flamboyant over-the-shoulder hairstyle and a short tunic that showed off her shapely legs was a lovely creature, indeed, but she wasn't the delicate Adana. Jason flipped to a fresh page and stared vacantly at the expanse of white paper.

Allowing his mind to float, Jason's skilled hand moved of its own volition, and before he was really aware of what he'd done, the image of Rachael Hubbard appeared on the page. A pair of huge, haunting eyes stared up at him from a delicate heart-shaped face. It was a beautiful, but disturbingly sad face, and Jason wasn't at all surprised that she'd finally surfaced on paper.

But what was he going to do about her? Roger was convinced that Jason should somehow make her take the job as his assistant, but it simply wasn't possible to force her to do something against her will. Rachael claimed she was happy where she was at Animators, but Jason was positive that was a lie—an unintentional one, perhaps, but a lie nonetheless. Rachael Hubbard was very *un*happy; not necessarily with her job, though.

In a way Jason thought he understood why she was content as a breakdowner. The job demanded nothing from her except total concentration. By filling her mind with the immediate task at hand, Rachael could keep her mind preoccupied and avoid thoughts of her late husband.

In that respect Roger was right. Rachael was running away. Grief had to be met and dealt with before the long healing process could begin. Of course a period of denial was inevitable, even natural. Jason had gone through it himself. It had been a period of total nonproductivity because he had clamped down on his feelings. He'd survived each day exhibiting no more emotion than a robot, yet he had continued to function with an appearance of normalcy. Everyone had marveled at the way he was "handling" Molly's death, but Jason had known he wasn't handling anything. He was simply existing, forcing himself not to feel the pain because it hurt too much. Eventually he'd been able to face the pain a little at a time, taking small, halting steps back toward something that resembled a normal life. Having Lorna to take care of, to nurture and to love had probably hastened his recovery, but it had still been a long journey.

What portion of that journey was Rachael on? Jason wondered. Was she still in that pitifully empty period of denial, submersing her emotions to avoid the pain? Everyone healed at their own pace, but two years was a long time to suffer so much. Roger was right; Rachael did need help. Maybe someone who understood what she was going through—who'd been there himself—was exactly what she needed. Maybe that was what Roger had really been trying to tell Jason. Rachael needed a friend who understood and could help her deal with her grief.

But would she accept help and allow Jason to be her friend? That was the most important question of all. Rachael had deliberately cut herself off from her family. She was alone by choice, he reminded himself. It was hard for him to imagine why anyone would want to be alone—completely alone. Jason enjoyed moments of solitude—he'd even been known to take off by himself for a whole week of camping in Yellowstone, or sight-seeing in the restored gold rush towns in the Sierra Nevadas. But he also enjoyed people, and he treasured leisurely hours spent with good friends, many of whom were his co-workers. Rachael had formed no such attachments at work, according to Robb. And if that was the case, it was likely that she kept to herself at home, as well.

Jason wished he'd thought to ask Roger if Rachael had always been a recluse. Had she—

"Whatcha drawing, Grandpa?" Bored with her butterfly, Emily rose to her knees on the couch and draped herself against Jason's side.

Pulled away from his thoughts, Jason looked down at the three-year-old. "I'm *supposed* to be drawing a beautiful princess."

Emily frowned as she studied the sad-eyed drawing of Rachael. "Princesses don't wear glasses, Grandpa," she told him seriously.

Jason hid a smile. "You're absolutely right, sweetie." He quickly applied an eraser to Rachael's eyeglasses, then reconstructed the eyebrows he'd accidentally erased in the process. "There. Is that better?"

"Ummm..." She made a so-so gesture with her narrow shoulders. "Princesses have long hair."

"Of course." With a few deft strokes, Jason added a long mane of hair that cascaded down to the princess's waist.

Emily laughed gleefully at the transformation. "Make her smile! Make her smile!" she exclaimed, jumping up and down with excitement.

"Your wish is my command," Jason said, chuckling as he made the appropriate changes. He eradicated the lines around Rachael's eyes that saddened her gaze and gave her lips the tiniest hint of a smile.

Emily cooed over the magical improvement, but Jason's smile vanished as he stared at the altered drawing. This was how Rachael had looked six years ago when Jason had met her so briefly at an awards banquet. Only her smile had been broader, happier, and her eyes had glistened with love every time she'd looked at her husband. The memories he hadn't been able to recall until after he'd talked to Roger now came back to him clearly, and he saw Rachael as she'd been that night.

One part of his memory hadn't been hazy. He *had* studied her then; not because she was the most beautiful woman at the banquet, or even the most unusual. It was the look of complete trust and adoration she'd bestowed on her husband that had captivated Jason. He'd watched her from a distance, noting that when she'd been looking at anyone but Sander, she was merely a lovely woman; but when her enormous, expressive eyes turned to her husband, she had taken on a glow that was magnificently radiant. Her love for Sander had been so obvious that Jason remembered having felt a pang of envy. He had missed Molly terribly that night.

"—story, Grandpa!"

"What, sweetie?" Jason looked down at his granddaughter, amazed that he'd been able to forget that the little wiggle worm was still there.

"Tell me the princess's story!" the little girl insisted, rapping her hand impatiently against the drawing of Rachael.

"Oh, Emily..." Jason often entertained her with improvised fairy tales, complete with illustrations. Emily thought they were wonderful. Jason thought they were exhausting.

"Pleeeeeeeeese."

Jason sighed with resignation, unable to refuse the child anything, just as he'd been unable to refuse her mother. Both girls were spoiled rotten. "All right, sweetie. One short fairy tale, coming up." He turned to a clean page of the sketch pad and quickly drew a picture of the long-haired Princess Rachael in a flowing gown, riding a huge black stallion.

"Once upon a time there was a beautiful princess named Rachael who lived on a mountain so tall that only the enchanted eagles could reach her." Magically, a mountain complete with a turreted castle appeared behind the princess, and two majestic snow-white eagles soared over her head.

"The princess had a lovely home, with a roaring fireplace and a dozen servants in every room—" a second drawing took shape, depicting the scene "—but she was very lonely."

"Why?" Emily asked, already engrossed in the tale.

"Because she had no one to love. Every day she would leave her lonely castle and wander along the cliffs overlooking the green valley below her. The eagles would soar along beside her, their huge wings catching the currents of warm air from the valley, and the princess would watch them rise and rise, until they could barely be seen. And then she would watch them come down, down, down, toward the castle, toward the cliffs, lower and lower until they were sailing down the mountain toward the valley where the princess could never go."

"Why?" Emily asked, her voice taking on the same sad quality as Jason's.

Why, indeed? Jason thought. "Because she couldn't fly, and no one had ever shown her the secret path that led down the steep mountain to the village in the valley."

"Why?"

"Because the path started in the heart of a deep, dark forest the princess had never dared enter." Jason turned to a new page and created a dark but nonthreatening forest. The story of Princess Rachael was sad enough for a three-year-old without adding menacing shapes that might give her nightmares. He would make sure this story had a happy ending, for Emily's sake, but as he continued to weave the tale, Jason wished that he could give the real Rachael a happy ending as well.

He shifted the scene of the story to the valley and introduced a brave young man who dreamed of taming the enchanted eagles that lived on the mountaintop. With his father's blessing, the young man collected everything he would need to make the treacherous journey through the forest. The young hero started into the woods as Jason turned to yet another new page, but there the story ground to an abrupt halt.

"Damn it, Lorna, that's not true and you know it!"

"I know no such thing! And keep your voice down. Daddy will hear you!"

Daddy certainly will, Jason thought grimly. Lorna and Cole were obviously making it an early evening—due to the latest in a long series of arguments. Jason had no idea what the couple argued about, since Lorna refused to discuss—or even admit that they were having, problems—but he knew his daughter's marriage was in trouble.

Jason hadn't approved of Lorna's decision to marry Cole Washburn only a few months after she'd graduated from high school, but there had been little he could do to stop her. Cole was three years older than Lorna and had just completed his junior year in college. They had dated for several years, and Lorna had been so certain that their love would last. Whenever Jason had insisted she wait, Lorna had reminded him that he had been younger than Cole when he got married, and Molly had been exactly Lorna's age.

Jason had often wondered if his daughter was really in love with her childhood sweetheart, or if she was in love with the idea of emulating what she thought was her parents' storybook-perfect marriage.

At the time he'd given Lorna away at the altar, Jason had convinced himself that Lorna was really in love. Now, though, he wasn't nearly as sure. Already it appeared that her four-year-old marriage was heading for the rocks.

The voices in the hall grew hushed as the quarreling couple headed for the family room, but it was apparent from even the low tones that the fight wasn't over. Unconsciously Jason tightened one arm around Emily, and it was then he noticed that the little girl was practically cowering. She heard her parents' voices rise briefly in anger, then grow hushed again, and she crawled into Jason's lap, the fairy tale forgotten.

The little girl wrapped her arms around her grandfather's neck, holding on for dear life, and a swell of fury rose up in Jason, so potent it almost choked him. Obviously Emily had heard her parents fight before—many times, probably—and she was terrified.

"Hello, Daddy." Lorna stepped into the family room with a falsely cheerful smile affixed to her delicate features. The bright red hair she'd lamented as a child was darkening to a rich auburn, but she'd had no such luck with the freckles she detested. They splattered haphazardly across her nose and onto her high cheekbones, but rather than detracting from her beauty, they added an air of mischievous innocence. It was that innocent air, so similar to Molly's, that constantly bedeviled Jason. One look from his daughter's wide blue eyes was all it took to mold him to her bidding.

Even tonight, as angry as he was, with Emily clinging to him, Jason couldn't bring himself to scold Lorna. But neither could he let go of his anger and concern for the child in his arms. With one hand supporting Emily, he rose to greet his daughter and son-in-law. "Lorna. Cole. I see you made an early night of it."

His terse tone caused Lorna's smile to slip a little, and she wondered what was wrong with him. "Cole and I both have to be up early in the morning. Did Emmy give you any trouble?" She gave him a curious look as she rose on tiptoe to kiss his cheek.

"None at all."

"Good." She slipped her arms around Emily and the little girl transferred her stranglehold from her grandfather to her mother. "What's the matter, honey? Are you sleepy?"

Emily's head, buried against Lorna's neck, shook vigorously.

"We'd better get her home to bed, Lorna." Cole stepped to his wife's side and rubbed a comforting hand across Emily's back. "Thanks for keeping her, Jason. She loves staying with you. I'm sure she'll talk about it for days."

Jason settled a hard look on his twenty-five-year-old son-in-law. "I love having her here, and it's good to know she's someplace where she feels safe."

"Yeah, right," Cole replied tentatively. He was as puzzled as Lorna about Jason's bad mood. "Come on, Lorna. Let's go."

"Is something wrong, Daddy?" Lorna asked, ignoring her husband.

Jason looked at the three of them and decided he couldn't let this pass. "Honey, why don't you take Emily on out to the car. I want to have a word with Cole."

"All right." She shrugged helplessly. Jason gave both his girls a good-night kiss, and Lorna headed out of the room. "Oh, by the way—" she stopped at the door "—the company picnic is at the end of the month, isn't it?"

Jason nodded. "Three weeks from this coming Saturday."

"Great. I'll call you tomorrow to find out what I can do to help."

"Gretchen's been in charge of everything so far, honey. Why don't you give her a call and see what she needs."

"No problem. I know you couldn't get by without me as your hostess." She puckered her lips to throw him a kiss. "'Night, Daddy."

"'Night, honey."

Lorna breezed through the arched doorway, leaving the two men behind—one distinctly uncomfortable, the other downright mad. "What did you want to talk to me about, Jason?" Cole asked when his father-in-law just glared at him.

Jason took a deep breath, fighting to keep his anger under control, but the memory of the way Emily had clung to him in fear made it difficult. "Cole, on the day you and Lorna got married, I made a vow that I wasn't going to interfere in your relationship. I've done my best to keep that vow. I've tried to be supportive, but at the same time give you two the space you need to make your marriage work."

"I know that, sir. Lorna and I both appreciate it," the young man said respectfully, wary of what was to come.

"Don't speak too hastily, son. You may not appreciate what I'm about to say."

"I'll be happy to listen to anything you want to tell me, sir."

Jason sighed irritably. This would be a whole lot easier if Cole weren't so damned polite. "My daughter is unhappy, Cole. I've known for some time now that you two were having problems, but I've tried to stay out of it. Lorna knows that if she needs me I'm here for her, but she's a grown woman and I keep hoping she'll be able to solve her problems on her own. But when those problems start adversely affecting my granddaughter, I can't in good conscience keep quiet."

Cole's eyebrows shot up in surprise. "Emily? What's wrong with Emmy?"

"I'll tell you what's wrong! Her mother and father came into this house tonight shrieking like a couple of banshees, and it scared her to death! And it's obviously not the first time. That's why she was cowering like a whipped puppy. We were having a splendid time until she heard the two of you quarreling. Again!"

Cole looked down at the carpet, unable to meet Jason's angry gaze any longer. "I'm sorry, Jason. We didn't mean to involve you in our fight."

"*I'm* not the one you should be worried about—*yet*!" Jason said heatedly. "You're a parent now, for crying out loud. When you and Lorna got married and conceived that child you took on the responsibility of nurturing her, loving her and providing her with a sheltered, secure environment. As I see it, you're falling woefully short."

Cole's eyes shot back up toward his father-in-law's. "Now wait a minute, Jason—"

"No, you wait a minute, Cole. You've *got* to find a way to settle whatever problems you and Lorna are having, for Emily's sake, at least."

Cole shook his head in disbelief, wondering why he was receiving the brunt of Jason's anger while Lorna was sitting in the car, unscathed. "*I've* got to settle the problems? Jason, you may not realize this, but it takes two to make a quarrel. Maybe Lorna is the one you should be talking to!"

"I intend to do just that," Jason replied tightly. "I didn't want Emily to hear this—that's why I sent Lorna on to the car." He turned away abruptly and paced toward the floor-to-ceiling windows overlooking the faintly lighted swimming pool.

"Cole, I don't want this...discussion to cause a problem between us. You're a fine young man, and I've always felt we had a good relationship." He turned toward him. "But on Lorna's wedding day I entrusted you with her happiness, and I expect you to do whatever it takes to live up to that—for both Lorna *and* Emily."

Cole gnawed at the underside of his lip, valiantly trying to control his temper. Jason was only expressing a well-founded concern—he and Lorna *had* been fighting too much lately, and Emily had undoubtedly heard some of those quarrels. Whatever it took, Cole knew he would have to find a way to insulate his daughter from the problems he and Lorna were having.

What made Cole angry was Jason's apparent willingness to blame the entire situation on his son-in-law, entirely ignoring the fact that his spoiled, willful daughter bore a share of the responsibility, too. At the moment, Cole wasn't sure it would be wise to express that thought to his father-in-law, so he held his temper. It was going to be interesting to see if Jason lived up to his promise to have this discussion with Lorna.

"I'll do the best I can, Jason," Cole finally answered. "And I appreciate your concern for Emily."

Jason looked at the young man wryly. "When Emily's a little older, I'm sure you'll appreciate and come to understand my concern for Lorna, as well."

Cole managed a little smile. "I expect I might, at that." He extended his hand. "See you, Jason."

Jason gladly accepted the peace offering and grasped Cole's hand firmly. "Good night, Cole."

Jason watched his son-in-law leave, wondering if their discussion would have positive results. He also wondered exactly what it was that Lorna and Cole had been fighting about. For the past year he'd rarely seen them when there wasn't some kind of unspoken tension in the air. He suspected that part of their problems had to do with money, but whenever Jason brought up the subject with Lorna she invariably replied that they were doing fine. He hadn't dared mention the subject to Cole for fear of damaging the boy's pride.

But if money wasn't the problem, Jason had no idea what it could be. Cole had a decent job at a mortgage banking firm, and Lorna had worked her way up to assistant buyer for an exclusive boutique in Beverly Hills. Neither of them was making a fortune, but their combined income was adequate. It bothered Jason to think of his daughter pinching pennies when she had a father who was as rich as Croesus. But he was determined to let her live her own life.

Though Jason had told Cole that Lorna knew she could depend on her father for anything, he had to wonder if that was really true. Frankly it surprised him that she refused to confide in him about her problems. Before Molly's death father and daughter had been very close, and afterward they had become inseparable. Even in her awkward teen years Lorna had been comfortable discussing anything with Jason. Now, though, she seemed determined to pretend nothing was wrong with her marriage, even though Jason had made it clear he knew otherwise.

Was it pride, he wondered, that kept Lorna from confiding in him? When she'd told Jason she and Cole were going to be married and live happily ever after, she'd been so certain she was speaking the truth. Was she ashamed now to admit that she'd made a grave mistake?

With a worried sigh Jason wandered around the family room picking up Emily's toys, coloring book and crayons, tidying the room. Mrs. Ramos, his housekeeper, came in twice a week, and she wasn't due back until Friday, so he policed the area carefully. He stowed Emily's gear in her toy chest, tuned his television to the all-news station and stretched out on the sofa.

"Oh, Molly, what should I do about our little girl?" he asked the empty room. Despite the droning babble of the TV, the silence of the house settled around Jason like a stifling cloak. He automatically picked up his sketch pad, propped it upright on his abdomen, and looked at the fairy tale he'd been improvising for his granddaughter. He studied the pictures one after the other, remembering the story he'd invented, and realized that the beautiful Princess Rachael wasn't the only one who was lonely.

Retrieving his pencil, he picked up the story where he'd left off, with the brave young hunter entering the mountain forest, unaware that more than enchanted eagles awaited him at the end of the treacherous journey.

CHAPTER FIVE

RACHAEL PUSHED ASIDE the remains of a microwavable carton of soup and propped her book on the small cafeteria table. Around her the room was quiet, just the way she preferred it. For two years now she had deliberately chosen this late lunch shift because it was the one least chosen by others. For similar reasons she always sat at the same table, in the deepest corner of the room where no one would bother her. Having a routine was an important part of maintaining the precious balance of her life.

Normally she doodled in her sketch pad to wile away the hour, but today she had left the pad at home. After her encounter with Jason Burgess the previous day, she had decided it was a good idea to find another way to fill her spare time at work. Today she had brought a seven-hundred-page best-seller, but it could just as well have been the Los Angeles phone book for all the enjoyment she was getting out of it. The words on the page melted into one another, forming an image of Jason Burgess's face when she'd refused his job offer that last time.

He'd been thrilled by what he'd seen in her sketch pad, but the real clincher had been the drawing he'd asked her to design according to his specifications, in his style. Though she cursed herself for it now, it had never occurred to Rachael at the time to do less than her best. It would have been safer by far to have simply botched the sketch, thereby convincing her employer she wasn't qualified for the job he wanted her to take. But Rachael had always been a perfectionist, particularly where her art was concerned, and she'd reacted on instinct. Her father had always demanded the best from her, as had Sander, and it was the fear of disappointing someone that kept Rachael constantly striving for perfection. The last thing she needed in her life right now was someone else to disappoint... one more chance to fail.

"Hello, Rachael."

Startled from her thoughts, Rachael glanced up sharply at the man who had approached without her realizing it. Jason Burgess stood across the table from her, watching her expectantly, and Rachael's heart began to race. "Mr. Burgess."

"I wish you'd call me Jason," he offered with a reassuring smile.

"All right... Jason." She glanced down, wishing the earth would open and swallow her whole.

"May I join you for a minute?"

Rachael's heart continued its irregular beating. "I... Of course... but I really should be returning to work."

Jason flashed a smile Rachael didn't see. "Don't worry about that. You're with the boss—what could be safer?"

Being at my desk. Being home alone. Being anywhere but here, she thought, hating the frantic, fearful pounding of her pulse. It had taken all the courage and control she possessed to face Jason yesterday, and there was precious little of either left in reserve for this unexpected rematch.

When Rachael didn't respond, Jason suddenly doubted the wisdom of cornering her like this. He'd spent most of the night wrestling with the dual problems of Lorna's rocky marriage and Rachael Hubbard's identity. When he'd finally decided there was nothing he could do to help Lorna until she asked for his help, the accompanying feeling of impotence he'd experienced had made him all the more determined to help Rachael. But seeing her so obviously distraught by his mere presence at her table made him wonder if he had the right to interfere in her life.

It was Roger Lampasat's conviction that Rachael didn't have a life that finally reinforced Jason's determination to offer her his friendship. He cleared his throat and glanced around the nearly deserted cafeteria. "Rachael . . ."

"Yes?" She took a deep breath and looked at him.

"After you left my office yesterday I looked over your employment application and called Roger Lampasat."

To her credit, Rachael brought a fleeting stab of panic under control quickly. "Oh? I assumed my previous employment had been verified when I was hired," she said warily.

"It probably was."

"Then why did you feel it necessary to call Mr. Lampasat?" she asked softly.

"I was having a hard time understanding why anyone would refuse a promotion they were obviously qualified for," he told her truthfully. "I thought Roger might know why."

Fighting alarm and the impulse to tell Jason Burgess to mind his own business, Rachael managed to keep her voice calm. "What did he have to say?"

"That he wants you to come back to work for Lamplight."

Rachael looked down again—somewhat guiltily, Jason thought. "That's not possible. I'm very happy here in L.A."

"Are you?" he asked her seriously, then dropped the question as Rachael's eyes snapped sharply up to his. "Never mind. That's irrelevant. The type of work you did for Roger can be done anywhere, even out of your own home. You don't have to go into the New York office."

Rachael held her breath. Was Jason playing a game with her? Did he know the truth? Roger had sworn he wouldn't tell, but that promise had been made two years ago. Lately he'd been calling her more often, putting on more unwanted pressure, but surely he wouldn't have betrayed her like this.

Carefully expelling her pent-up breath, she told Jason evenly, "That only applies to a comic's principal artist, not inkers."

"As I said, Rachael, that's irrelevant—" he met her gaze evenly "—because you and your late husband *were* the principals on *Ravenmede*."

Rachael went perfectly still, as though the fragile sparks of life in her had suddenly been siphoned off. "Roger promised he wouldn't tell anyone."

The deadness in her eyes almost made Jason wince. He was going about this all wrong, but it was too late to turn back. "Roger kept his word, Rachael. While you were in my office I realized I'd seen you somewhere before. Talking to Roger jogged my memory. Had you forgotten that we met at an awards banquet six years ago?"

Rachael looked down again, feeling sick inside. She'd gambled on Jason's faulty memory and had lost. "No. I just didn't think you'd remember."

"Rachael, look at me." She did. "That brief meeting six years ago notwithstanding, how long did you think you could keep your talent hidden?"

"Talent is a relative term, Mr. Burgess, and whether I have it or not, whether I *hide* it or not, is my decision."

Jason gave her a short, acknowledging nod. "True enough. But can you be happy not using the gift you were born with and worked so hard to perfect?"

"I've already told you I am," she answered quietly, unable to hold his gaze any longer.

"I don't believe that, Rachael. I think you're dying inside a little more each day—not just as an artist, but as a person."

Rachael's jaw stiffened. "I'm not going back to Lamplight Comics," she said tonelessly, telling herself his astute observation was untrue. It was only possible to die once, and she had already experienced a death of the soul so complete that she had nothing more to lose.

"Then if you won't go back to *Ravenmede*, work for me, Rachael. Be my assistant. I need you. I need your creativity, your talent. And I think you need this job as much as it needs you." He reached out and touched her clasped hands. They were as cold as ice. "You can't grieve like this forever."

His voice and his hand were so incredibly gentle that Rachael felt the hard-won shield of numbness surrounding her grief begin to crumble. Fighting to maintain rigid control, she withdrew her hand from his, closed the book in front of her and stood. Her dark eyes captured his lighter, searching ones that threatened to destroy her with their innate kindness.

Her voice was shaking when she spoke. "I'm sure you mean well, Mr. Burgess, but you can't possibly understand. I just want to do the job I have now and be left alone. When my husband died, the entity known as Garrett Mallory died as well. I'd appreciate it if you wouldn't tell anyone otherwise. And I'd appreciate it even more if you'd accept that fact yourself." She plucked her purse off the back of her chair. "Excuse me. I have to get back to work."

She moved from behind the table and headed briskly toward the door. Irritated with his own clumsiness, Jason turned to watch her go. Again today she was wearing dark, somber colors—the colors of mourning. Her delicate body moved with a natural poise and grace, but her squared-off shoulders were not an indication of good posture. Rather they were a rigid frame that kept her fragile body upright, as though she feared that otherwise she might fold in on herself and collapse. Somehow Jason didn't think that was true. Rachael was holding herself in—and holding herself back—because she didn't realize that she had the strength to move forward. She was alone and afraid, just as he had been after Molly's death. As he still was some days.

An emotion far stronger than pity swept through Jason and forced him to his feet. Without giving a thought to what else he might say, he hurried out of the cafeteria to catch up with the woman who touched him so deeply.

"Rachael?" The doors swung shut behind him and the outer hall was already empty. He turned right, then left, then right again, and finally caught sight of her in the long hall outside the sound department.

"Rachael!" He quickened his pace, noting that his quarry reluctantly slowed hers. "Rachael, please. Let me talk to you."

She stopped completely, and Jason moved to her side. She turned to face him, and for a moment there was a kind of agony written on her lovely face that was almost more than Jason could bear. "*Please*... leave me alone," she begged in her always-soft voice.

Jason reached past her and pushed open the door to a vacant sound studio. He gestured for her to precede him, and Rachael's brows drew together in a grimace as she tried to make up her mind whether or not to obey.

"Rachael, please. Just hear me out."

She wavered with indecision for just a moment, then entered the darkened studio. Behind her Jason switched on a light, illuminating the soundproof, acoustically perfect room that housed an array of musicians' chairs, microphones, and beyond one glassed-in wall, a darkened control booth. Closing the door behind him, Jason moved into the room, but made no attempt to close in on Rachael. She needed space and he was already invading too much of it. "I'm sorry about what happened in the cafeteria, Rachael. I'm afraid I handled the whole situation badly."

She refused to look at him and faced the dark control booth, instead. "Why is it so important to you that I take this job?"

"It's not the job that's important, Rachael, it's you."

She did face him then. "Me? You don't even know me!"

Jason nodded. "In one way, you're absolutely right. I don't know you—I only know about you." He took a step toward her. "But in another way, I know you very well. Fourteen years ago I lost my wife to cancer, and I wanted to die, too. Long before I recognized you, I recognized that same deep well of sorrow in your eyes."

Rachael glanced back at the darkened glass wall. "If you understand that much, you must know why I want to be left alone."

He stepped toward her and suddenly Rachael could see his reflection in the glass. "For how long?"

She looked at him questioningly. "How long?"

"That's right." He returned her mirrored gaze. "How long are you going to allow yourself to suffer like this? How long are you going to insulate yourself from the world?" Gently he touched her shoulders and turned her toward him. Her dark, fathomless eyes stared up into his. "Rachael, the pain doesn't go away until you confront it, acknowledge it and let it heal. You need help, and—"

His hands were still resting lightly on her arms, and the weight of his words and his touch were suddenly too much for her. Two years of keeping her emotions in balance went out the window, and she threw her arms up, angrily pushing his hands aside. "Don't tell me what I need! Who made you God omnipotent?"

Jason refused to recoil from her attack. "I'm not God, Rachael, but I do understand—"

"You understand nothing! *Nothing!*" Once the floodgate had opened, Rachael was unable to force it closed. "I don't need your job, or your help. I just want to be left alone! Try to *understand* that!"

"You've been left alone too long, Rachael," Jason insisted, feeling his own composure slipping a little. "You've cut yourself off from friends and family, you're doing a job that's so far beneath you it's criminal and you're only doing it so that you can keep busy—keep your mind occupied so that you won't have to think about everything you've lost."

A memory struggled to the surface of Rachael's consciousness, the memory of a tiny face with huge hazel eyes and a mop of sandy curls. With all her might, Rachael forced the memory away, because no matter what, she was not going to break down and cry in front of Jason Burgess. Instead, she threw up the strongest barrier she could erect against him and shouted, "What's wrong with that? What's wrong with keeping busy?"

"Nothing, Rachael. It's important to keep busy, but eventually you've got to start challenging yourself again, start creating again. You can't stagnate like this forever. Eventually you've got to face the fact that your husband is dead and you're still alive."

Rachael drew back as though he'd slapped her. She took in a sharp breath, and all color drained from her face. "I face that fact every day of my life," she told him coldly.

"I know that, Rachael. Believe me, I know it. I face it, too," he said gently, aching for her. "But you won't always hurt as badly as you do right now. You won't always feel this alone if you'll just let the wounds heal."

"What do you know about my wounds?" she demanded, fighting an intense pain that battered at her. The memories she tried to keep locked away came rushing up again, and suddenly escape was the only thing she could think of. She had to escape the memories, the pain and Jason Burgess, most of all, before he completely destroyed what little was left of the protective wall she'd spent two years building.

"Rachael—" He reached out to her, but Rachael hurled herself away from him.

"No! Just leave me alone! You have no right to do this to me. I don't even know you!"

"I just want to help."

"Then leave me alone!" she shouted, rushing for the door. "Just leave me alone!" The slamming door punctuated her panicked request.

Frustration carried Jason several steps toward the door in pursuit, but he stopped short of his goal. *You can't help someone who doesn't want help, or who isn't ready to be helped,* he reminded himself. All he'd succeeded in doing was causing her more pain.

The part of Jason that was deeply touched by Rachael demanded that he go after her, but another part demanded that he leave her in peace. Rachael's problems were her own, and he couldn't solve them, no matter how much he might want to.

Saddened, remorseful and more than a little depressed, Jason returned to his office.

"WHAT THE HELL did you say to her?" Robb Weston charged into Jason's office without knocking and planted himself righteously in front of his employer's desk.

Jason looked up, startled by the attack, but it wasn't necessary to ask Robb to whom he was referring. "I was trying to convince her to take the job she refused yesterday," he replied irritably. He was still chastising himself for the abominable way he'd handled the situation, and he was in no mood to have someone else chastise him, too.

"Well, you did a fine job," Robb drawled sarcastically.

Jason's frown darkened. "I figured that out for myself, thank you."

"Good. Maybe you can figure out how to get her back!"

"Back?"

"She's gone! She came back late from the cafeteria where I saw the two of you together, marched into my office as pale as a ghost and told me she was quittin'. Effective immediately."

"Damn!" The force of the curse brought Jason to his feet and he began pacing furiously. It hadn't occurred to him that Rachael might actually quit her job because of what he'd said.

"You know, Jason, I was prepared to lose Rachael if it meant promoting her, but this is something entirely different! What happened between the two of you, anyway?"

Jason ran one hand down his face and tugged at his beard in frustration. He wanted very much to confide in his old friend, but to do so would be betraying Rachael's secret, and he'd done enough damage already. "It's personal, Robb," he said finally.

"Personal? How the hell could it be personal? You didn't even know the woman two days ago!"

"Well, I know her now," Jason replied cryptically.

Something about the defeated slump in Jason's shoulders took the wind out of Robb's sails. He clamped down hard on his irritation and sat in the chair at the front of Jason's desk. "You wanna explain that remark?" he asked.

Jason turned to him and shook his head. "I'm sorry, Robb. I can't. Let's just say I screwed up and leave it at that."

"That may be fine for you, but I'm now missing one damned good artist. If she's not going to be your assistant, I'd like her back."

"Then tell her that."

"Me? I'm not the one who got her so riled up that she felt she had to quit!"

"Which is exactly the reason I can't talk to her," Jason shot back. When he'd returned to his office, Jason had been determined not to interfere in Rachael's life any further. He intended to abide by that decision.

"So you're just going to let her go."

"It's her life," he said tersely, recalling Rachael's insistence on that point. And she was right. He shouldn't have stuck his nose in where it didn't belong.

Robb looked at his boss curiously. He was silent for a long moment before he finally told him, "This isn't like you, Jason. You're one of the kindest, most caring men it's ever been my good fortune to know—even if you are a Yankee." He grinned. "You can be a tough son-of-a-gun when the situation calls for it, but I can't imagine any situation that would call for you bein' tough on sweet little Rachael Hubbard. I can't believe you came down on her just 'cause she refused a promotion."

Jason shook his head and sat in the leather swivel chair behind his desk. "Robb...it's very complicated. If I say any more than that I'll be betraying a confidence, and I know you wouldn't want me to do that."

Robb nodded sagely. "You're right, I wouldn't. But I don't want that woman to quit, either. Do you?"

"No, of course not. But I don't know what I can do about it at this point."

"How about apologizing?" Robb suggested. "I've never known that to do any harm, and it might do some good."

Jason leaned back in his chair, making a steeple out of his clasped hands. "I'll think about it, Robb."

Rachael's distraught, pain-filled face floated before his mind's eye, and he wondered if he had a right to say anything more to her.

No right, he decided. *No right at all.* But that probably wouldn't stop him.

CHAPTER SIX

IT WAS MID-AFTERNOON by the time Rachael let herself into her apartment. She'd managed the long bus ride home with her shoulders squared and her emotions held rigidly in check, but once she closed the door to her sanctuary a fit of uncontrollable trembling overwhelmed her. She barely managed to make it to the sofa before her legs gave way beneath her. She tried to control her anger, but the memory of the things Jason had said to her made it impossible.

You have to face the fact that your husband is dead and you're still alive.

Damn him! Didn't he think she knew that? Did he really believe she could forget it? For eleven years, Sander Hubbard had been the center of Rachael's life. His love and patience had taken a shy, awkward college co-ed and made her someone special—his partner, his wife and ultimately, the mother of his child. Sander's ambition and drive had made *Ravenmede* and Garrett Mallory famous, and he'd taken Rachael along on that ride to success. More importantly, though, he'd given her a home and the stability she'd never known as a child. And he'd given her Micah. Sweet, innocent little Micah.

As always the thought of her son brought tears to Rachael's eyes and pain slicing through her heart. These past two and a half years since the accident, Rachael had gradually learned to cope with a life without Sander, but she still hadn't found a way to cope with the loss of her son. Did

Jason really think that work was a cure for that kind of pain?

As far as Rachael was concerned, there was no cure. Other wives had lost husbands; other mothers had lost their only child. Many had lost both in one tragic moment, and they suffered no more or less than Rachael. But grief was a private thing, and pain was uniquely personal. No one could share it. No one could take it away. Rachael was coping as best she could, by keeping her life simple, focusing on a daily routine and clamping down on her emotions in order to keep the pain at a controllable level. What right did Jason Burgess have to tell her she was going about it all wrong?

The right of someone who just wanted to help you, Rachael, a quiet voice seemed to say to her. *He was just trying to be kind. He was concerned.*

Strangely it was the memory of Jason's kindness that finally helped Rachael bring her anger under control. He had meant well. He hadn't intended to hurt her or upset the delicate balance of her life. He was a nice man who'd thought he was doing the right thing, she finally decided.

Calming herself, pushing away the pain that always accompanied memories of her lost son, Rachael tried to recapture the blessed numbness that made her life bearable. It settled around, enveloping her, but for the first time she discovered that the numbness was not comforting. For just a moment it felt alien—a thing to be rejected, not welcomed like an old friend.

Was that Jason's fault, too? she wondered. Because of his interference, she'd been forced to quit her job, and now her life would be turned upside down again. It was no longer possible for her to go on as she had before, because the unvaried routine that kept her life in order no longer existed.

Two years earlier, escaping the Vermont home she'd shared with Sander and Micah and starting over had been necessary to preserve her sanity. But the thought of going through all that a second time paralyzed her with fear. At one time, learning to get around in a new city and coping with the demands of a new job had been a welcome distraction. Doing the same thing now was terrifying. Without the stabilizing routine that allowed her to function, her life would descend into emotional chaos again.

But there was no way to avoid it. She couldn't go back to Animators, not after quitting today. Pride had nothing to do with it. By now Jason had told Robb Weston who she was, Robb had told one or two of her co-workers, and word was spreading like wildfire that the reclusive Rachael Hubbard had once been part of the Garrett Mallory team. And once word had spread through the Animators studio it would miraculously skip over to Disney and on to Hanna-Barbera and all the other animation houses in Southern California.

Anywhere Rachael went to look for a new job, the truth would precede her or follow shortly thereafter, and the whispers would start. Pitying looks would abound. Questions would be asked. And worst of all someone like Jason Burgess would start pressuring her to "live up to her potential." Someone else would feel sorry for her and try to coax her out of her shell. But Rachael didn't want to be coaxed. She just wanted to be left alone.

Which meant that moving on was inevitable. She'd have to leave L.A. and find a new line of work. The idea of moving was so devastating that Rachael found it easier to concentrate on the problem of finding another job. The comic book industry was out, of course. She'd known that two years ago and it still held true. Animation and comics were distantly related cousins in the world of fantasy art, and Rachael had felt safe that her real name and face would be unfamiliar in the animation end of the industry. In comic book publishing, however, too many people had worked with Rachael and Sander Hubbard in the early days before

Ravenmede became successful. Too many people knew that the names Rachael and Sander Hubbard equalled Garrett Mallory. Too many old friends and acquaintances would start pressuring her. She couldn't go back to comics, and she couldn't stay in animation. But what did that leave?

There was print work, of course. Science fiction book covers and fantasy magazines could keep her busy, but that was all done on a free-lance basis. She would have to set her own routine and make the contacts necessary to find each new assignment. Self-employment was not a nine-to-five job.

But on the other hand, a second voice argued, *it would be challenging.* She would be doing more than copying someone else's work. She would be doing original paintings, she could use her creative—

Damn! Rachael bolted upright on the sofa, cursing Jason once again. This was all his fault! She'd rejected that damnable job of his because she hadn't wanted to be challenged; she no longer had the heart or the vision to be creative. Yet because of Jason she was thinking how nice it would be to create again, and not just as a means of filling the incredible void in her life.

Muttering a soft expletive, Rachael went into the kitchen, splashed cold water on her face and poured a glass of iced tea. She returned to the living room and commanded herself to concentrate on the problem of moving.

Again a feeling of panic assaulted her, but she fought it down the way she had as a child every time her father came to her and said, "Get packed, girls. I've been transferred again." For someone as painfully shy as Rachael, moving had been torture. If her mother had been alive, or if her sister had been closer to her own age, the move from one Air Force base to another might have been easier. But her mother had died when Rachael was two, and her sister, May, was seven years older. May had been able to take much of the responsibility for packing and organizing the moves, but she hadn't been able to help shy little Rachael make friends or adjust to her frightening new surroundings. Consequently Rachael had grown up with an overpowering need for stability.

But she had moved before—many times—and it hadn't killed her. She could do the same now if necessary. It would be hard to leave her comfortable little apartment, but she could do it if she had to. She reviewed the steps she'd have to take if she planned to relocate, and it finally occurred to her that it really wouldn't be hard at all. Leaving L.A. would be as simple as packing her clothes. One extra box would be enough to hold all her personal items—if an incomplete set of china, a few glasses and some pots and pans could be called personal. It might take a second box to hold her sketch pads and the few framed photographs that sat on her nightstand, but other than that there was nothing in the furnished apartment that was hers to take. Moving would be simple.

Too simple, she reflected sadly. She could pick up and leave tonight and no one would even realize she was gone. There were no friends at work to say goodbye to, no neighbors to bid a tearful farewell. Rachael Hubbard could disappear from the face of the earth, and not a soul in Southern California would know the difference.

That's not sad, Rachael thought suddenly. *That's pathetic. That's...sick.* For the first time in two years, Rachael forced herself to take a long look at her life. What she discovered was nothing to be proud of. She'd worked so hard at just getting by from day to day that she had dropped out of life completely.

Because she was such a shy person by nature, Rachael had never been fond of socializing. Back in Vermont, she'd had many casual acquaintances, but few close friends. Sander had understood her shyness and had never tried to force her to be more outgoing. He'd been content, as she was, to concentrate on the work they shared and on raising their son. Sander had understood Rachael's deep-seated fear of change and had kept their lives secure and stable. But his sudden, tragic death had changed all that.

At first Rachael hadn't known how she could possibly survive without him. Aside from the emotional balance he'd given her life, there were also practical considerations she'd never had to contend with. Sander had taken care of the monthly bills, handled minor household repairs and kept their car serviced—all the routine things that fell under the antiquated category of "men's work." And when *Ravenmede*'s popularity had finally made them wealthy, Sander had hired an excellent business manager to handle their investments.

During their entire marriage, Sander had been the one to direct their careers, make all the right contacts, meet all the right people. Sander had been dynamic and driven to succeed. Rachael had been too shy to push ahead toward success. Together they had made a perfect team.

As husband and wife they had been good together, as well. No magazine would have named them "Liberated Couple of the Eighties," but Rachael believed that her marriage was sound. She was old-fashioned enough to believe that a woman's place was in the home, and she considered herself fortunate that her career allowed her to work and be a full-time wife and mother, too. She had the best of all possible worlds—until a freakish spring snowstorm claimed the lives of her husband and son.

Rachael's sister had taken time away from her job and family to be with Rachael during those first hideous weeks. Eventually, though, May had been forced to return to her family in Connecticut. She'd begged Rachael to come with her, but Rachael hadn't been able to leave just then. Sander and Micah were gone, but leaving the home they'd shared would have been admitting that the most important part of her life was over. Staying in the house had been a way of keeping them with her, keeping them alive.

For months Rachael rattled around alone in the huge barn that they had converted into a home. Spring slipped into summer, summer into fall, and with the change of the seasons, Rachael slipped deeper and deeper into a dark depression. When autumn began giving way to winter, Rachael reached her lowest point. Entire weeks passed when she thought of nothing but taking her own life.

On the day she awakened to a light, early snowfall Rachael knew she could stand no more. In utter despair, she had taken a blade from Sander's razor and raised it to her wrist.

Even now Rachael still didn't know what had stopped her. It hadn't been fear of the blood, or even fear of death, because there was no life left in her. Something inside her had simply said, "No."

With a strength she hadn't known she possessed, Rachael had thrown the razor blade into the trash and started packing. Within two days her summer clothes were in suitcases, a moving company was boxing up the entire contents of her home for storage, and the house itself had been placed on the market with a local real estate broker.

Thinking only of escaping the house and the coming New England winter, she had bought a plane ticket to Los Angeles, found a job, located an apartment, and settled quickly into a safe, secure routine that demanded nothing from her. And for the next two years, she had simply existed.

It had never occurred to Rachael that changing her life as completely, abruptly and efficiently as she had was a major feat of strength in itself—just as making the decision to live had taken more courage than the simple solution of suicide. In Rachael's mind, she had simply done what she had to do in order to survive.

But is surviving enough? she asked herself now as the late-afternoon sun began casting long shadows through her apartment.

You're still alive, Jason had said. *You can't stagnate like this forever.*

A sudden flood of memories brought tears to Rachael's eyes, and she wrapped her arms around herself to hold in the pain. With crystal clarity she could see her sunny office in the loft of the old barn. She saw the slanted drafting tables and the color layouts of *Ravenmede* on the board in front of her. She saw herself at the table working frantically to meet a critical deadline, while opposite her, Sander was laying out the story for the next month's edition. She saw her hand creating the familiar fantasy world of Ravenmede Castle, but more than that, she could actually *feel* the joy she'd derived from her creation. She'd been alive then, not just because of her husband and son, but because her work had fulfilled a part of her that was separate from the devoted mother who cherished her family.

For two and a half years Rachael had grieved for the loss of that family, not realizing that her deep mourning had cost her something that was intrinsic to everything she was. Through the lonely, painful years of her childhood, the need to draw, to paint, had made her life bearable. The worlds she created on paper and canvas had been her lifeline. Even now she filled sketch pads with drawing after drawing. But that was simply busy work with no focus. She was accomplishing nothing. For a few short years, Sander's ambition had given her art a purpose and a life of its own.

Rachael knew she could never go back to *Ravenmede*—that was Sander's dream, Sander's vision. Without his ideas to guide her she could never live up to the demanding standards he had set. But as she sat in the dark and wept,

Rachael finally realized that somehow, some way, she was going to have to find a dream of her own and make it happen, or her creative soul would eventually wither away to nothing. For Rachael, that would be a death as certain as her husband's and son's.

When Jason Burgess had offered her a chance to create again, Rachael had told herself that there was no creativity left in her. Perhaps a year ago, even six months ago, that had been true. But even as she cried, Rachael could feel the need to create blossom within her again. The need may have been repressed along with all her other emotions these past years, but it hadn't died as she'd once thought. It was still there, clamoring to be set free.

For nearly an hour Rachael wept as though her heart was breaking, but when the tears finally ran their course, something inside her was, at long last, reborn.

CHAPTER SEVEN

FORTY-EIGHT . . . forty-nine . . . fifty. Jason finished his last lap down the length of the pool, grabbed onto the side and allowed himself to float there for a moment. He wasn't particularly tired or out of breath; it simply felt good to drift in the warm, disembodying water. His mind hadn't been focused on his daily workout this evening, so he hadn't pushed for speed or forced himself into a few additional laps. Today he'd just have to settle for the minimum daily requirement.

A childhood bout with rheumatic fever had done some minor damage to his heart, and since then, daily exercise was an unbreakable ritual. The once-sickly kid was now as healthy as a horse, and his doctor swore Jason would live to be a hundred—if he kept to his exercises, diet and medication. Jason liked living well enough to conform unfailingly to the doctor's prescription. Rain or shine, winter or summer, he swam at least fifty laps. And then he floated for a few minutes.

As they had all day, thoughts of Rachael Hubbard surfaced and Jason chastised himself for putting off the inevitable. He had to go see her. His conscience wouldn't allow anything less. He'd pushed her so far today that she'd actually quit her job, and Robb, quite rightly, wanted her back. Jason wanted her back, too, but he seriously doubted that his wishes would carry any weight with Rachael. He would go to her and apologize anyway, though. He'd promise to leave her alone if only she'd come back. He'd tell her that he'd had no right to pry into her background, and if she was content as a breakdowner, then that's where she could stay until she was ready to move up or on.

That's what he'd say to her, Jason had decided. The only problem was that despite his remorse for the things he'd said, Jason didn't want to retract them. He hated to see such a phenomenal artist waste her talent, nor did it sit well that such a beautiful, loving woman was wasting her life. But as Rachael had pointed out, he wasn't God; he couldn't tell her what to do.

Which brought him back full circle to the necessity of apologizing. As he'd left work for the day, Jason's mixed feelings had convinced him to postpone a visit to Rachael's apartment until later in the evening. He procured her address from her personnel file, then drove home, telling himself he was only delaying because he had to take his daily swim. Even at the time, he'd known it was a flimsy excuse, and now it seemed even more so. The pool wouldn't have dried up just because he delayed his laps an hour or two.

Knowing he couldn't put it off any longer, Jason grabbed on to the side of the pool and hoisted his body out of the water. Just as he reached for a towel, the intercom from his security system buzzed, and he padded across the deck toward it with some surprise. He wasn't expecting a guest, and Lorna had her own key to the electronic gate that guarded his privacy.

He punched a button on the unit, which also served as an outdoor telephone. "Yes?"

"Mr. Burgess?"

It was a woman's voice, but the intercom distorted it too much to make it recognizable. "This is Jason Burgess. May I help you?"

There was a slight pause. "Mr. Burgess...this is Rachael Hubbard. If it's not inconvenient I'd like to speak with you."

For just a moment Jason was struck speechless. Rachael was *here*? Jason viewed life as one continuous string of surprises, and this definitely confirmed the accuracy of his philosophy. It took a second for him to recover. "Of course, Rachael. Please come on up." He hit the switch that opened the electronic gate and punched a second switch that would flood the front lawn with light. Returning quickly to the pool, he snatched up his short, white terry cloth bathrobe and slipped into his rubber-soled sandals, then headed around the side of the house toward the driveway, in time to see Rachael emerging from a taxi. She spoke to the driver, then looked up, her eyes widening in surprise as she caught sight of Jason in his thigh-length robe. The security gate was closing, and Jason guessed that Rachael had instructed the driver to wait for her.

"Hello, Rachael."

Even in the artificial light, Jason could see an embarrassed blush creep up her cheeks. "I've obviously come at a bad time."

"Not at all," he hurried to assure her. "I just finished a few laps in the pool. This is not the way I normally greet guests, I promise you." He grinned, but doubted that she noticed since her gaze was directed downward. Coming here hadn't been easy for her, he realized.

"It won't take a moment—"

"Don't be silly, Rachael. Please come on into the house where we can talk. Actually you saved me a trip."

She did look at him then, and Jason flashed her another reassuring smile. "Saved you a trip?"

He nodded. "I was just about to come over to your apartment."

"Dressed like that?" she asked with a shy smile. The unexpected, almost tentative attempt at humor caught Jason completely off guard and he laughed. It was a deep, rich, distinctly masculine sound that Rachael found herself automatically responding to.

"No, I don't go calling like this, either."

Just a few yards away the cab driver was watching them with a look of bored indifference, and Jason gestured toward him. "Why don't we send the cab on, Rachael? I'll be happy to take you home after we've had a chance to talk."

Rachael forced herself to concentrate on the reason she was here rather than on his wonderfully kind smile. "That's not necessary, Mr. Burgess. I couldn't put you out. This won't take long—"

"It wouldn't be putting me out, Rachael, since I was going to your place anyway. And I think we'd both be more relaxed without a meter timing our conversation." She seemed to hesitate for a moment, and Jason added, "If you'd be more comfortable taking a taxi home we can always call one later."

Rachael hesitated a moment longer, then nodded. "All right."

Jason automatically reached for his wallet, intending to do the gentlemanly thing and pay for her cab, but his swim trunks were conspicuously lacking a pocket. Rachael seemed not to notice the train of his thoughts, though. She returned to the cabby, paid him, and Jason stepped forward to tell him he'd open the security gate once he returned to the house.

With Rachael at his side, Jason retraced his route around to the back of the house. On the deck, he released the gate and turned off the floodlights, then gestured toward the doors that led into the family room. Rachael preceded him nervously, pausing just inside the door until he joined her.

"Please make yourself comfortable, Rachael," he said invitingly. "I'm going to get out of this soggy suit. I'll be back in just a minute."

Unable to stop herself, Rachael watched him leave, fascinated by the easy, athletic way he moved. He was a big man—tall, broad-shouldered and thick-thighed—and yet he had a masculine grace that was very pleasing. All the time they'd spent standing uncomfortably on the driveway, the artist in Rachael had been aware of the perfect conformation of his bone structure and musculature. But as she watched him leave the room, his belted terry robe barely skimming his thighs, the woman in Rachael responded to his incredible masculinity, which would have been almost frightening to her had it not been tempered with such a gentle personality.

When he was gone, she remembered too clearly the fine dusting of damp golden hair that had been visible in the open V of his robe, and the way his beard had glistened with tiny drops of moisture from his dip in the pool. Jason Burgess was an extremely attractive man.

Disturbed by the direction of her thoughts, Rachael turned her complete attention to Jason's home. The informal family room, with its vast square footage and high vaulted ceilings took a moment to survey, but Rachael found it a delightful surprise. Despite its size, the room seemed warm and cozy. It had a personal, lived-in look that was enormously appealing. Sander had insisted that the converted barn in Vermont be a showplace. She'd accomplished that with a rustic country decor that would have made for a wonderful layout in *House Beautiful* magazine. This room, on the other hand, would never be featured anywhere, but it was all the more inviting for its lack of organization.

By far the most surprising aspect of it was the crowded but uncluttered corner that had obviously been designated as a child's play area. Pint-sized bookcases housed a collection of cuddly dolls and stuffed toys as well as books. There was a good-sized play table and a lovely Victorian dollhouse. Fascinated, Rachael found herself drawn toward the pretty, obviously feminine corner.

Does Jason have a daughter? she wondered. He'd said his wife died fourteen years ago, but he could have remarried. And he was certainly young enough to start a family with his second wife.

Rachael couldn't help but wonder how long it had taken him to put his life back together and risk loving someone again. For herself, she couldn't envision that time ever arriving, and yet something that felt suspiciously like hope wormed its way into her heart. Maybe that was something else Jason had given her. Yesterday she'd had nothing; today she was beginning to feel hope for the future.

"That's my granddaughter's inner sanctum."

Startled, Rachael turned to find Jason just inside the arched entrance to the hallway. He had changed into a pair of comfortable-looking stone-washed jeans and a short-sleeved sweatshirt. His hair was still a little damp, and its curly disarray made him look much younger than his years. So much younger, in fact, that Rachael couldn't help asking, "You have a *granddaughter*?"

He nodded and smiled proudly. "Emily. She's three."

Three. Micah had been three. In Rachael's memory he would never grow any older. That disturbing, sad thought temporarily diverted Rachael from her purpose and she quickly clamped down on her feelings. Her histrionics that afternoon had already embarrassed her in front of this man. She wouldn't damage his opinion of her any further by bursting into tears for no apparent reason.

"Can I get you something to drink?"

"No, thank you." Rachael stepped away from his granddaughter's play corner. "As I said before, I don't want to take up much of your time. It was presumptuous of me to just drop by like this, but your phone number is unlisted. All

I had was your address on the flyer about the company picnic that was included in our last pay envelope."

"Rachael, there's no need for you to justify how or why you came. I'm just glad you're here."

"I had to come to apologize," she explained. "I'm sure Robb Weston told you that I quit today."

Jason nodded. "Yes, he told me."

Uncomfortable, Rachael turned away and wandered toward the patio doors, only vaguely aware of the pool and lawn beyond the windows. "That was unforgivably unprofessional of me."

"I don't think so, not when you take into consideration the way I pushed you—the things I said. They weren't particularly professional, either. You had every right to be angry with me for sticking my nose in where it didn't belong."

"I was angry at first," she admitted, turning to find that he'd quietly joined her at the window. Though their height difference wasn't *that* great, he seemed to tower over her, but Rachael found nothing threatening about his size or his nearness. "You made me do some serious thinking, though. That's the other reason I came here—to thank you for trying to help."

Standing closer to her than he had since she arrived, Jason finally saw the unmistakable evidence of the tears she'd shed because of him. Her eyes were still faintly red and puffy, and she seemed so vulnerable that he wanted to wrap her in his arms and take away all the pain that was reflected in her soft brown eyes. Something about that desire bothered Jason, and it took a moment to realize that what he was experiencing was more than compassion. It wasn't an employer-employee feeling, or a friend-to-friend emotion, or even his empathy with her pain. This was a man-woman thing—an attraction and a wanting that had no place in any conversation with Rachael Hubbard.

Clearing his throat nervously, Jason put a little distance between them. "Why don't we have a seat?"

"I really can't stay—"

"Please, Rachael, don't run off just yet. You've said your piece, but I still have a couple of things I need to say to you."

Rachael remembered then that Jason had said he'd planned to visit her tonight. Was he going to put more pressure on her? she wondered. She'd known that was a possibility when she'd come here, but facing him now she wasn't quite sure how to handle it. Still, she discovered that she wanted to hear him out.

"All right." She moved to the chair Jason indicated and he sat on the sofa across from her.

"Robb was very upset because you quit, Rachael. And naturally, so was I. He told me he'd been prepared to lose you to a promotion, but he wasn't willing to give you up for no reason."

Rachael looked down at the plush tan carpeting. "So you told him why I quit."

Jason looked at her with some surprise. "No, of course not. I pried into your personal life when it was actually none of my business, but I would never reveal what I discovered, Rachael. That's your decision to make, not mine."

"Then Robb doesn't know that—" she faltered over the words "—doesn't know who I was?"

"No." Jason leaned forward, his elbows resting on his knees, his hands clasped in front of him. "Don't answer this if you don't want to, Rachael, but... why is it so important to you that no one know you were one of the creators of *Ravenmede*?"

She averted her gaze and it was a moment before she made up her mind to answer him. She couldn't have said why; talking to Jason just seemed right. Maybe she just needed to talk, period, and anyone would have done, but it was Jason who had asked the question. It was Jason who was so kind and seemed so willing to listen.

"My husband's name was Sanderson *Garrett* Hubbard. My maiden name was Rachael *Mallory*. When we became partners we chose the pseudonym Garrett Mallory because it was a part of both of us, just as the work was." She looked at Jason, wondering if he could understand. Somehow she knew he would. "When Sander died, Garrett Mallory ceased to exist."

"But your talent didn't die, Rachael."

"No. It's still there, but..."

"But it's hard to create when everything inside you feels withered and empty."

He did understand. "Yes."

"Oh, Rachael..." Jason desperately wanted to reach out and take her hands into his, but he knew instinctively that that was a bad idea. He would have to settle for what he hoped would be comforting words. "That emptiness you're feeling isn't always so overpowering. Little by little that wasteland starts to grow green again, like the coming of spring."

"I hope you're right, Jason," she said, not realizing how very easy it had been to cross that ambiguous line between thinking of him as Mr. Burgess, her former employer, and Jason, a newfound friend. "The things you said to me this afternoon made me realize that I've spent too long in a barren winter. You made me acknowledge that a part of me still needs to create."

He smiled gently, but inside he was turning cartwheels. Maybe he hadn't messed things up quite as badly as he'd thought. "I can't tell you how happy that makes me, Rachael. After my wife, Molly, died, I did very much the same thing you've done. I shut down all systems and just... functioned for a while. I had been doing children's books at the time, and I just didn't have the heart to continue."

"But you did, eventually."

Jason shook his head. "Not exactly. I never wrote another children's book, anyway."

"Why not?" Rachael asked, genuinely interested in something outside herself for the first time in a long time. It felt good. She knew that several of Jason's books were now classics, but it had never occurred to her to wonder why he'd stopped writing them.

Jason sighed expressively. "For pretty much the same reason you feel you can't go back to *Ravenmede*," he explained. "Molly never did any of the actual work on my books, but she was the inspiration for everything I did. Every time I tried to put an idea on paper, Molly's memory haunted me, and it was too painful to continue."

"So you went into animation instead."

"Yes. I'd been considering it for a long time, and had even been approached by a producer who wanted to turn the *Castle of Dreams* trilogy into an animated feature. I convinced him I had a better idea, one that would appeal to both children and adults, and presto, a new career was born."

"You found a new vision . . . a new dream," Rachael said softly.

Jason smiled. In some ways, he and Rachael understood each other very well. "Exactly."

"I have to do that, too, Jason. You made me see that today," she told him honestly, then glanced away from his soft, penetrating gaze. She stood and wandered to the windows. "I don't know what it will be yet, but maybe someday I'll figure it out."

Realizing what a tremendously positive admission she was making, Jason rose and moved to her. "Rachael, I don't mean to press or to push—I've done enough of that already—but if you'd like a chance to do something different, something challenging while you're searching for that new dream, I'd be proud to share mine with you. I still want you to be my assistant."

Rachael turned to him and found a measure of strength in his encouraging, hopeful smile. "The job is still open?"

"You spoiled me. I just couldn't reconcile myself to hiring less than the best."

"Jason, I'm not the best—"

"Don't kid yourself, Rachael, and don't sell yourself short," he said a trifle sternly. "You may not be the best, but I've never seen better. Will you take the job?"

That wasn't the reason Rachael had come to see him. In fact, accepting his job offer had been the farthest thing from her mind. She'd only meant to apologize for her unprofessional behavior and to thank Jason for shaking her out of the cocoon she'd been hiding in. But the job—that was something she hadn't considered because she'd been convinced that Jason had revealed her identity.

Knowing that he'd kept her secret shed a new light on the situation, though, and Rachael was suddenly confronted with a difficult question. Was she really ready to change her life, or had she merely been giving lip service to the desire to change?

Being Jason's assistant wouldn't be easy. The hard work would be welcome and challenging, just what she wanted and needed, but it would also mean greater contact with people. She wouldn't be working in a vacuum; she would be required to attend meetings and story conferences. She would be expected to contribute.

The thought was frightening. Only she and Sander knew just how inept she was when it came to having fresh, original ideas. Through the years that she and Sander had worked together, he'd shown her time and time again why her suggestions on their *Ravenmede* stories were unworkable. And because rejection and criticism had always been so hard for her to accept, Rachael had ultimately given up making suggestions. She had simply drawn the stories as Sander wrote them, and had been happy doing so.

But she couldn't tell Jason that and make him understand. He would say she was selling herself short again. Maybe the only way to convince him that she wasn't good assistant material was to prove it by taking the job. To do so would be risking rejection, but it was time she took some risks. She was thirty-three years old and she'd lost everything in her life that was important to her. When it came right down to the bottom line, what else did she have left to lose?

Jason watched as she wrestled with her decision. She had come so far today. Was it asking too much of her to take this one extra, gigantic step?

He was on the verge of offering her more time when Rachael finally looked up at him. "I'd like to give it a try."

Jason offered her one of his gentle, encouraging smiles. "I don't think you'll regret that decision, Rachael."

"I hope you don't either, Jason."

CHAPTER EIGHT

THE NEXT MORNING, promptly at nine, Rachael presented herself to Jason's secretary and was escorted to a small office adjacent to the Bull Pen. Jason's office was two doors down the hall. The large conference room was in between, and the three rooms were conveniently interconnected so that Jason could reach his assistant without having to go out to the corridor.

The secretary, who introduced herself as Gretchen Wixted, took Rachael on a guided tour through the wing devoted to Jason's directorial staff. She pointed out the offices of the assistant director, who helped Jason coordinate all aspects of the film's production; the layout lab, where each scene of the movie was broken down into its individual camera shots; the sound supervisor's office; the background supervisor's office; and several more. The directorial wing was one big "think tank." If work ground to a halt here, the entire company would fold like a house of cards.

"Jason will introduce you to the staff later," Gretchen told Rachael once they had completed their tour and returned to Rachael's new office. "He's over at Ink and Paint right now, working out some color problems that came up yesterday, but he asked me to give you this." Gretchen handed Rachael a leather-bound copy of the script for *The Quest*. "It's a wonderful story, but I expect you'll be sick of it by the time we get finished."

Rachael tried to return the woman's friendly smile. "I hope not."

Gretchen laughed as she stepped to the door. "Well, if you aren't, you'll be the only one. Listen, if you have any problems or need anything at all, just let me know. One of my many jobs is to requisition the supplies, and Jason likes everyone to have whatever they need." She pointed to the slanted lightboard that sat next to the window. "It's fully equipped, but if you'd prefer anything different—even a different brand of pencils—I'll be happy to get them for you."

Rachael glanced at the setup, unable to imagine what else she might need. Everything seemed in perfect order. "I'm sure this will be fine."

Gretchen's smile broadened as she recalled the way Jason's previous assistant had waltzed into this office and imperiously demanded that everything be changed. If she would just unbend a little, Rachael Hubbard would be a pleasant relief from the obnoxious Paul Harris.

As an afterthought, Gretchen showed Rachael how to use the telephone intercom to reach her, Jason, or any of the department heads, and once that demonstration was out of the way, she left.

Alone, Rachael wandered around inspecting the lightboard more fully and checking the contents of a small oak credenza. It contained paper and other supplies, and again, Rachael could find nothing missing. The room's walls were bare, but she could see nails and faint rectangles where paintings or prints had once hung. Apparently her predecessor had been invited to decorate the office to his own taste and had taken his decor with him when he left.

The naked walls reminded Rachael of her own bare apartment, and she vowed that over the coming weekend she would make an effort to find some prints that would give the office a little more character. And while she was at it, she might even look for a few for her apartment, as well.

Moving to the windows that took up most of one wall, Rachael glanced out into the courtyard for the first time. The Animators complex was hexagonal in shape. It was like a huge wheel with the courtyard as its hub. The purpose of the design was to provide as much natural lighting to as many offices as possible. Rachael's section in the animation department had been located on the outer side of the hexagon, so she'd had little opportunity to enjoy the pastoral beauty of the courtyard.

Trees and shrubs hid much of the complex opposite her window, but she had an excellent view of the fountain that was surrounded by a rainbow-splash of flowers and tropical plants. The whole courtyard was something of a jumbled jungle, and it was the nonformal appearance of the area that lent it an air of pastoral serenity. It was beautiful to look at, and she suspected it would be just as lovely to walk through.

But she wasn't getting paid to stare out the window, Rachael reminded herself, picking up the copy of *The Quest* Gretchen had left her. She settled behind the desk that sat perpendicular to the windows and began reading.

Having had little previous experience with movie scripts, she found the format distracting at first, but before long she became engrossed in the tale. There were bursts of humor here and there—enough to keep an audience entertained—yet there was also a message. *The Quest* was the story of one man's triumph over adversity, but it was also a story about honor and about finding the hidden strength that resides deep in all human souls.

Captivated, Rachael finished the manuscript quickly and was satisfied that she understood at least part of what Jason hoped to accomplish with the film. Having familiarized herself with the plot and characters, she then went back to the beginning and started reading again, this time paying even greater attention to the descriptions of settings and the myriad details outlined in the script. She read slowly this time, visualizing each scene, attempting to break it down into its individual components. She might not have the ability to add fresh, new ideas to Jason's creation, but she could learn the script by heart so that she would be ready to perform whatever assignment he gave her.

She was only halfway through the second reading when a knock at her door drew her attention from the manuscript.

"Come in."

The door opened and Jason stuck his head in. "Good morning."

He was smiling at her like the cat that swallowed the canary, and Rachael found it impossible not to return the smile. "Good morning . . . boss."

Jason's grin broadened and he stepped into the room. "I like the sound of that—especially coming from you. Welcome aboard."

"Thank you. Gretchen showed me around and tried to make me feel at home."

"Tried? You mean she didn't succeed?"

He was still smiling, so Rachael realized he was teasing her, but she had never had the knack for smooth banter and witty repartee. Her eyes slid away from his. "She was very kind, but . . . well, I guess it will take me a while to get used to everything."

Jason sat on the corner of her desk and told her seriously, "No one expects you to set the world on fire today, Rachael. Or tomorrow, for that matter. Take your time."

"But time is the one thing you don't have, Jason," she reminded him. "You need an assistant who can pick up the ball and run with it now, not tomorrow or the next day. If you want to change your mind—"

"I'm not going to change my mind. I know you can do the job, and deep down you know you can do it, too, or you wouldn't have accepted it."

Rachael nodded slightly and glanced down at the script. "I do want to try."

Jason smiled again. "Then that's all that's necessary. The rest will come automatically once you get a grasp of what needs to be done."

"I hope so."

"I *know* so."

Something about his ultra-positive outlook struck Rachael as funny and she grinned. "Have you ever been wrong about anything?"

Jason laughed, wondering if Rachael realized what a big step she'd just taken. She was teasing him, and she was also giving him an unforced, genuine smile. It was a little shy, still, but it was a smile nonetheless... and it was beautiful. "As a matter of fact, I was wrong once. I think it was April—no, May of 1971."

"Was it a big mistake?"

"Terrible," he said with mock gravity. "I wore one brown sock and one black sock to a formal dinner dance. I was so embarrassed I couldn't show my face in public for weeks."

Rachael grinned and glanced down, wishing she could think of a clever response that would keep their banter going. She'd forgotten how good it felt to smile like this, and she wanted the moment to continue. But she couldn't think of anything to say, and after a moment, Jason changed the subject.

"Oh, well, enough of my true confessions. How are you coming with the script?"

Rachael picked up the manuscript. "It's wonderful."

"I'm glad you think so. There are a lot of rough spots to be worked out, but it will eventually come together."

"What would you like me to work on first?"

"Just familiarize yourself with the story," he told her. "That's your main priority at the moment. It will help me considerably if you know the story backward and forward—in your sleep."

Rachael nodded in understanding. "What about the character sheets? If I could take a look at the ones that are finished it would help me get a better idea of the texture you're looking for. My section of the animation department was responsible for Phoenix only, so I have no concept of what any of the other characters are supposed to look like."

"Done," he declared succinctly, pleased that she'd thought of that herself. "And we'll go over to Backgrounds sometime today so that you can take a look at what they're working on."

"Good."

"Oh, and one other thing—" He paused for a moment. "I hate to throw you to the lions like this, but every Tuesday and Thursday—as in today—we have a story conference with all the directorial staff in the Bull Pen right after lunch. It should give you a really good idea of where we are and what I need you to work on."

A staff meeting with Jason's upper echelon. This was what Rachael had dreaded most about her new job. She was uncomfortable in groups, yet she was going to have to fit in with this one. She would have to work hand in hand with Jason's dynamic creative staff. They would contribute their ideas and their talents, and they would expect her to do the same. The thought terrified her.

Some of her trepidation must have shown on her face, because Jason's voice took on a wonderfully soothing quality. "Rachael..." Something about his tone forced her to look up at him, directly into his eyes. Though she couldn't have said why, what she found there took most of her fears away. "You'll do fine. All that's expected of you today is just to listen and learn."

"I'm a good listener," she said, making an attempt at a smile.

"I know," Jason answered, wishing he could tell her all the other wonderful qualities she possessed. She was soft and sweet and gentle—almost too gentle for the world she lived in. She was strong, but she had no tough, protective outer shell to shield her from life's cruel bumps and bruises.

Again Jason was overwhelmed by the urge to be her protector, to be her shield against the world. It was a dangerous urge, not just because he had no right to feel that way, but because protecting anyone in that manner was wrong. Rachael's late husband had probably shielded or sheltered her, and because he had done so, his death had nearly destroyed the very thing he was trying to protect.

Rachael had to learn to survive, not just *in* this world, but *with* it, as well.

Resisting the urge to become her self-appointed guardian, Jason instead took on the more appropriate role of patient employer. As he had suggested earlier, they left Rachael's office and headed across the compound to the Background department where Rachael had a chance to study the paintings that would form the basic backdrop for each scene of the movie. Many elements of each background painting would require animation—the rustle of leaves through trees, sparkling sunlight reflecting off a lake, or the rolling clouds of a thunderstorm—but the basic paintings would give her the feel of the few scenes that had already been designed.

With Jason always at her side, Rachael was introduced to various members of the Background department, many of whom she'd seen on the grounds or in the cafeteria, but had never had the opportunity or the inclination to speak to. Now, though, she forced herself to greet them all. Jason expected it of her, and not only that, as his assistant, she would need to know these people. She would have to learn who did what, and who was capable of doing whatever job needed to be done. When Jason had explained the job to her in the Bull Pen on Tuesday, Rachael had known there was more to it than simply drawing what he told her to draw. To be an effective assistant, she was going to have to learn as much as she could about the way Animators operated.

After Rachael had thoroughly studied the backgrounds, Jason escorted her back to her office, then left her alone with the stack of model sheets he'd had Gretchen locate.

While Jason went back to the Ink and Paint department to check on the problems he'd been trying to iron out earlier, Rachael studied the model sheets that showed *The Quest*'s characters in various costumes and poses. She worked back and forth between the sheets and the manuscript, making a few rough sketches of her own, until she was satisfied that she could accurately draw the characters in any pose or situation Jason might suggest.

She became so engrossed in her work that she hardly noticed the passage of time, and she was quite surprised when Jason stuck his head into her office and informed her that it was time for lunch.

"Already?" She looked up at him with a dazed expression Jason recognized. It was the same one he got whenever he was traveling back in time to one of his mythical kingdoms.

He smiled and glanced at his watch. "Actually it's about ten minutes past already. Come on—we'd better head down to the cafeteria now if we're going to eat lunch and make it back to the Bull Pen for that one o'clock meeting."

The invitation flustered Rachael. She hadn't expected that she'd be invited to dine with the boss, and she wondered if it was mandatory that she do so. "I, uh, brought my lunch today," she told him. "I thought I'd just eat in here so I can keep on working."

"And have everyone accuse me of chaining my new assistant to her desk?" He grinned. "Are you trying to ruin my reputation as the best boss in the world, and a prince of a guy, to boot?"

Rachael couldn't keep from smiling at his infectious good humor, but that didn't change the fact that she didn't want to go with him to the cafeteria. She was completely inadequate in social situations, informal though this one would be; but more than that, she needed all the time she could get to prepare for the staff meeting that would commence in less than an hour. Jason had promised that no one there would be judging her, but Rachael knew otherwise. Every person in the room would be looking curiously at Jason's new assistant, wondering what it was that had made him choose her over who-knew-how-many other candidates.

Intentionally or not, they would all be waiting to see if Jason had chosen wisely. The very thought of it was enough to make Rachael regret her decision to take on this job.

And then she looked at Jason. His encouraging smile and wonderfully kind eyes reminded her that she had made a conscious decision to get on with her life, and some instinct told her this was the way to do it.

But she still didn't feel up to the pressure of having lunch with him. "I am truly sorry if your reputation will suffer because of me, but I still think I need to stay here and work."

Jason opened his mouth to protest, then shut it quickly. He was at it again, trying to play protector when only a couple of hours ago he'd sworn he wouldn't fall into that trap. Rachael was a big girl. She'd been going to the cafeteria here for two years, and she'd probably been eating lunch for most of her life. She was perfectly capable of doing so today without his help.

He sighed heavily, pretending to be crushed. "All right, have it your way, but if I don't get a present from the staff on Boss's Day, it'll be on your head. See you at one."

He left and Rachael went back to studying the script with every good intention of eating her lunch while she did so. Somehow, though, she never got around to it. Before she was even aware that any time had passed, the sounds of voices and laughter from the room next door brought her out of Jason's mythical fantasy and into the real world. She checked her watch and discovered it was, indeed, time to brave the den of lions.

Quickly gathering up the manuscript, several sharpened pencils and a pad of paper, she moved to the Bull Pen door and took a deep breath as panic attacked her. She wasn't ready for this. She had taken on too much. She should never have let Jason Burgess's kind eyes and warm smile convince her to take this job.

There was a brief knock at the door, and Rachael realized she must have made some sound, because it opened and there was Jason, smiling.

"Are you ready to meet the gang?" he asked.

"I suppose so," she answered.

Jason saw the apprehension in her wide, dark eyes, and something inside him melted. Unable to stop himself, he reached out and tenderly stroked her pale cheek. "You're going to do fine, Rachael."

Her eyes grew even wider, but she didn't draw away from his light, gentle touch. "That's a big comfort coming from a man who once wore mismatched socks to a dinner dance," she said softly. Jason threw back his head, laughing with surprise and delight, and this time it was Rachael who melted. The sound made her happy, which was quite something considering she'd been convinced she'd never feel that way again. . . .

CHAPTER NINE

"EVERYBODY—I'd like you to meet my new assistant, Rachael Hubbard." Jason got everyone's attention with the announcement, and as Rachael expected, seven pairs of eyes immediately focused on her. She did have to admit, though, that they were seven friendly pairs. Everyone smiled and offered a greeting as Jason introduced them all individually, and Rachael shook every hand held out to her. Robb Weston, of course, needed no introduction, but Rachael did her best to memorize the names and faces of the others.

"Robb's told us a lot of good things about you, Rachael," Dan Eisenberg, the background supervisor said with an encouraging smile. "Welcome aboard."

"Thank you," Rachael replied in her quiet voice. "I hope I'll be able to live up to the faith Mr. Weston and Mr. Burgess have both shown in me."

"We only use first names in here, honey," Deanna Hedges, the character stylist, told her wryly as she carried a huge mug of coffee from the coffee maker to the oval table. "If you show Jason too much respect he starts acting like he owns the joint."

A couple of the men laughed as they took their seats, and Jason guided Rachael around to the head of the table and gestured toward the chair next to his. "What is this, Dee, Pick on the Boss Day? I finally find an assistant who shows me the reverence I so richly deserve and you want to go and spoil it."

"Don't worry about it, Jason," Todd Frasier, the layout chief, quipped. "You should know by now that we're all devoted to seeing that you get *exactly* what you deserve."

As he sat, Jason eyed Frasier with mock suspicion. "Why does that not make me feel all warm and fuzzy inside?"

"Maybe it's because you're a little too fuzzy on the outside," Robb drawled, scratching his own chin to clarify his reference to the beard on Jason's.

Rachael took her seat as the lighthearted banter continued. This was obviously a group of professionals who had worked together for a long time and had enjoyed the relationship. A feeling of easygoing camaraderie pervaded the room, and Rachael wondered how she would ever learn to fit in with this friendly, garrulous group.

Jason allowed the teasing to continue a few minutes longer as his staff settled around the table, but when they were all finally in their seats, he called the meeting to order.

Tuesday's meeting had been brief because Jason had been interviewing prospective assistants, so they had a lot of ground to make up today. All the supervisors presented him with packets of drawings that needed his approval, and he glanced through them quickly, approving some and setting others aside for further study after the meeting. Deanna's set of model sheets were passed around the table, and everyone was invited to critique them. Some passed with flying colors, but a few were deemed unacceptable for one reason or another.

Deanna made copious notes so that she could keep track of the changes she would have to make before submitting the drawings again, and Rachael marveled at the way the young woman took the criticism. Artistically all of the drawings were very good, but it didn't seem to faze her in the least that her work was being picked to pieces.

"This one is great," Todd said, indicating a drawing of Phoenix in a flowing golden cape. He held the color sketch up to the group and everyone murmured agreement. Rachael was seated to his left, and he passed the sketch on to her. She held it out to Jason, but he didn't reach for it.

"What do you think of it, Rachael?" he asked.

Her hand trembling ever so slightly, Rachael looked at the drawing again, acutely aware that everyone's attention had shifted to her. She didn't feel qualified to register an opinion yet, but Jason had asked, and she had to answer.

"Is this the cloak Phoenix is wearing when he enters the netherworld?"

"Yes," Jason confirmed. "It's the one Zahara gave him for protection."

"And we all know the oh-so-lovely Queen Zahara is not to be trusted," Robb interjected. "It goes up in flames shortly after he enters the fire pit."

Rachael nodded, appreciating their attempt to clarify the story and characters for her. More than anything, though, she was grateful for the time she'd had to study the script. "It's a beautiful costume. I can visualize the way it will flow around Phoenix when he moves...."

"But...?" Deanna said with a smile that encouraged Rachael to say what she really thought.

"But...well...I wonder about the color. I gathered from the script that the fire and flames of the netherworld will be depicted mostly in golds, yellows and reds. A gold cape..."

Jason saw where she was leading and picked up her train of thought. "A golden cape won't exactly stand out against the background of the fire."

"That's a good point," the background supervisor said appreciatively. "We're going to need some contrast."

"White, maybe?" Deanna suggested, looking to Jason.

"Rachael?" Jason threw the ball back in Rachael's court. He could tell she was scared to death, but she was doing great so far, and he felt it was important to prove to her that she could contribute. And, too, he really wanted to hear her opinion.

Rachael knew exactly what Jason was doing, and she privately acknowledged his right to put her on the spot. She'd come this far, she might as well go all the way. "I thought maybe silver might work. It would contrast with the fire, but as Phoenix travels deeper into the netherworld it would also pick up and reflect the colors around him."

"That's perfect!" Jason exclaimed, envisioning the dramatic moment when the cape would burst into flames. "When Zahara gives him the cape it's a nice, shiny, cool silver, but when he passes through the gates of hell it begins changing, until finally it's as red-gold as the fire around him."

Everyone was instantly enthused by the idea. "Aside from being visually dramatic, the gradual transition from silver to gold could also help reinforce Zahara's treachery in the minds of the audience," Robb pointed out.

Deanna laughed. "I take it I need to redo this sketch in silver." She reached for the rejected drawing.

"Definitely," Jason told her. "Do it in silver, and then get together with Dan on the netherworld backgrounds to see if you can capture some of the color changes the cape will undergo."

"The netherworld backgrounds are very rough, Jason," Dan reminded him. "We still haven't fleshed out the exact sequence of events once Phoenix enters."

Jason glanced at the nearly empty storyboards behind him. The netherworld scene came near the end of the movie, but it was such a complicated, critical segment that he estimated it would take a full year just to get it right. That meant they had to begin giving it top priority now. "How well I know," he said ruefully. "Don't worry about it. Rachael and I will hit that hard next week. In the meantime, let's back up to scene seven and see if we can't come up with some ideas for the banquet scene at Zahara's fortress."

Script pages rustled as everyone turned to the scene in question, and in a matter of minutes Rachael was dizzy from the rapid-fire exchanges taking place around her. The script merely stated "Phoenix enters the Great Hall and is introduced to Zahara's court," but it was not nearly as simple as that. Every staff member at the table had a different concept of how the scene should be depicted, and Rachael knew she was way out of her league. These people had been studying the script for months, and they'd known for days that this particular scene would be under discussion. She could barely keep up with the flow of the conversation, let alone voice an opinion—not that she had one.

"No, the size of the Great Hall will have more impact if we start that segment with a long shot from the lower entryway," Dan argued, taking issue with something Todd had said. "We need to see the room from Phoenix's point of view first."

"But it would also be effective from Zahara's perspective—from the throne looking across the Great Hall toward Phoenix, who's dwarfed by the arched entry," Lloyd Pope, the assistant director insisted, supporting Todd's idea.

"Personally," Deanna interjected, "I'd like to see the scene from Adana's point of view. She's hiding up in one of those lovely minarets, looking down at the whole scene. From her POV she can see her captor, Zahara, and Phoenix—the man she's loved since childhood."

Jason nodded at the idea. "That has possibilities," he said, and they went on, heatedly discussing the pros and cons of the three alternatives.

Recalling the background sketches she'd seen of the Great Hall, Rachael did what she'd been hired to do. Visualizing the hall from the three perspectives suggested, she quickly drew a rough sketch of each one. The others were so engrossed in their argument that no one noticed what she was doing until she laid the three drawings side-by-side in front of her.

When Todd glanced down for a moment and saw the drawings Rachael had just laid out, he exclaimed, "Wow! This is fantastic. Look at these!" He quickly shifted the drawings to the middle of the table, and the others rose, jockeying for the best position to view them.

"That's great!" Dan exclaimed, picking up the drawing of the Great Hall from Phoenix's point of view. "See what I mean about how well this shows the majesty of the room? This is wonderful, Rachael."

The others chorused their agreement, then began using Rachael's drawings to illustrate their various viewpoints. The argument grew more heated as bigger and better ideas were expressed, and Jason leaned back in his chair, letting the chaos roll on around him.

This was the part of his work he loved most. He'd chosen his staff carefully for just this purpose. They all had consistently good ideas, and they argued them with such gusto that the net result was an influx of even better ideas, better ways of doing things. Yet they argued completely without ego or rancor. He'd never known any member of this group to leave the Bull Pen resentful or carrying a grudge because his or her idea had been thoroughly trounced on.

Of course, he reflected, that hadn't been entirely true when Paul Harris had been part of the conclave. Paul's point of view had been the *only* point of view, and if the entire group hadn't agreed with him he'd left the meeting in a royal snit. Naturally that disruptive attitude hadn't emerged overnight, but now Jason saw that he should have dismissed the young man much sooner. His staff was back to normal again, and he liked it that way.

And what about Rachael, he wondered, watching her as she rapidly completed another sketch implementing a suggestion Deanna had made. She didn't say much, and Jason suspected that she would never be as vocal as the others, but already she was becoming a part of the group by her incredible artistic talent. That was the one area in which she had no fears about her ability to perform well, it seemed. On the surface she was modest, but deep down she knew she was good or she never would have displayed those first sketches so readily.

Forcing his thoughts away from Rachael and back to the story conference, Jason settled the argument. "Actually I think the best way to do it is start with a shot of Phoenix being escorted by Zahara's guards down a long corridor. He turns at the archway of the Great Hall and the entire expanse stretches out in front of him, with Zahara on her throne in the center of the shot." He stood, taking Rachael's drawings to the storyboard and arranging them in the sequence he liked best.

Todd still had reservations about that particular order of shots, but Jason had made a decision and that was the way it would be done. They moved on, discussing the scene, shot by shot, and Rachael continued to draw rough sketches of each idea proposed. Several were rejected, but most of them went up on the storyboard, and by the time the meeting was finished, everyone agreed that they had accomplished an amazing amount of work—thanks to Rachael's quick, adaptable hand.

Based on the day's work, Jason handed down assignments to all the supervisors—Deanna would do costume sketches for Zahara and members of her court, Robb's department would begin rough animation sketches of Phoenix's short trip down the corridor and into the Great Hall, Dan would finalize the background paintings for the Hall, and so on. Just that one short scene would require weeks of painstaking work, but now that everyone knew the direction they were to take, the work could commence in earnest.

"Any questions?" Jason asked when he was satisfied everyone knew what they should be doing. No one responded, so he went on. "Okay, next Tuesday we'll concentrate on Adana's entrance into the Great Hall. Give it some thought between now and then, and we'll see what we come up with."

"Speaking of Adana..." Deanna said cryptically, leaving the sentence hanging, and the other supervisors chuckled as they turned expectantly toward Jason.

Rachael knew this must be some sort of inside joke, but she had questions of her own about the mysterious princess. Moistening her lips nervously, she looked up at Jason who was standing next to her. "Excuse me, Jason, but... what does Adana look like? I didn't find any model sheets of her in the pile you gave me this morning."

The question brought a burst of laughter, and Rachael's face flushed with color.

"Yes, Jason, what does Adana look like?" Todd asked with a smirk.

"Yeah, we'd all kinda like to know the answer to that one, boss," Lloyd said.

"All right, all right! You've made your point," Jason snapped with feigned irritation. He gave Rachael a sheepish grin. "The reason there are no character sheets on Adana is because I haven't come up with a design for her. She has eluded me at every turn."

"Do you think you'll come up with something soon?" Deanna asked.

"I'm trying, folks, believe me." Jason shook his head, frustrated. "Nothing I put on paper works, and I can't figure out why. I've *never* had this much trouble conceptualizing a character before."

The room erupted with laughter, and Rachael looked around, startled by the boisterous, mocking mirth.

"Is that right?" Robb drawled, still chuckling. "Jason, old boy, I got a news flash for you. You have this very same problem every single time we start a film. And usually, it's with the same character."

Deanna rose, gathering up her sketches. "Robb's right, Jason. You have this mental block when it comes to creating your heroines." She grinned at him. "Wonder why that is?"

"Maybe you need a flesh-and-blood heroine in your life to inspire you," Lloyd suggested with a teasing smirk.

Rachael held her breath and darted a glance at Jason. Last night he'd told her that his late wife, Molly, had once been his inspiration, and in light of that confession, Rachael didn't think Lloyd's joke was too funny. But Jason only laughed with his friends, apparently unaffected by the reference. He threw out a quick quip that warned everyone to mind their own love lives and not his, and the meeting broke up.

Rachael started gathering her own things as the others filed out, but Jason placed a light hand on her shoulder to stop her. "Hang around for a minute, Rachael. There are a couple of things we need to go over."

She nodded, and Jason flagged Dan down for a brief conference. They talked for a moment, then Dan started for the door. He stopped just short of his objective and turned back. "Rachael! Great work today. It's good to have you aboard."

"Thanks." She watched him leave, then turned her attention to Jason who was standing just inside the door watching her.

"He's right, you know. You did great work today."

"I'm glad you think so."

Jason grinned. "You think so, too. Come on, admit it. You know you did a good job."

Embarrassed, Rachael went back to gathering up her belongings. "It was...nerve-racking—" she looked at him, unable to stop a smile from spreading "—but it was exciting, too."

There was a hint of an impish sparkle about her that Jason had never seen before, and as he looked into her soft, shining eyes, his mouth went as dry as parchment. His heart slammed smack into his rib cage, and he had to turn away quickly to keep Rachael from seeing his surprising reaction to what was really nothing but a shy, pretty smile.

"That's us, we're an exciting bunch—a real thrill a minute," he babbled, moving toward the storyboard they'd worked on today. He wanted to turn back to her and soak up more of her newfound effervescence, but what he was feeling was beyond his immediate comprehension, so he didn't dare. Instead he forced himself to concentrate on business.

"Thanks to you, we accomplished more in one session than we have in a long time," he told her.

Rachael found it hard to understand how that was possible, but she was undeniably pleased by Jason's praise. He was at the storyboard with his back to her as he numbered the sketches she'd done. "Do you want me to formalize those drawings?" she asked when he started taking them down and carefully stacking them in numerical order.

Jason nodded and placed the drawings in front of her. "Yes, we'll need them cleaned up, and of course they'll have to be transferred down to four-by-six sheets rather than these nine-by-twelve. Also, they'll need some minor changes. Here...and here..." He bent over beside her, pointing out the slight variations he wanted her to make. He'd gone no further than the third sketch when he realized his mistake. Rachael's head was bent and her short, sable hair hid none of her long, slender neck. The skin on it looked soft and smooth and eminently kissable, and her hair smelled of sunshine and flowers—just tantalizing enough to make a man want to bury his lips in it.

Mentally Jason cursed himself roundly and tried to concentrate on the instructions he was giving his assistant. *That's right, Jason—assistant,* he reminded himself. *This is your assistant, not your lady-friend or your lover—just a shy, talented, fragile, grief-stricken assistant who would probably go flying out the door permanently if she knew what you were thinking, so get a grip!*

Edging away from her ever so slightly, Jason forced himself to focus on the work to be done and not the woman who was going to do it. He finished as quickly as possible, and was greatly relieved when he could finally put some distance between them.

"I'm going to be out of the office tomorrow, and probably most of Monday as well. Do you think you can have those sketches ready for next Tuesday's meeting?" he asked, shuffling the folders the supervisors had left with him.

Rachael looked at him in surprise. "Tuesday?"

"If you need more time, that's fine—"

"No, I don't need more time, Jason," she told him. "What I need are more assignments. I can probably have these finished before I leave today. But what should I work on after that?"

Jason laughed, delighted by her eagerness. "Sorry. I forgot how fast you are. I'm going to start calling you Quick Draw Hubbard."

She smiled at him shyly. "I've never had a nickname before."

"Really?" Jason said with surprise. "I've had several, but none that I'd care to have repeated. Do you like yours?"

Rachael glanced down. "Not particularly."

"Then I'll work on something else."

She looked up at him, her eyes dancing. "Don't put yourself to any trouble on my account."

"No trouble at all," he said, chuckling devilishly.

They looked at each other for a moment and some special, unspoken communication passed between them. Jason couldn't have said what it was, nor could Rachael, but they suddenly seemed a little closer than they had been a minute before.

Rachael was the first to break the wonderful, yet unsettling, eye contact. Picking up the bound script of *The Quest*, she asked, "You mentioned that we need to work on the netherworld sequence. Is there anything I can do on my own?"

Jason frowned, wondering what he should say. During the meeting when he'd said he and Rachael would work together on the netherworld scene he'd regretted the suggestion immediately. Phoenix's visit to the dark regions of hell was not going to be an easy segment of the movie to produce—especially for someone who was going through Rachael's own particular brand of hell. Due to the nature of the scene, he was a little worried that it might be too much for her to handle just yet.

"No, Rachael, I don't think so. I'll take care of that myself. Why don't you continue with the banquet scene."

"But without Adana—"

Jason groaned. "Right, right. We can't go any further into the banquet until I create a heroine. I'll get it done this weekend, I swear."

This time it was Rachael who frowned. "Jason, is there some reason you don't want me to work on the netherworld scene?"

It seemed to Rachael that her question made him uncomfortable, and she immediately regretted asking it. After all, if he didn't think she was qualified to work on that particular scene, it wasn't her place to question why.

"It's not that I don't *want* you to work on it, Rachael," he told her, his voice solemn. "But it's asking a lot of you. Maybe too much, too soon."

Part of Rachael wanted to let the subject drop, but she couldn't. "I don't understand what you mean."

Jason sat in the chair next to her. "Rachael... Phoenix's journey into the netherworld is one of the darkest, most emotionally revealing scenes I've ever attempted to do. He's convinced that Adana is dead and his life has no meaning without her. Everything he does is a reaction to his grief."

Rachael went still, suddenly feeling very cold inside. "Just as everything I do is a reaction to *my* grief, you mean."

"No, I—"

"Yes, Jason, that is what you mean. You don't want me working on that scene because you're afraid I can't handle it emotionally." She stood, trying to ignore the sudden trembling of her limbs. She was angry, and she didn't really understand why—she just knew that she was. "I should appreciate your concern for me, Jason, but I don't. My personal life has no bearing on my job, and if my emotions get in the way of my work, then I shouldn't be here."

Jason came to his feet slowly. He was sorry he'd upset Rachael, but more than that, he was amazed at this flash of temper she was displaying. He wouldn't have thought she had that kind of fire. "Nothing is so black and white, Rachael, and no one I know has ever been able to completely separate their personal lives from their jobs."

"But you need an *assistant*, not an emotional cripple—and obviously that's what you think I am."

"Of course I don't think that," he insisted hotly. "But you're going through one of the most horrible ordeals any person can ever suffer."

"So I deserve special consideration—the kid-glove treatment."

"You deserve an employer who understands that you're going through a rough time. That's not the *kid-glove* treatment, that's just simple human compassion. I'd like to believe that I'd show the same consideration to anyone."

Rachael knew he was right, and she knew she was overreacting, but that didn't change the fact that Jason Burgess pitied her—and pity was the one thing she couldn't tolerate. She forced herself to calm down and told him, "My personal life has to be separate from my job, Jason, or I won't be able to work for you. If there's something that needs to be done, you tell me what it is and I'll do it. I don't want to be coddled, and I especially don't want to be pitied."

Jason nodded, understanding, but he couldn't keep from issuing one last word on the subject. "There's a big difference between compassion and pity, Rachael. This netherworld scene—" he picked up the script "—this whole movie, in fact, is very personal. There's a lot of Molly and me in the romance between Phoenix and Adana, and there are a lot of my...emotions in the telling of how a man copes with losing the thing he holds most precious. It's taken me fourteen years to be able to put this story on paper, and even now it's so cloaked in drama and medieval fantasy that I doubt anyone who knows me would recognize it for what it is.

"But it's a story about loving and losing, Rachael. Phoenix is reunited with his lover in the end because my audiences want happy endings, but it's still a story about loss. And the netherworld scene most particularly is about the kind of hell people like you and me go through. Job or no job, I don't have the right to ask you to suffer more just for the purpose of getting a movie to the screen."

Rachael felt tears welling in her eyes, and the last of her anger dissipated. Jason's personal revelation touched her so deeply that she wanted to cry. "I'm sorry. I didn't realize..."

He smiled gently. "Don't feel sorry for me, Rachael. I don't want pity, either. I learned to cope with my loss of Molly a long time ago, or I never would have been able to write this script. I just didn't want you to be angry with me."

"I'm not," she said, looking at him in a new light—not as her employer, or as the artistic genius he was said to be, but as a man who had suffered a great deal and who cared a great deal more about others who were suffering. "Thank you for telling me what this story means to you."

"I told you because I knew you'd understand."

"I think I do." She looked down at the table, not to avoid his wonderfully kind eyes, but because she needed to look into herself. "On Tuesday when I saw that netherworld sketch in here it touched me personally, and I wanted to run away from what it represented." She looked at him again. "But when I took this job, I stopped running, Jason. Maybe I need to confront your netherworld so that I can better understand my own."

Jason took a deep breath, fighting an emotion he didn't dare acknowledge. He'd known Rachael had courage, but he hadn't known how much. He'd realized he was attracted to her, but he hadn't known the feeling could be this strong. "Then I'll expect to see some sketches from you on Tuesday."

"I'll have them ready."

She picked up her sketch pad and her banquet drawings, then left, quietly closing the door to her office behind her.

When he was alone, Jason sank into his chair at the head of the big, vacant table and wondered what the hell he was going to do, because falling in love with Rachael Hubbard would be the biggest mistake of his life.

He just wasn't sure how to keep from making it.

CHAPTER TEN

THE SKETCH PAD on his lap forgotten, Jason stared blankly at the sunlight shimmering off the surface of his pool. Useless drawings of Adana littered the patio table beside him, and for the moment, at least, he had given up all thoughts of getting any constructive work done. In fact, since the staff meeting two days ago, Jason had accomplished next to nothing because all he could think about was Rachael Hubbard.

You cannot be in love with a woman you've known for less than one week, he told himself for the hundredth time. *What you're feeling is empathy, compassion, or maybe even some of the pity she accused you of feeling, but you are* not *falling in love.* The notion was too absurd to even consider. Jason had always been sensitive to the feelings of others, so it was only natural that he would feel close to Rachael because they had so much in common—not just the loss of a spouse, but their mutual drive to create.

He also knew what it was to be shy and a little afraid of the world. As a child, he'd always been the outsider. Because he couldn't keep up with the other kids, he'd been left out of everything. Loneliness had sucked at him like a bottomless pool of quicksand. Molly had changed all that, with her zest for life, her insatiable curiosity and her limitless imagination. Even as a little girl, Molly O'Hurlehy never met a stranger; everyone she encountered was a friend.

It had taken years, but the sense of security she gave Jason had finally enabled him to reach outside his protective shell and welcome life rather than fear it.

He saw so much of himself in Rachael, he reasoned, that it was only logical to feel a great fondness for her. But that didn't mean that he was falling in love with her. Rachael was only now, two and a half years after her husband's death, coming to grips with her loss. It would be a long, long time before she was ready to risk loving someone else. Until then only a masochist or a martyr would think of her as anything but a friend, and Jason was neither.

So why couldn't he get her out of his head? Why, after forty-eight hours, was the scent of her hair still with him? Why, every time he closed his eyes, did he see her lovely, delicate face? Why did his heart turn over in his chest every time he thought about how magnificent it was to watch her learning to smile again? And why was it so important that he be the one who taught her?

Because you're falling in love, Jason, an obnoxious little voice in his head answered.

"Wrong, wrong, wrong," he muttered, flipping to a fresh page of his sketch pad.

"Daddy, are you talking to yourself?" Lorna eyed her father suspiciously as she climbed the two shallow steps that led to the pool's cedar deck.

Surprised by her unexpected appearance, Jason twisted around to see her. "Hi, honey. What brings you out to my neck of the woods?"

Exasperated, Lorna tossed her purse and a thick file folder onto the patio table and dropped into a chair. "Daddy, are you getting senile or something? I told you I'd be by to discuss the final arrangements for the company picnic, remember?"

He did remember now, and he was mightily embarrassed that he'd forgotten. "I'm sorry, honey, it completely slipped my mind. I've been a little preoccupied lately."

"Woman trouble?" she asked smugly.

The question startled Jason so much that he almost dropped the sketch pad. Lorna knew him very well, but he hadn't realized that he was so transparent she could read thoughts like the ones he'd been having about Rachael. "Why would you assume that?" he asked cautiously.

Lorna waved her hand across the drawings on the patio table. "Because you always have a problem getting your heroines right." She leafed through the discarded sketches. "What's this one's name?"

"Adana," he said with considerable relief. He had absolutely no desire to talk to his daughter about his recent obsession with a grieving widow.

"Oh, Daddy, this one's beautiful," she said, fingering a portrait-type drawing. She held it up, and Jason had to agree; the woman in the sketch was beautiful. The only problem was that it was a lovingly drawn picture of Rachael Hubbard. "She has such magnificent sad eyes."

"Yes, she does," Jason replied softly.

"So, is this going to be your Adana?"

"Not exactly," he told her. "But I may try for something similar."

Lorna put down the drawing and looked at her father wistfully. "We used to do this all the time, didn't we? You'd spend hours telling me the plot of your movie and drawing the characters for me.... You even asked for my opinions and took my advice." She looked out over the pool and when she spoke again, there was a tiny crack in her voice. "I miss those times, Daddy...."

Jason reached over and took his daughter's hand. "So do I, sweetheart. More than you can imagine."

Lorna's breath hitched in. "Oh, Daddy... why isn't life like the stories you used to write for me? What happened to all those happy endings?"

"The happy endings are still there, honey. I have to believe that. It's just the happily ever after that's elusive. Life is one long series of beginnings and endings, and it's up to us to make the most of them." He released her hand and touched her chin gently, turning her face to his. "Tell me what's wrong, Lorna. You've been unhappy for such a long time."

For just a split second Jason thought she was going to break down and confide in him as she had in the old days, but he was wrong. The moment passed and she plastered on a bright, false smile. "Don't be silly. I'm not unhappy. I just got a little sentimental there for a minute."

"Damn it, Lorna," Jason cursed softly, leaning back into his chair heavily.

"Daddy!"

"Honey, I want to help you, but I can't if you don't confide in me."

"There's nothing to confide!"

"Of course there is! Lorna, I'm not deaf, blind, or stupid. You and Cole are having problems—"

"No, we're not!"

Jason tried to quell his frustration. "Oh really? Then what were you and Cole fighting about when you came in last Tuesday night to pick up Emily?"

Lorna sighed heavily, realizing she'd opened a can of worms she'd been hoping to avoid. "It was a stupid argument, Daddy. I don't even remember what it was about. All couples fight, you know."

"Yes, Lorna, all couples fight, but not all of them make a career out of it."

"That's a horrible thing to say!"

"But it's true," he insisted. All week long, Jason had dreaded having to confront his daughter the same way he'd confronted Cole on Tuesday, but the subject was out in the open now, and he couldn't put if off any longer. "Honey, what you and Cole do with your lives is your business, but I saw something last week that made me so angry that—"

"This is about Emily, isn't it?" Lorna asked, cutting him off.

"That's right."

Lorna nodded. "Cole told me what you'd said to him, and it upset me, too. I had no idea Emily had heard us fighting." She reached over and patted her father's hand patronizingly. "It won't happen again, Daddy, I promise."

"Honey, you can't keep it from happening again unless you get to the root of your problems with Cole."

"We don't have any problems!" she insisted hotly.

Jason held up his hands as though to ward off his daughter's anger. "I give up. I surrender. End of discussion. When you're ready to talk, I'll be right here waiting."

"And when there's something to talk about, you'll be the first to know," she told him. "Now—" she opened the file folder she'd brought "—shall we get on with the picnic plans?"

"Sure," he said with a resigned sigh, unable to imagine why she couldn't confide in him. Maybe there really wasn't a problem. It could be that Lorna and Cole were one of those rare, unenviable couples whose relationship thrived on conflict—which wasn't a happy thought. If that was the way Lorna wanted to live, Jason could accept it, but he wasn't thrilled about the prospect of his impressionable, defenseless granddaughter growing up in an armed camp.

But there didn't seem to be anything he could do for the time being, so he turned his attention to the arrangements for the ninth annual Animators picnic.

As usual, Gretchen had everything so well organized that there was very little for Lorna to do once she decided to step in and "take over." Since the first year, Lorna had been his official hostess, and Jason suspected that she was far more interested in maintaining that position than actually helping organize the backyard barbecue. But he listened patiently as she described how the activities had been planned and how they would be executed.

A caterer specializing in old-fashioned Western shindigs would set up an open-pit barbecue, and provide enough food to feed an army. Clowns, magicians and Disney cartoon characters would keep the children entertained in a tent on the east lawn while the adults mingled, and later there would be family participation games followed by the Annual Animators Softball Fiasco.

If the picnics of previous years were any indication, it would be a fabulous day, one that would be remembered fondly until the next one rolled around.

"It sounds as though everything is well in hand," Jason commented when Lorna closed her file.

"Yes, it is. Daddy, you really ought to give Gretchen a raise. I could never have done any of this without her."

That was an understatement, considering Gretchen had done all the work. Jason had to smother a grin. "I'll keep that in mind."

"You do that."

"So, are we all finished?"

Lorna nodded and checked her watch. "Yes. I've got to get over to the Washburns' and pick up Emily."

"How are Vic and Becky?" Jason asked. Cole's parents were nice people, but he rarely had occasion to see them.

"Oh, they're fine. They wanted to keep Emily this afternoon, but they were adamant about me picking her up by five so they could get ready for some party they were attending tonight. Listen, Daddy, why don't you chuck all this—" she gestured toward the discarded sketches "—and come home with me tonight? I'll make us something special for dinner and we can play cards later."

She had a smile that was so bright and hopeful he hated to refuse her, but he had no choice. "I'm sorry, honey, I can't. I have tickets for a play that's opening at the Pavilion tonight."

"Who are you taking?"

"Belinda Matheson."

Lorna frowned. "I thought that thing between you and Belinda ended years ago."

Jason smiled indulgently. Lorna and Belinda had never really hit it off, but then, Jason's daughter had never really hit it off with any of the women her father had dated. "That *thing*, as you call it, did end a long time ago, but we're still good friends."

"Well, I hope that's all there is to it," Lorna said, taking a tone that was usually reserved for parents lecturing their children, not vice versa. "Belinda Matheson was never interested in anything but your money. I thought you'd figured that out."

Jason frowned because the accusation was not only untrue, but unfair. Belinda was a lovely lady with a sparkling sense of humor, and she'd inherited a multimillion dollar business from her father. "Actually, Lorna, what I've figured out," he said firmly, "is that one of these days you're going to have to reconcile yourself to the fact that I might remarry."

The comment rolled off his daughter like water off a duck's back. "Don't be silly, Daddy. You'll never find anyone you could love the way you loved Mother."

"Maybe not, but there are different kinds of love. Whether you believe it or not, your grumpy old father is just as entitled to finding happiness as anyone else."

That got Lorna's full attention and she leaned forward anxiously. "Daddy, are you unhappy?"

It was a good question, one Jason had thought about a lot in the past few years. "No, honey, I'm not *un*happy, but it does get pretty lonely around here sometimes—particularly since you flew the nest."

Lorna's head lowered thoughtfully, and she seemed to consider her next question carefully. "Are you trying to tell me that you're getting serious about someone? That you really are thinking of remarrying?"

"There's no one in my life right now, if that's what you mean. But I haven't ruled out the possibility, and neither should you."

"Okay!" She brightened considerably, said a hasty goodbye and left to go pick up her daughter. Jason wondered if her parting smile was genuine.

When he'd started casually dating again a year or so after Molly's death, Lorna had nearly come unglued. Jason had only been seeking companionship and a way to start living a normal life again, but Lorna had seen it as a betrayal of her mother. Jason had honestly understood how she felt; it had taken him a long time to overcome that same feeling. As years had passed and time began to heal the wounds, Lorna had become a little more tolerant of her father's casual dinner companions. Or maybe she'd just gotten better at concealing her animosity toward them—Jason wasn't sure which.

Knowing that his dating upset his daughter, who'd already lost so much, Jason tended to keep his relationships light so that Lorna wouldn't feel threatened. It hadn't been a problem for him thus far because remarrying wasn't something he'd ever considered.

But Lorna wasn't a child any longer—and Jason wasn't her security blanket. And though he hadn't given it much conscious thought until now, he suddenly realized that he was very serious about starting a new life, finding a new love.

An image of Rachael Hubbard popped into his mind, and Jason told himself sternly that there was absolutely no correlation.

THE MUSICAL, a road show with the original Broadway cast, was excellent, but as Jason exited the theater with Belinda Matheson on his arm he felt as though he'd just taken a severe beating.

"What's wrong, Jason, you look a little dazed," Belinda commented as they wove their way through the crowd.

"Sondheim always does that to me," he told her with a grin. "His lyrics are amazing, but they're so intricate I sometimes feel I need an interpreter to simplify them for me."

Belinda laughed. "They say when you get *old—*" she dragged the word out for effect "—the attention span is the first to go."

"What is this with my age today?" he asked with feigned irritation. "First Lorna accuses me of being senile and now this...." They reached the crowded walkway outside the theater and Jason handed his parking stub to one of the valets. "White Mercedes."

The valet, a harried young Chicano, looked at Jason as though he was from Mars. "Thanks man, that narrows it down a whole lot. In this crowd the only people who don't drive white Mercedes' are the ones who drive black ones," he joked as he went off to look for the car that matched the license plate number written on the parking stub.

Jason and Belinda exchanged amused looks and the petite blonde told him, "At least it wasn't a crack about your age."

"Thank heaven for small favors."

Belinda's gaze wandered through the crowd, casually looking for anyone she might know, but her voice held an odd note when she asked, "So how is Lorna these days?"

As far as Jason was concerned, that was the sixty-four-thousand-dollar question for which he had no answer. Under other circumstances he might have welcomed the chance to discuss his worries about his daughter, but he couldn't see getting into a heavy discussion in the middle of a chaotic sidewalk. "She's fine," he lied.

"And Emily?"

Jason positively beamed. "She's wonderful. I usually have her over at my place once a week, and it's not nearly enough. Sometimes I actually envy Lorna and Cole."

That got Belinda's undivided attention. "You sound as though you'd like to have another child of your own."

He considered her comment and realized it was true. He was only forty-one years old; that wasn't too late to start a family. "I suppose I would like that . . . someday."

"Do you have any candidates for Mother of the Year in mind?"

Jason looked at Belinda closely. There was a time, a few years ago, when he would have been able to read something more than casual interest in her question. Of all the women he had dated since Molly's death, Belinda was the only one he'd felt he might have been able to build a life with. Somewhere along the way, though, the intensity of their feelings for each other had dissipated and the moment had passed. Now there was no hope for herself in Belinda's question, just friendly curiosity.

"Not at the moment," he told her with a grin. "But I'm keeping an open mind." He changed the subject, inquiring after Belinda's fifteen-year-old son, and they were safely inside Jason's Mercedes by the time his date finished bemoaning her son's escapades as lead guitarist in a rock band.

It took over an hour to escape the traffic and get to Belinda's Bel Aire neighborhood. They chatted from one subject to another like old friends with a lot of catching up to do, and they were both laughing as Jason pulled up in Belinda's driveway. She waited patiently for him to open the car door for her, and they mounted the stairs to her porch with Belinda's hand tucked snugly in the crook of Jason's arm.

"I had a wonderful time, Jason," she told him fondly as she fumbled for her keys.

"So did I. We need to do this more often."

"You have my number."

"And you have mine," he reminded her.

"True. Would you like to come in for a nightcap?" she said invitingly.

Jason considered the question for a moment, then declined. "I don't think so—it's getting pretty late. Us old folks need lots of rest."

"Speak for yourself, wise guy." Smiling, Belinda placed one hand on Jason's shoulder and stretched up to meet his lips for a friendly good-night kiss. Jason placed his hands at her waist to steady her and pull her close as his mouth closed over hers. She smelled wonderful and felt even better as she pressed against him, and it was the most natural thing in the world for Jason to deepen the kiss.

A spark of passion flared between them, and what was supposed to have been a simple good-night kiss took on an entirely different meaning. Jason plied at her lips as their bodies strained to get closer, and he felt a piercing sting of arousal. Somewhere in the back of his mind, he realized it had been a long time since he'd been intimate with a woman, and he wondered if that could account for his misplaced attraction to Rachael Hubbard.

The thought worked its way to the front of his mind, and he broke away from Belinda with a groan when he realized that the desire he was experiencing wasn't for his old flame, but for his new assistant. The last thing in the world Jason would ever do was use one woman to assuage his need for another one.

Still keeping one hand on Jason's shoulder, Belinda settled back and tried to control the breathless, dizzy feeling she always had when this man touched her. They could have been so good together, but it hadn't worked out and she had long ago accepted the reality that it never would. The most she could ever have with Jason was a comfortable friendship. She'd learned to settle for that, but having him kiss her as though he couldn't get enough didn't help her state of mind.

But then, he hadn't been kissing *her*, Belinda reflected sadly, or he wouldn't have pulled away like that. Nor would he be looking at her with such guilt, now. Despite his disavowal earlier, there was a woman in Jason Burgess's life.

Swallowing her disappointment and keen feelings of rejection, Belinda captured Jason's eyes and managed a reassuring smile. "You wanna talk about her?"

Jason should have been surprised that Belinda had realized what had just happened to him, but he wasn't. She was a good friend and she understood. He wished he did. "No, I don't think so. I'm sorry."

"No harm done," she said wistfully. "Who is she?"

He glanced away, looking off into the dark night. "Someone you don't know," he admitted softly. "Someone I can't have."

Belinda placed a comforting hand on his arm. "Don't underestimate yourself, Jason. There aren't enough nice guys in this world to go around. Your lady-friend would be a fool to let you get away."

"Flatterer." He grinned at her, and for a moment Belinda was tempted to tell him it wasn't just flattery. She wanted to tell him that she'd give anything to be able to turn back the clock and recapture what they'd lost. She'd gotten over her love for Jason Burgess a long time ago, but it would be so easy to fall for him again. Of course she wasn't going to tell him that. Letting him know how much he meant to her would destroy their comfortable friendship, and she didn't want to risk having Jason embarrassed by her admission and pull away from her.

So instead she accepted a platonic kiss on the cheek and let herself into the house. From the living room window, she watched him return to his car, admiring the easy, graceful way he moved and the broad set of his shoulders. He was a devastatingly handsome man, but without a hint of conceit or cunning in him. He made a woman feel safe. He could make a woman feel wanted. Jason Burgess was a very special man.

For just a moment, Belinda felt a stab of envy for the woman who so obviously occupied his thoughts—and probably even his heart. But then she remembered Jason's possessive, willful daughter, Lorna, and her envy turned to pity.

Jason had dealt admirably with the ghost of his late, beloved wife, but his selfish daughter was another matter entirely. Any woman who wanted Jason Burgess was going to have to get past Lorna first.

Belinda hadn't been able to do it. She wondered if Jason's new ladylove would have better luck.

For Jason's sake, she hoped so.

CHAPTER ELEVEN

CAT SAT ON the ottoman, watching his mistress suspiciously. In his considered opinion She was behaving very strangely, even for a human. Yesterday he'd watched as She'd rearranged the furniture to make room for an annoying new table that was unlike any he'd ever seen. It sat in a sunny corner near the door to the patio, and had a stool in front of it that Cat had no objection to; it was nicely padded and comfortable to sit on. But the table really confounded him. It was so sharply slanted that he couldn't possibly jump on it, and if it wasn't useful to Cat, he didn't see any need for it to be in his apartment at all.

He'd been pleased last night when Her aberrant behavior had ended and She'd finally settled down with her pencil and paper as usual, but today She was at it once more. She was attaching things to the walls that, again, he could find no useful purpose for. They were different and moderately interesting to look at, but, like the slanted table, he had no idea what he was supposed to do with them.

The only additions to the apartment Cat found acceptable were the lovely green plants She'd acquired for him. Those would provide him countless hours of enjoyment scratching in the dirt, and in the case of an emergency, he could always use them for a between-meal snack. As for the rest of the stuff, She could just as well have saved Herself the trouble.

Rachael stepped back from the print she was hanging and glanced at Cat, wondering how he felt about the changes in the apartment. She'd caught him watching her several times when he thought she wasn't looking, but so far he hadn't given her any indication of whether or not he approved. If he didn't like the changes, well, that was just too bad, because Rachael was very pleased with what she'd done in only two days.

Yesterday she'd gone on a shopping spree unlike any she'd ever indulged in before. A trip to the art supply store she frequented had yielded a drafting table, and at a gallery nearby she'd found five museum prints that she couldn't resist. Two were now hanging in her tiny living room, one was in her bedroom, and the remaining two would be on the walls of her office first thing tomorrow morning.

She'd had the drafting table delivered and had carted the prints home in a cab, and then she'd taken off again to hit the department stores on Wilshire Boulevard. Her simple wardrobe had been perfectly acceptable for the casual atmosphere of the animation workroom, but as Jason's assistant she felt she should begin dressing a little more upscale. And besides, most of her wardrobe predated her move to Los Angeles and she could use the new clothes and a slightly new look to go with her new life.

She'd purchased several comfortable, conservative pantsuits, coordinating blouses, and even a couple of dresses. In addition, she'd bought a couple of potted plants and a few odds and ends to dress up the apartment. When Martin Chomsky, the financial genius who handled all her money and her business affairs, received the credit card receipts he would probably have a coronary. Certainly she could afford the expenses, and he wouldn't begrudge her a penny of the amount, but Rachael so rarely bought anything that the shock might very well kill him.

Satisfied with the placement of the print she was hanging, Rachael stepped onto the patio and pulled one of the wrought-iron chairs out of the shade into a small patch of late-afternoon sun. She'd accomplished a lot in two days, but her greatest achievement had little to do with the changes in her apartment. She was actually enjoying things for the first time in two and a half years. She felt good about herself, and about her life in general. Her new job was intimidating, but that would lessen in time, and she could already sense the surge of excitement that was growing by leaps and bounds when she thought about working alongside Jason Burgess.

Rachael had suppressed her emotions for such a long time that emerging from her shell did, indeed, feel like the coming of spring Jason had promised her.

THE NEXT TWO weeks were a revelation to Rachael. She'd never known any life—let alone hers—could change so quickly. And all the changes revolved around Jason Burgess. The man was a good-natured ogre, a slave driver of the highest order, but one who made the slave happy to be driven. He worked tirelessly and expected the same of his staff, and the resulting chaotic activity created a whirlwind that Rachael quickly came to find exhilarating.

Nothing was the same two days in a row. Once Jason realized she was serious about accepting all the work he could give her, Rachael was never without a stack of assignments that even she had trouble keeping up with. They worked together and separately on various aspects of the storyboard, and before her first full week was out, one new section—sixty drawings in all—was complete.

Thanks to Rachael's input, the netherworld scene began to take shape, and Jason was able to tell Robb Weston to assign an animation team to that critical segment of the movie. Jason finally came up with a design for Adana that made her an ethereal, beautiful blonde, in contrast with the raven-haired Zahara. Everyone who saw the model sheets of the heroine noted that, except for the hair color, she bore a striking resemblance to the boss's new assistant, but they all kept the observation to themselves. Things had run so smoothly since Rachael's promotion that no one cared in the least if something romantic was going on between Jason and his new right hand.

Unaware of the speculation about her relationship with Jason, Rachael began to thrive on the tumultuous activity that enlivened her days. For someone who'd always worked in relative solitude, it amazed her that she enjoyed the pressure and diversity so much. But, of course, Jason made it easy for her. He was so supportive and encouraging that she learned she could express a new idea or prepare a drawing from a perspective opposed to his own without fear of ridicule. He didn't always adopt her ideas, but he never made her feel stupid for having submitted a suggestion. Instead, Jason made her feel as though she was an important part of a team, as though she was working *with* him, rather than *for* him. It was a liberating feeling that allowed her to blossom.

But there was also something disturbing about Jason's openness, and Rachael was having a difficult time confronting it. Too often she found herself comparing Jason to Sander, and though she had yet to admit it, her late husband did not fare well in the comparison. Sander had never encouraged her to express her ideas. She had drawn what he'd told her to draw, and he had never allowed her to forget that *Ravenmede* was *his* brainchild.

On an intellectual level Rachael had always known that her own artistic ability exceeded Sander's, but she had never resented the way he utilized her talent. *Ravenmede* had been a cooperative effort—she and Sander had been partners, sharing the work and the benefits equally. Or so she had convinced herself.

But now, though she was just an employee, Jason made her feel like a partner. He made her feel valued, respected, needed. This from a man who had become a legend in his field without any help from Rachael Hubbard and would continue to excel whether she was his assistant or not.

Sander Hubbard, on the other hand, would never have achieved the heights he'd reached as Garrett Mallory if it hadn't been for his wife, yet he'd made her feel like a hireling. Through all the years of her marriage, Rachael had accepted Sander's attitude of superiority because she'd honestly believed that the only thing she had to contribute to the comic book was her ability to draw.

Jason was allowing Rachael the freedom to express ideas and proving to her that she had more to offer than just her artistic hand. Each time he solicited her opinion, each time he praised an innovative drawing, Rachael discovered a growing resentment for her late husband that was unnerving. Flaws and all, she'd kept Sander on a pedestal. Now that the platform was crumbling she felt disloyal, as though she was betraying her husband and the life they had shared.

The emotion was so disquieting that Rachael found it impossible to confront. Sander was dead; it was unfair to find fault with him when he wasn't able to defend or redeem himself. And more importantly, on a deep subconscious level, Rachael knew that if she allowed herself to acknowledge her late husband's imperfections it would mean accepting that her marriage was not the utopia she'd been clinging to.

Without realizing it, she'd come a long way in these past two years, and an even longer way in only the past two weeks, but she wasn't nearly ready to give up the illusion of her perfect marriage. She repressed her disloyal feelings by telling herself that Jason really wasn't as wonderful as he seemed, and that he was only humoring her because he felt sorry for her. It was a weak excuse that did a great disservice to Jason and to herself, but it was the only rationalization she could come up with that allowed her to keep the memory of her late husband untarnished.

"Yo, Rachael!" After a perfunctory knock on her door, Jason stuck his head in and Rachael placed her pencil into the trough of her lightboard, slipped off her glasses, and looked at him expectantly. She'd been wondering when he'd make his first appearance of the day, and it was difficult for her to admit just how eager she'd been for him to show up. Nothing was ever boring around Jason Burgess, and that was particularly true since he'd begun his joke crusade.

He seemed to take some perverse delight in making her laugh, and not a day went by that he didn't pop into her office unannounced, say something comical, then disappear as quickly as he'd come.

Rachael found his hit-and-run tactics far more amusing than the jokes he told, which were usually awful. After a while, when it became obvious that he was serious about making her laugh, Rachael decided that she shouldn't make it so easy for him. As a joke of her own, she began pretending that she didn't find him in the least amusing, and the contest was on. The harder Rachael tried not to laugh, the harder Jason worked to crack her up.

"Two penguins were sitting in a bathtub," he had said without preamble one afternoon when he'd popped his head into her office. "The first penguin said to the second penguin, 'Pass me that bar of soap,' and the second penguin replied, 'Get it yourself. What do you think I am, a typewriter?'"

Rachael had stared at him blankly. "Is that it? That's the punch line?"

"Yes."

"I don't get it."

He grinned. "Good." And with that, his head disappeared, the door closed, and he was gone.

The ridiculous, pointless joke had stayed with Rachael all day, and the longer she thought about it, the funnier it became, until she was finally forced to laugh. That afternoon she'd left a note on Jason's desk that had read, "The penguin joke gets you one point for originality. Score: Jason one; Rachael zero."

After that Jason posted a sheet of paper in the Bull Pen to keep track of their scores, and this morning—the end of her second full week of work—they were tied at eight each.

"Good morning, Jason. What can I do for you?" she asked, though she knew very well from his mischievous grin that he was about to launch another joke attack.

"What did the stove say to the refrigerator?" he asked as he stepped into the room, closing the door behind him.

"I have no earthly idea. What did the stove say to the refrigerator?"

"Dick Tracy."

The look of disbelief she gave him was so comically droll that Jason had to laugh. He came into the room and sat on the corner of her desk. "You don't look amused, Rachael. I guess that means I don't get points for this one," he said, still chuckling.

"Not even for originality."

"Shucks."

"That's nine to eight in my favor, Jason. You're going to have to get on the ball or you'll be eating my dust."

"What can I say? It's been a long, hard week," he commented lightly, still amazed at the transformation he was seeing in Rachael. She came out of her shell a little more every day, and the woman he was discovering was a rare, priceless jewel.

As an assistant she exceeded all his expectations. It was impossible to imagine how he'd gotten along without her. Not only did she make his job easier, she made it a constant joy, as well. Somehow just her presence made the problems that cropped up daily a little easier to handle. An employer couldn't ask for a more perfect employee.

The changes Jason had noted in her as a person pleased him, too. Gradually she was learning to speak her mind freely, without fear of scorn, either from Jason or any of his staff. It was a wonderful development, but it had caused Jason some concern. The very fact that she was afraid to voice an opinion indicated that sometime in her life, someone had subjected her to so much criticism that she'd simply learned it was less painful to keep her mouth shut.

He had speculated endlessly on who might have instilled that insecurity in her, and the most frequent answer he came up with was her late husband, Sander Hubbard. But that didn't make much sense. Rachael obviously revered Sander. If he'd belittled her and made her feel inadequate, how could she have loved him so much? Why would she have continued to grieve for him so long?

Despite the transformation in Rachael, that was the thing that hadn't changed; she was still grieving. Occasionally when they were working together in her office or in the Bull Pen he caught her in an unguarded moment and he could see that she was remembering something from the past. At those times Jason often wondered if she was remembering how she and Sander had worked side by side.

The thought that she might be comparing him to her late husband disturbed Jason. He knew it would only be natural for her to do so in their work environment, but it was in the personal aspect of their relationship that Jason discovered he didn't want any comparisons made. He remembered only too well the way Rachael had looked at Sander six years ago at the banquet they had all attended. He'd never seen a woman so much in love, and Jason knew he could never compete with the ghost of her husband.

He kept trying to tell himself that it was ridiculous to worry about being compared to Sander. His association with Rachael was purely business, nothing else.

But as much as Jason tried to deny having any feelings for Rachael, the feelings persisted. She was seldom out of his thoughts, and his preoccupation with her was growing daily. He forced himself to think of her only as his valued assistant, but it was becoming harder and harder not to think about how wonderful it would be to hold her in his arms and press her body close to his. He tried not to imagine a time when she would trust him, confide in him and look to him for something other than her next assignment.

"So, what's on the agenda for today, boss?" Rachael asked, drawing Jason away from his inappropriate thoughts.

"I thought we might adjourn to the Bull Pen and see what we can come up with for the Wizard's Lair segment. Deanna and Dan are breathing down my neck for some roughs to work from."

"All right. I'll gather my stuff and meet you there in five minutes," she told him.

"Great." Jason bounced off the desk, started toward the Bull Pen door, then stopped and turned back to her. "Rachael—"

"Yes?" She looked at him, waiting, and noticed that the teasing light had left his eyes. In its place was a tender, thoughtful look that did funny things to her heart.

"Have I told you recently what a pleasure it is to work with you and how much easier you make my job?"

Rachael glanced down, disturbed by both his look and his words. She would have liked to believe that she was indispensable to him, but he'd gotten along without her too well for her to accept his compliment unconditionally. "It's very nice of you to say so, Jason."

"It's true," he insisted, already regretting that he'd broken their lighthearted mood. Only a moment ago she'd been smiling her wonderful smile that was becoming more natural and relaxed with every passing day. Now she was retreating into her shell again, and Jason was cursing himself.

When was he going to learn that Rachael was only comfortable as long as their relationship stayed on a certain level? She could handle whatever comments he made about her work, and she tolerated his meager attempts to make her laugh, but when he spoke seriously, personally, she reverted to the same shy, insecure woman who'd entered the Bull Pen several weeks ago.

"Why do you do that, Rachael?" he couldn't keep from asking.

"Do what?"

Jason moved toward the desk and sat on the outer edge, facing her at the lightboard. "Why do you retreat every time I pay you a compliment?"

"I didn't realize that I did," she answered softly, though she knew very well it was a lie. She did pull into herself, particularly at times like these when he was so close to her, speaking about personal things.

"Of course you know it, Rachael," Jason argued, careful to keep any hint of frustration or irritation out of his voice. "You can laugh and joke and speak your mind freely until I take our conversation to a personal level, and then you freeze on me. You'd think I was yelling at you rather than complimenting you."

"Maybe...maybe that's because you pay me too many compliments," she said quietly.

"Too many compliments?" Jason was stunned. "Rachael, don't you think I know how lucky I am to have you here? I've got one of *the* most talented fantasy artists in the country working as my assistant—and doing a better job of it than any other *two* artists could do! My God, Rachael, I ought to be dancing in the streets and singing your praises from the rooftops."

She wanted to smile at the tribute, but too many years of uncertainty had built a nearly impenetrable wall around her fragile ego. "I'm not that good, Jason. No one is. You... just say things like that because you feel sorry for me—you want to build my confidence."

Jason was astonished—and more than a little irritated. "I don't believe this! I though we settled this ridiculous *pity* issue weeks ago. Who did this to you, Rachael?"

His vehemence startled her, but she didn't try to retreat from him. "Who did what?"

"Who gave you this inferiority complex? Who convinced you that you're a marginally talented, brainless idiot."

"I am not a brainless idiot!"

"Oh, but you *are* only marginally talented, right?" he said sarcastically.

Rachael glanced away from him to stare blankly into the courtyard outside her window. It was a moment before she answered, "I have talent, Jason. I know that. But I'm not the Eighth Wonder of the World you like to make me out to be."

Knowing he was pushing too hard, Jason softened his voice, but he couldn't give up completely. "Rachael, were your parents—" he struggled to find the right word "—were they critical of you when you were a child?"

With a small, resigned sigh, Rachael looked down at her lightboard. "My mother died when I was very young—I hardly even knew her."

"And your father?" he asked gently, praying that she would confide in him so that they could get past the invisible wall that seemed to be standing in the way of their friendship.

Rachael moistened her lips. "My father was a very strict disciplinarian. He was an Air Force captain who really didn't know what to do with the two daughters he had to raise on his own. He remarried several times, but none of the marriages lasted long."

Jason gleaned a great deal from just that small piece of information. He formed an image of a shy little girl who'd had no one to nurture her and give her a sense of self-worth.

Though he knew he would be treading on shaky ground, he couldn't keep from asking, "What about your husband, Rachael? Didn't working with Sander on *Ravenmede* prove to you how extraordinary your talent is?"

"Leave Sander out of this!" Rachael said sharply. Jason was encroaching on areas that couldn't stand up to close scrutiny, and though she knew she was overreacting she couldn't seem to quell the surge of anger that welled up in her. "I told you once that my personal life and my job here are to be kept separate, and I meant it, Jason."

"I'm sorry. I didn't mean to upset you," he apologized, wondering what nerve he'd just struck. "But you accomplished so much with *Ravenmede* that I just don't understand why that didn't build your confidence. Sander—"

"I said I don't want to talk to you about Sander!" Rachael practically shouted, coming to her feet. "He was a wonderful artist—*Ravenmede* would have been nothing without him! I won't listen to anyone say otherwise."

Jason stood, barely able to believe that their conversation had gotten so out of hand. It was obvious that despite her denials, Rachael had a great many conflicting emotions about her late husband bottled up inside her. "I didn't say Sander wasn't a good artist. It took both of you to create *Ravenmede*, I know that."

"Then you have no right to criticize him!"

"I wasn't criticizing him, Rachael."

"Yes, you were, and I won't stand for it," she said, coming to the brink of tears, knowing she was being irrational, but unable to stop herself. "Sander was a brilliant artist, a wonderful husband and a kind...loving...father." The tears

CHAPTER TWELVE

JASON STARED at Rachael's folder, so deep in thought that it took him a moment to realize his intercom was buzzing.

"Yes, Gretchen, what is it?" he asked, his mind completely absorbed with the new puzzle Rachael had just presented him with. Had Rachael lost her husband *and* her child in the accident? Just the thought that it might be true made Jason ache inside, as though a tight, unyielding fist had taken hold of his heart. The pain of losing a child was too terrifying to even comprehend.

"Jason, you have visitors," Gretchen told him. "Your daughter Lorna—"

"Lorna!" Jason tossed the phone receiver into its cradle and flew toward the door. Lorna never came to the office unannounced unless it was an emergency. "Honey, what's the matter? Is Emily sick?" he asked as he entered the reception area and saw Lorna standing beside Gretchen's desk with Emily in her arms.

"No, Emily's not sick," Lorna said irritably as she swept past Jason into his office. "Lord, you wouldn't believe what a horrible day I've had, and it isn't even noon yet!"

"Sweetheart, I'm in no mood for riddles. Just tell me what's wrong," Jason instructed gently. Now that he knew this wasn't a serious emergency, his thoughts shifted automatically back to Rachael and the way she'd run out of her office. He needed to locate her so that they could talk, so that he could find out if what he suspected was true.

"What isn't wrong!" Lorna told him melodramatically. "An hour ago I got a call from Mrs. Davina, Emily's sitter, telling me I'd have to come get Emily immediately. Her little boy was being taken to the hospital with appendicitis or something. All the kids she keeps had to be picked up."

Lorna sat down, and Emily immediately crawled off her mother's lap and headed for Jason. He picked her up, placing a kiss on her cheek, and returned to his desk, waiting for Lorna to continue. "And..." he prompted.

"And, I called Cole, but he's out of the office all day in meetings at the Reseda branch. I've called every sitter we've ever used, I've called Cole's parents—no one can keep Emily. Daddy, I hate to ask it, but I'm desperate."

Lorna wanted him to keep Emily. On any other day, he probably would have been able to oblige, but this was not any other day. "Honey, can't you take off—"

"No! This is the day I leave on a buying trip to Chicago, remember?"

Jason nodded. "That's right. I forgot."

Emily turned a pitiful, elfin face up to Jason's and milked the situation for all it was worth. "Can't I stay with you, Grandpa?" Her lower lip jutted out as it always did when she thought it would help her get her way, and Jason had to laugh.

"I tell you what, princess...why don't I call Mrs. Ramos? I'll bet she'd be tickled pink to have you help her clean Grandpa's house today. And I'll see if I can get off work early and we'll do something special together, okay?"

"Okay."

"Thank you, Daddy," Lorna said, rising. "I didn't even think about Mrs. Ramos."

"Can you drop Emily by the house?"

"Sorry, I can't. I've got to pick up my luggage and get to the airport or I'll miss my flight." She moved to Jason behind the desk and gave him a quick peck on the cheek.

"Give Mommy a hug, sweetie," she instructed Emily. "You be a good girl while I'm gone, and I'll see you on Sunday."

"With a surprise?" Emily asked, planting a wet kiss on Lorna's cheek.

"Of course! Thanks a million, Daddy." She departed, leaving Jason feeling as though he'd been hit by a hurricane.

He picked up the phone and got his secretary on the line. "Gretchen, call my house and ask Mrs. Ramos if she'd be willing to take care of Emily for a few hours."

"All right."

"Thanks." He hung up the phone and looked at his granddaughter. "Well, Miss Emily, what am I going to do with you in the meantime?"

Emily considered that for a moment. "I could help you work," she suggested.

"An excellent idea," he said, rising with her in his arms. He moved into the Bull Pen, seated her at the table, and found a box of colored pencils in a supply cabinet. "Here you go. You draw some pictures for Grandpa and I'll be right back."

"Okay."

With a last look over his shoulder to be certain she was staying put, Jason hurried to his secretary. "What did Mrs. Ramos say?"

"Sorry, Jason, but I couldn't reach her."

Jason frowned. "Damn! She must be out doing the marketing."

"I'll keep trying. But in the meantime, you've got a call on line one. It's Glasner, the special-effects man you've been trying to reach."

"I don't believe this!" Jason snapped. Everything was happening at once. It was vital that he take this call, but it was also important that he speak to Rachael—and he had a three-year-old granddaughter in the Bull Pen who needed supervision. "Did you see Rachael leave her office a few minutes ago?"

Gretchen nodded. "She went down the hall to the ladies' room."

That was a relief. At least she hadn't fled the building. "All right, I'll talk to Glasner. When you see Rachael, ask her to wait for me in her office. And would you do me a favor and check on Emily every few minutes? I'll finish this call as quickly as I can."

"Sure. Don't worry about the kid," Gretchen said, wondering what had Jason so rattled. Normally he handled a dozen concurrent emergencies with incredible aplomb. Something unusual was obviously going on, and apparently it had something to do with Rachael Hubbard.

"Thanks." Jason disappeared into his office and Gretchen walked to the Bull Pen door. She peeked in and found the little girl sitting exactly where Jason had left her. Everything seemed under control except the switchboard, which was lit up like a Christmas tree, so Gretchen returned to her desk and tried to restore order.

She was still juggling phone calls a few minutes later when Rachael came back down the hall, her face pale and strained. "Oh, Rachael..." Gretchen put a caller on hold and flagged her down. "Jason wants to see you in the Bull Pen when he gets off the phone." The secretary altered Jason's instruction slightly, thinking she could kill two birds with one stone. Rachael would be where Jason could find her, and little Emily would have someone to keep her entertained.

"All right," Rachael answered quietly. She stepped into her office and began collecting the things she would need for her work session with Jason. She was mortified by the way she'd spoken to him, and not at all sure how she was going to face him. Once she'd fought back the bout of weeping that had threatened to overcome her, she'd realized that she'd overreacted, but she couldn't bring herself to question why. Again it was just a matter of Jason's well-meaning concern getting in the way of business, and she was going to have to find a way to convince him that she wouldn't tolerate any more prying into her personal life.

With her emotions barely under control, Rachael went into the Bull Pen prepared to tell Jason that the subjects of her husband and her past were off-limits. She would suggest that they forget their discussion had ever taken place, and get down to work. When she stepped through the door, though, her hastily prepared speech flew right out of her head.

Sitting where she'd expected to find Jason was a little girl of three or four years of age, with carrot-colored hair pulled back into a braid that only barely constrained her wild, curly tresses. She was kneeling in the chair, with her slender torso bent over the table and her face contorted into a grimace of fierce concentration.

Rachael froze just inside the doorway, feeling as though the wind had suddenly been knocked out of her. She couldn't handle this—not right now, not when she was still shaking inside from her argument with Jason. She hadn't yet learned how to deal with young children; just seeing them brought back a flood of painful memories. They all reminded her of the sweet little boy she'd lost.

Realizing that someone else was in the room, Emily looked up from her "work" to study the newcomer, pinning Rachael with her pale blue eyes. "Who are you?"

Rachael moistened her lips. "My name is Rachael," she answered softly. She wanted to turn and run as she always did, but something seemed to have rooted her to this spot.

Emily's face lit up. She knew she'd seen this lady somewhere before. "Princess Rachael!"

She gave the little girl a tremulous smile. "No, I'm not a princess."

"Yes, you are!" Emily insisted. "Grandpa told me the whole story, all about your castle and your pretty white eagles. Only I made him give you long hair because all princesses have long hair. Why did you cut yours off?"

Rachael's hand automatically went to the back of her neck, lightly touching the hair that had once fallen to her waist. "It kept getting in the way," she answered. Apparently, this was the three-year-old granddaughter Jason had told her about weeks ago. Somewhere in the back of her mind she was wondering if Jason really had drawn a picture of her, or if his grandchild just had a fanciful imagination. It must have been her imagination; Rachael couldn't think of any reason Jason would want to draw her.

Emily considered Rachael's answer and touched her own long hair, bringing the frayed braid over her shoulder. "I know," she said with a resigned sigh. "Mommy wants to cut mine sometimes, but I won't let her. I'm Grandpa's princess, so I have to have it long."

Rachael felt tears forming in her eyes, but she fought them back. "Your grandpa is very lucky to have a princess like you."

"I know," Emily replied with the confidence of the very young and the very innocent. "Do you draw for Grandpa?"

Rachael looked down at the script and sketch pad she was holding tightly against her body. "Yes, I do. I'm Jason's assistant."

"I'm his 'sistant, too! See?" Emily pushed her colorful paper across the table, waiting expectantly for the praise she knew would come. Despite her growing need to flee, Rachael couldn't disappoint her. She moved to the edge of the oval table and set down her script and drawing pad.

"That's very, very good. Jason will like it a lot."

Emily grabbed the picture and slid out of her chair. "Can I put it up here?" she asked hopefully, pointing to an empty storyboard.

"Can I put it up here, Mommy?" Micah asked, his eyes shining with pride as he displayed a drawing of squiggly lines and clashing colors. "Can I put it with yours?"

"Of course you can. We'll put it right next to the big drawing of Ravenmede Castle."

The flashback startled Rachael and she was barely able to tell the little girl that it was perfectly all right to pin her masterpiece on the storyboard. Desperate to escape before she burst into tears, Rachael moved back toward the door to her office. "I have to go back to work now, honey. It was nice to have met you."

"My name is Emily."

"Well, it was nice to have met you, Emily." The need to run was becoming overpowering. Jason's bright, talkative little granddaughter reminded her too much of Micah. Just being in the same room with her hurt more than Rachael could bear.

"Don't go!" Emily pleaded when it became obvious she was about to be left alone again. "I can't do it myself." She was stretching up toward a thumbtack that was out of her reach.

With her short fingernails digging into her palms, Rachael moved to the storyboard and secured Emily's picture. "There you go."

"Thank you. Grandpa will like that."

"I'm sure he will." She headed back toward the door so that the child wouldn't see her tears.

"No, don't go," Emily insisted again. "I want you to stay and draw me a story like Grandpa does. Draw me the story of Princess Rachael and the white eagles."

"Draw me a story, Mommy," Micah demanded as he climbed into Rachael's lap. It was bedtime and he smelled of Ivory soap and childlike innocence. "Draw me the story about Mickelmoss Monster and the big black dragon. Draw it, Mommy, please."

Rachael leaned against the door, fighting back the sob that threatened to choke off her voice. "I'm sorry, Emily. I...I don't know that story." Somehow she managed to say goodbye, then fled into her office as the tears began in earnest. Grabbing her purse, thinking only of finding some private place where she could deal with the haunting memories of her son, she ran out of her office, past Gretchen's desk and down the corridor that would take her outside, as far away from Jason's granddaughter as she could get.

JASON PULLED UP at the stoplight and consulted the Wilshire-Western section of his Thomas Bros. L.A. map book. According to the map, he was only a few blocks from Rachael's neighborhood, but that wasn't close enough to suit him. He'd taken Emily to his house and left her in Mrs. Ramos's capable hands and now he had to get to Rachael.

"She just ran past me," Gretchen had told him over an hour ago when he'd finished with his phone call. "I'm pretty sure she was crying."

Confused, Jason had gone to check on Emily, and with her help the pieces of the puzzle fell into place. Rachael had gone into the Bull Pen, found his granddaughter, and after spending a few minutes with the child she'd run away in tears. If he'd needed any confirmation of his suspicion that Rachael had lost a child, this was surely it.

He placed a quick phone call to Roger Lampasat, and had learned that both Sander Hubbard and his three-year-old son had been killed in the same tragic accident.

Jason felt sick inside. All the things he'd said to Rachael about getting on with her life, accepting her loss, buzzed around in his head. He'd been so smug and all-knowing, giving her the benevolent benefit of his own experience, when in truth, he knew nothing about what she was going through. He could hardly bear to imagine the kind of pain she was living with.

He had serious doubts about whether Rachael would want to see him after their argument, but he couldn't turn around and go back to the office. He knew only that it was important that he find her, talk to her...comfort her. Most of all, he wanted to comfort her.

The traffic started moving again, and Jason wound his way through the streets until he found Rachael's apartment building, an eight-story Spanish-style stucco complex that was topped by an ornate bell tower. He whipped the Mercedes into a parking space along the curb, locked the door and headed toward the arched entrance to the lush green courtyard that hid the doors to the apartment from the street. There was no security system—not even a locked door—to prevent him from entering, and he quickly found Rachael's ground-floor apartment at the rear of the building. He knocked, waited a moment, then knocked again, praying she was home because he had no idea where else he might look for her. He knew nothing about her personal life; his impression was that she didn't have one. If she wasn't here, he'd just have to return to the lobby and wait for her to come home. He wasn't leaving until he saw her.

He raised his hand to knock a third time, but a subdued voice on the other side stopped him. "Who is it?"

"It's Jason." He waited for what seemed like an eternity. "Rachael, please... Let me talk to you." There was another long pause and Jason could almost sense Rachael on the other side of the door, trying to make up her mind. Then the security chain rattled, a bolt turned, and the door opened.

Surprisingly Rachael seemed far more composed than he'd expected, but it took only a second to see that her apparent poise had only a thin veneer of self-control over it. She was holding herself rigidly in check, her arms crossed protectively across her midsection as though she was afraid she might fly apart at any moment.

"May I come in?"

Wordlessly, she stepped back and crossed to the French windows that led to a small, enclosed patio. She stood at the windows, looking out, seeing nothing, as Jason closed the door behind him and moved silently to the center of the room.

"Are you all right, Rachael?" he asked, then cursed his stupidity. He hadn't gone to all the trouble of tracking her down just to ask dumb questions.

"I'm sorry I ran out of the office like that. I just couldn't... handle it."

"Rachael, I am so sorry...." he said, his voice filled with all the regret he genuinely felt. "I didn't know you had a son. After you told me what a good father Sander was, and then ran out after seeing Emily, I called Roger Lampasat. He told me about your little boy—he assumed from our first conversation that I already knew."

Rachael nodded without turning toward him, and when she spoke, her voice was barely audible. "I must have upset Emily a great deal. I'm really sorry. She couldn't have had any idea why I was behaving so strangely."

"No, she wasn't upset. She just wanted to know why Princess Rachael had such sad eyes," he said gently. "I told her it was because you had seen some very sad things."

There was a long pause before she asked, "Did Roger tell you that Micah was three?"

"Yes."

"Emily asked me to... 'draw her a story.'" Her voice broke and it was a moment before she could continue. Jason waited patiently. If Rachael was finally ready to talk, he wanted to be the one who listened. "Every night at bedtime, Micah would ask me to draw him a story, too."

"Oh, Rachael..." Feeling a small part of her pain, Jason took a step toward her, then stopped, not knowing whether it would hurt or help if he touched her as he so much wanted to do. He couldn't remember ever feeling so helpless.

"I haven't learned how to deal with children yet," she told him, sounding very far away. "Particularly not the little ones. To tell you the truth, I haven't even tried. I avoid the park and school yards. When I see a mother and child on the bus, I look out the window and pretend they're not there. I chose this neighborhood because it's mostly working singles, very few families. You must think that's very cowardly."

"No, Rachael, I think that must be very natural. I can't even imagine how I would have been able to cope if I'd lost my daughter."

Rachael leaned against the door frame, turning partially toward Jason, but still not looking at him. It was easier to talk if she couldn't really see him, and she did need to talk. It wasn't a need she recognized consciously, but somewhere inside, she'd known that Jason would come after her and that talking to him would ease the pain. She was so tired of being alone.

"Your wife, Molly...did she die suddenly, Jason?" she asked, her voice hushed.

He moved a little closer, coming to stand a few feet away from her at the French windows. "No. We knew she was terminal for about eight months. It hurt, knowing I was going to lose her, but at least I had the chance to say all the things I needed to say to her."

Rachael closed her eyes and felt scalding tears gathering. "The last time I saw Sander alive, we were quarreling. His family was meeting in New York to see his sister off for school in Europe, and I was supposed to go with him. I came down with a strep infection, and when the doctor refused to let me travel, Sander wanted to leave Micah at home."

Twin tears ran down her cheeks, but her voice was soft and clear. "I knew how disappointed his grandparents would be if they didn't get to see him, and I was too sick to really take care of him. I was afraid he'd get sick, too.... I had a lot of good reasons for insisting Sander take him, but he'd be... alive if I'd let Sander win that argument the way he won all the others we'd ever had."

"You were doing what you thought was best, Rachael. You couldn't have known what would happen."

"Micah was so bright and mischievous... so full of himself, so full of questions.... I'm learning to cope with Sander's death," she told him, her voice broken. "I don't wake up in the night and reach for him. I don't hear his voice... I don't *ache* quite so much when I think about never seeing him again, but... Micah..." Rachael covered her mouth as a wrenching sob caught in her throat. "Oh, God, I want my baby."

Jason wasn't surprised to feel tears on his own cheeks. He was only an arm's length away, and when he reached out to gently touch her, Rachael went to him. He pulled her close, holding her as tightly as he dared while she spilled out the grief she'd kept trapped inside.

"It's all right, love, let it out. It's all right..." he crooned, stroking her hair and rocking gently back and forth. "It's all right. I've got you."

Rachael let the tears run freely, holding on to Jason as she wanted to be able to hold her child—closely and securely, as though she would never let him go again. For a brief time the deep, empty well inside her didn't feel quite so deep, not half so empty. Jason had her cocooned in his warm, caring arms, and she wasn't quite as alone as she'd been before.

She cried for her lost son and for the parts of herself that she'd lost with him, and when the sobs began to subside, Jason led her gently toward the sofa. He sat, keeping her in his arms, pulled close to his side. It was a long time before either of them spoke; Rachael was drained by misery, and Jason seemed to know instinctively that when she was ready she would let him into the dark places she'd been hiding away. There were still things she had to say, feelings she needed to express, and he would hold her and listen for as long as she needed him.

Long after her tears had stopped, Rachael sat quietly in Jason's arms with her head cradled on his shoulder. He had so much strength that he seemed so willing to share, and she wanted the feeling of safety to last.

"Tell me about Molly," she requested softly. At this moment she felt an emotional bond with Jason that she couldn't remember feeling with anyone—not even Sander—and she needed to share in a part of his life so that she could be sure the bond wasn't just an illusion.

She felt Jason's chest rise and fall heavily as he sighed. "Molly was...something quite extraordinary," he told her. There was just a hint of sadness in his voice, but as he talked about his late wife, Rachael could tell that he'd learned to enjoy his memories, not fear them. "I came from a large family—three brothers and two sisters—but I was a sickly kid, which made me the odd man out. I couldn't keep up with my older brothers and the neighborhood kids because I always had some annoying childhood disease that kept me laid up most of the time," he explained in a soft, soothing, reflective tone.

"When I was twelve I developed rheumatic fever, and discovered what being alone was really all about. For the next year, my entire world consisted of a four-poster bed and a chair at my second-story window. For my thirteenth birthday, my folks gave me an artist's kit with colored pencils, watercolors, charcoal, chalk—everything imaginable in it—and I went wild. Well, at least as wild as a ninety-pound weakling with rheumatic fever can go," he said with a grin.

"I started drawing everything I could see from my windows—the trees, the houses across the alley, the kids playing—everything. And just when I started getting frustrated because I thought I'd run out of new things to draw, Molly showed up. She and her mother and father had moved into the house directly behind ours, and every afternoon after school Molly would play dress-up and hold high tea in her fenced-in backyard.

"One day she would be a duchess in a pillbox hat, the next, a movie star in a shedding feather boa. She had this wild, carrot-colored hair and the most incredible imagination I'd ever seen."

"Did she know you were watching her?" Rachael asked, visualizing the scene Jason described and knowing from her own lonely childhood what a ray of sunshine the imaginative Molly must have been to him.

"Not for a couple of weeks," Jason answered, pleased that Rachael was listening to him. For some reason it was important to him that she know about him and about his life. "She was such a fearless, outgoing person that she made friends very quickly, and pretty soon she had real friends to replace the dolls at her tea parties. One day I saw one of them point to my window, and I wanted to die of mortification when she turned and looked up at me. But that was nothing compared to what I felt when she calmly dismissed her friends, crossed the alley, and climbed the drainpipe up the side of my house! I opened the window and she slithered inside and bluntly asked, 'Are you Jason the Wimp?' "

Rachael could feel the rumble of a gentle laugh in Jason's chest, and she smiled at his distant memory. "You're making this up," she accused wistfully.

"I swear I'm not! That's exactly what she said," Jason insisted, raising one hand to punctuate his truthfulness. "I was already half in love with her, just watching her out the window, and that really sealed my fate."

"That's understandable. What man wouldn't love a woman who was beautiful, imaginative, painfully direct and could climb drainpipes without batting an eyelash."

Jason laughed. "Exactly."

"So what did you say when she asked if you were Jason the Wimp?"

"I said, 'No, I'm Sir Jason the Bold, fearless knight of King Arthur's Round Table.'" He stroked Rachael's hair without even realizing he was doing it. "And she said, 'Well, Sir Jason, I am Lady Gwendolyn, and King Arthur has decided that you and I will someday marry.' She was only joking, trying to shock me with her outrageous behavior, but I took King Arthur's decree very seriously. I knew that one day I would marry her. She saw the drawings I'd done of her, and she came back every day to see more, until she became my best friend, my confidant, co-conspirator in fantasy worlds we created and the inspiration for everything I did after that."

"And you never loved anyone else?"

"Never," he answered, and somewhere inside his head a voice said very clearly, *Until now.*

"You had something very special, didn't you, Jason?" Rachael asked, turning her face up to his. She reached up, touching her fingers lightly to his cheek, and it was everything Jason could do to keep from turning his lips to the palm of her hand and pressing a kiss there.

Something warm and wonderful passed between them, and Rachael seemed to sense his thoughts. She brushed her fingertips lightly across his lips as she raised her face to his,

CHAPTER THIRTEEN

JASON HAD NEVER KNOWN a single kiss could express so many emotions, so many needs. When their lips first touched it was only to seal the bond of real friendship that had just been born between them. It was a moment of giving and taking comfort, though who was doing the giving and who was doing the taking, he couldn't have said. Sweet reassurance was offered and accepted with no strings attached.

But as Jason's lips lingered over Rachael's and her body remained pressed against his, he felt her overwhelming sadness surge to the surface. He felt her desperate need to forget, if only for a moment; he felt her hunger for contact, for closeness, for someone to share the burden of her loss.... His lips pressed more insistently against hers, and she opened to him, welcoming his possession of her mouth and her other senses, as well.

The sweet kiss of friendship blossomed into an embrace of even sweeter passion. Rachael strained against him, needing everything Jason could give her. His arms were around her, one hand stroking her back, the other buried in her hair, and when he shifted her position, pulling her across his body, Rachael moaned. She arched her breasts tightly against his broad, rock-hard chest and felt the crests harden with a wonderful, painful ache that she had never expected to feel again.

As though he sensed what she needed, Jason cupped one breast in his hand, kneading it gently through the softness of her blouse and underclothes. She was small and firm, and she fit his hand perfectly, just as he knew instinctively she would. He'd never known a need to mate that was so strong and so right, and yet so wrong.

He wanted to make love with Rachael. Now—this minute. He wanted to carry her off to her bed and press himself into her until they were both lost in the promise of passion that was in this kiss. And Rachael wanted that, too. He could tell by her labored breathing and the soft moans that were lost in his mouth.

But though she wanted it now, in the heat of this moment, Jason knew that when the moment passed Rachael would never forgive herself. And she wouldn't forgive him, either, for having taken advantage of her. He didn't have to be told that she'd never slept with any man but her husband—not before their marriage or since—and if she let herself succumb to a passion that was born of need and grief, not love, she would experience more guilt than she realized.

She would feel that she'd betrayed Sander and had betrayed herself, and if she couldn't handle the guilt of that betrayal, she would blame Jason. He would lose her, and he couldn't allow that to happen. In the brief seconds before he released her, Jason realized he was going to have to stop fighting the all-too-obvious fact that he'd fallen in love with Rachael Hubbard. Whatever it took, however long he had to wait, he was going to have to make her his. Seducing her now wasn't the way to achieve that goal.

Slowly, very slowly, he loosened his hold on her and gentled their kiss until it was as soft as a long, lingering sigh. With one hand buried in her short hair, he moved his lips across her face, feathering kisses on her cheeks, her eyes and her forehead, and then finally he pressed her head into the crook of his neck. He held her cradled against his shoulder until their breathing began returning to normal, but it was still a moment longer before he spoke.

"I want very much to make love with you, Rachael," he told her in a voice filled with more emotion than he knew was wise to betray. "But I don't think you'd ever forgive me or yourself if we allowed that to happen now."

Rachael tried to summon a measure of guilt and shame for the wanton way she'd reacted to Jason's kiss, but she couldn't find any. It felt right to be in his arms; it felt right to kiss him and have him kiss her. The guilt might surface later, but for the moment it was blissfully quiescent. She was free to savor the pleasure and serenity of being close to him.

"I suppose you're right," she answered softly. "I'm sorry."

"You don't have anything to be sorry about, Rachael, and neither do I. We both needed the reassurance of that kiss. But if we ever do make love, it has to be because we're running toward something, not away from it."

Rachael nodded against his throat, more than content to be held as he was holding her, as though she was something precious to him.

"Tell me about your childhood," he suggested, knowing instinctively that Rachael needed emotional intimacy more than physical closeness right now. And he needed it, too. "Whatever you'd like me to know."

She sat quietly in his arms for a moment, and then she began speaking, telling him about her older sister and her father's military career that had dragged them all over the country. Though she never said so outright, Jason read between the lines and saw how difficult that kind of unsettled childhood had been for her. She'd needed security, not upheaval, and her father hadn't been able to provide that for his youngest daughter.

She described her love of art and the high school teacher who had recognized her talent and encouraged her to enter a national scholarship competition. Much to her surprise, she'd won the scholarship and had gone away to college. It was the first time she'd been on her own, and she'd been terrified.

"Had you always wanted to be a cartoonist?" Jason asked, praying that he wasn't encroaching on an area she would find difficult to discuss.

"No, I wanted to be an illustrator."

"Of...?" he prompted.

"Children's books. Maurice Sendak was my idol."

Jason chuckled. "Mine, too. What made you shift your focus?"

Rachael fell silent for a moment. "I fell in love with Sander Hubbard." The moment she mentioned her husband's name, Rachael no longer felt comfortable being so close to Jason. She needed to talk—she *wanted* to talk—but she couldn't stay wrapped in the warm cocoon of his arms to do it. She eased away from him and for just a moment Jason's hold on her tightened, as though he didn't want to let her go. But the moment passed and he released her, giving her the freedom she needed.

"Would you like something to drink, Jason?" she asked.

It was only a diversion, an excuse to put time and space between them, and Jason recognized the question for what it was. "That would be nice," he replied, remembering the sentimental adage, "If you love something, let it go. If it comes back, it's yours. If it doesn't, it never was." He didn't want to allow Rachael to put distance—neither emotional nor physical—between them, but if he ever hoped to build a relationship between them, he would have to do just that.

"Tea? Coffee?" They settled on iced tea, which Rachael served outside on her viewless patio.

Jason looked around at the characterless ten-by-ten-foot concrete cubicle, as he settled into one of the wrought-iron chairs. "I'm surprised you haven't painted a couple of murals on these walls to provide you with a little scenery."

Rachael smiled as she poured the tea into mismatched glasses she'd purchased at the Salvation Army store around the corner from her apartment. "Give me a break. It was only two weeks ago that I finally got around to putting something on the apartment walls." She glanced at the bare concrete. "It is a little characterless, isn't it?"

"That's the price you pay for privacy."

A small, companionable silence settled between them as Rachael took a seat across the little table from him. They exchanged amenities about how good the tea tasted, and finally Jason said, "You were telling me about college."

Rachael smiled wistfully and glanced down at her glass, toying lightly with the condensation that formed on the side. "No, I was on the verge of telling you about Sander."

"Do you want to?"

She looked at him, taking in the hard angles of his face that were softened and diffused by his beard and by the gentleness of his pale blue eyes. "Yes. If you want to listen."

He reached across the table and took her hand into his. "Rachael, you have to know by now that I care about you. Not just as a colleague or an assistant, but as a person. We're past the point of building walls and hiding what we feel. Friends share the good and the bad, and we are friends now, aren't we?"

Rachael felt tears stinging behind her eyes. "I've never been good at making friends, Jason."

"If that's true, it's because you were too afraid to open your heart to the people around you."

"And that doesn't make you think less of me?"

"No." He tightened his grip on her hand, squeezing it reassuringly. "It just means that you have a lot of this world—and yourself—left to explore. I rather like the idea of sharing some of that exploration with you."

Rachael laughed shortly. "You're a strange man, Jason Burgess."

"And that doesn't make you think less of me?" he asked with a grin.

"No."

"Then will you tell me how you met Sander?"

Sighing deeply, Rachael gently removed her hand from Jason's. "We met in college—in an art class, naturally. He was very handsome, but more than that he had this incredible air of self-assurance about him that drew me like a magnet. For over half a semester I watched him when I didn't think he'd notice. I was terrified he'd realize I had a crush on him."

"Did he?"

She smiled sheepishly. "Of course. I wasn't nearly as subtle as I'd thought I was."

"Did he ask you out on a date?"

"No. We were paired up by the instructor for an assignment. We were supposed to create a cartoon strip. I was completely at a loss, but Sander took charge and came up with an idea. He was a very intense person, very driven to succeed, and for some strange reason, we hit it off despite my shyness. By the time we finished the class project I knew all about his burning desire to be a comic book illustrator, and he'd started trying to convince me that I should be one, too.

"We began dating, and I fell so madly in love that I'd have done anything in the world for him. When he came up with the idea for *Ravenmede*, he asked me to help him illustrate it and I immediately said yes. It was a way to be with him, to be part of his life. I wanted to be indispensable to him."

And you were, Jason thought, remembering what Roger Lampasat had told him about Sander's artistic ability. As she continued, Jason formed an image of their relationship that was not very pretty. Without Rachael, Sander would never have been anything but a second-rate hack, and even in those early days in college, he had to have known it. He'd seen Rachael's incredible talent and lack of self-confidence as his ticket to success, and had used her without ever giving her the credit she deserved or making any attempt to strengthen her fragile ego.

In faet, it occurred to Jason that Sander had done just the opposite. He'd made Rachael feel lucky to be doing his work for him; it had been to his advantage to keep her subservient, dependent and oh, so grateful.

Rachael said nothing like that to Jason, of course—he simply applied his own interpretation to the facts she related about their marriage immediately after graduation, and the lean years they spent together before they finally sold *Ravenmede* to Lamplight Comics. Intellectually Jason knew that he was probably being unfair, subscribing such devious motives to Rachael's late husband, but he couldn't quell his instinctive dislike for the man. It was obvious that despite the air of self-confidence that had attracted Rachael to him, Sander had had big ego problems. Had he been more secure, he would have nurtured Rachael's talent and ego, building her up and making her truly a partner. But that wasn't the way their relationship had worked, and Jason couldn't keep from resenting the weakness in Sander that had kept Rachael from becoming strong.

Part of his dislike stemmed from simple male jealousy—a primordial, instinctive hatred of one man for another over the possession of a woman. But Rachael wasn't an object to be possessed, and Jason wasn't a caveman. Nor was he going to place himself in competition with a dead man. If Rachael was ever going to love again, she would have to make peace with her memories of Sander, learn to treasure them, and find a place for them in whatever new life she chose. Jason already knew he wanted that life to be with him, even though he had no idea how long it might take for her to be ready.

Rachael's narration finally turned to the birth of her son, and Jason watched her closely, softly asking questions when it seemed appropriate, and allowing long silences when she needed time to adjust to the emotion of her memories. She talked about Micah's first step, his first tooth, his first word, and she cried, but there were no wrenching sobs, just gentle, cleansing tears.

They talked for hours—until late afternoon—but it seemed like much longer. The bond that gradually formed between them was one that many people never achieved after years of friendship.

Cat showed up for dinner, immediately suspicious of the stranger encroaching on his territory, and his antics broke the contemplative mood of the afternoon. Jason could see that Rachael was exhausted, both emotionally and physically, and he reluctantly told her he had to be going. Mrs. Ramos would be waiting for him to take charge of Emily, but more importantly, Rachael needed time to be alone.

"Thank you, Jason," she said with heartfelt sincerity as she walked him to the door. "Thank you for coming after me, thank you for listening, thank you for..." She searched for the appropriate words, but she had so much to be grateful to him for that nothing quite seemed to do the trick. "Thank you for being you. You're a very special man, Jason."

Unable to resist, he reached out and stroked her cheek. "I don't feel special, Rachael. But I'm very glad you think so. I'll give you a call tomorrow, but if you'd like someone to talk to before then, you've got my number, right?"

Rachael nodded. When Jason had learned that she did a lot of her work for *The Quest* at home, he'd given her his number in case she ever needed to ask a question. "I'm fine now, Jason. Really. Please tell Emily that I'm sorry I didn't know the story of Princess Rachael and the eagles."

He smiled, hoping that all the fresh, deep emotions he was feeling for her didn't show too plainly in his eyes. "I hope someday you'll feel up to meeting Emily under better circumstances."

"I hope so, too, Jason. I can't run from children for the rest of my life."

He took her hands in his and pulled her close. It pleased him immensely that she came to him so willingly. "Have you ever thought about having another child?" he asked her quietly.

Rachael put her arms around Jason, grateful for the contact. "Until you stampeded into my life, I'd been doing my best *not* to think about anything."

"No one will ever replace Micah in your heart, Rachael."

"Or Sander," she added softly.

"Or Sander," Jason allowed, feeling a constricting tightening of his heart. He pulled back slightly and lifted her face so that he could see her eyes. "But that doesn't mean you can't love again."

"You couldn't," she reminded him.

"Ah, but I'm a hopeless romantic who believes in fate and love everlasting. Somewhere in this world there's a woman looking just for me."

"A woman like Molly?" Rachael asked, wondering why her heart felt as though a fist was squeezing it, and realizing that it was because nobody could have been more different from Jason's late wife than she was. She wasn't ready yet to examine why that knowledge made her feel an emptiness like none she'd ever known.

But as quickly as the emptiness had come, it vanished as Jason told her, "No, not like Molly. I don't think I'd ever make the mistake of trying to replace her. She was the friend I needed as a boy, and the wife I needed as a young man. I like to believe that if she'd lived, we'd have grown up together and become even stronger in our love for each other...but I'm a different person than I was then. I have different needs."

"What do you need, Jason?" she dared to ask.

"I need someone warm and soft and gentle to fill some of the empty corners of my life." *I need you,* he wanted to add, but didn't dare.

"I hope you find her soon."

"I hope so, too."

CHAPTER FOURTEEN

THAT NIGHT PROVED to be a very long one for Rachael. Her head was filled with memories, but for the first time since the accident, she wasn't afraid she'd fall to pieces if she took the memories out and explored them. She allowed herself the sadness she was entitled to, and she cried some more, but the horrible weight of her grief wasn't nearly as oppressive as it had been before Jason had uncorked it and held her while it spilled out.

From somewhere she found the strength to examine her relationship with Sander and the resentments she'd been suppressing. It was no longer possible to convince herself that Jason's praise of her was only pity. She had to face the truth. Jason Burgess was a man so strong and sure of himself that giving credit to others, nurturing talent, didn't threaten him. Sander had been weak in that respect.

Strangely, once Rachael allowed herself to accept that judgment about her late husband, she found that it didn't diminish her memory of Sander. He had been an imperfect man, but she had still loved him, and whether he'd given her the credit she deserved or not, she would never have achieved the level of success she'd attained without him. That success had not come overnight; alone, she wouldn't have had the courage or the fortitude to persist as Sander had. By herself, she could never have conceived an idea as original and innovative as *Ravenmede*. She had needed Sander, and he had needed her. Their marriage had been based on a symbiotic relationship that had benefited both of them.

Rachael had been happy during the years of her marriage, and admitting to herself that Sander had flaws did not take those happy years away from her.

Late that night, when sleep wouldn't come, Rachael went to her bedroom closet and pulled out a large artist's portfolio, the only possession other than her clothes that she'd brought with her when she'd left Vermont. The portfolio was full of drawings, but there was one in particular she needed to see. It was a large chalk portrait she'd done of Micah shortly before his death. The soft, diffused pastels had captured his innocence and sweet purity, but her artist's hand had also captured the twinkle of mischief in his smile.

She studied the portrait a long time, and when she finally returned the portfolio to her closet, she left the picture out on her bureau. She went back to bed, drifted peacefully to sleep and dreamed of her son.

Rachael spent Saturday in much the same way she'd spent the previous night. As she went about her weekend chores her thoughts were filled with Sander and Micah, and Jason was buzzing around inside her head, too. He lurked pleasantly on the fringes of her consciousness, comforting her with his presence.

He stayed with her as she did her grocery shopping and through a quick trip to the art supply store, and by late afternoon when her phone rang she knew that he would be on the other end of the line.

"How are you, Rachael?" Jason asked seriously after they had exchanged hellos. He held his breath, praying that after all they had been through yesterday there would be no need for game playing or beating around the bush. They'd broken down so many walls, and he wasn't sure he'd be able to bear it if she'd resurrected them.

But he needn't have worried. "I'm fine, Jason, truly. I've been a little sad, but I'm not falling apart or anything."

"That's because you're a lot stronger than you give yourself credit for."

"Having strong friends helps."

Jason chuckled. "If that was directed at me, thank you."

"It was."

"So, how have you occupied your day?" he asked. "What does an animator's assistant do in her free time?"

Rachael laughed. "She does all the things normal people do, I suppose. Housecleaning, laundry, shopping..." She looked across the room at the picture of Micah that was leaning against her drafting table. "And I just finished framing a picture."

"Did you get a spurt of inspiration and create a new masterpiece?"

"No, this is an old masterpiece," she told him. "It's a portrait of Micah I did several years ago."

"You *have* been productive today," he said gently, and they both knew he was referring to more than what she'd accomplished in the physical sense. He was acknowledging an emotional growth and healing, and Rachael found it amazing—and very comforting—that he could know her so well.

"And what have you done today?" she asked, turning the tables on him.

He wanted to tell her that all he'd done was think about her, but that didn't seem wise. Instead he told her how he'd been trounced in a tennis game at his health club, and about a couple of new ideas he'd come up with for the Wizard's Lair scene in *The Quest*.

"Would you like me to work on them tomorrow?" she asked after he'd explained the new concept in detail.

"Definitely not," he said firmly. "I have other plans to keep you busy tomorrow."

"Oh?" She couldn't imagine what he meant. The Wizard's Lair was their next major project.

"Have you ever been to Catalina?" he asked. Even over the phone, he could tell that he'd taken her completely by surprise.

"Catalina? The island?"

"The very one."

Flustered, Rachael fumbled for an answer. "Umm...uh, no."

"Good. Then I'll pick you up at seven tomorrow morning and we'll drive down to San Pedro to catch the eight o'clock ferry. We'll spend a quiet day sight-seeing and I'll have you home by eleven tomorrow night."

Rachael was still in a state of shock. She certainly hadn't expected anything like this. "Jason, that's very nice of you, but—"

"Nice has nothing to do with it," he said, cutting her off before she could think of a dozen excuses not to come with him. "I need to get away from the city for a while, and Catalina is so beautiful and peaceful it regenerates me. Besides, I'd like to share it with you. Do you already have other plans?"

"No," she admitted.

"Are you afraid of the ocean?"

"I've never been on it, so I can't really say."

"Then I'll bring the Dramamine, you bring a wide-brimmed hat so you won't get sunburned, and we'll go to Catalina." He paused a moment, realizing that despite his good intentions he was putting more pressure on her than he'd intended. "I'm sorry, Rachael. I wasn't trying to bulldoze you into going with me. If you'd rather not—if you need time to be alone, I'll back off."

Time to be alone. Rachael considered that for a moment. She'd had two and a half years of being alone; that was more than enough.

"I would love to explore Catalina with you, Jason. Thank you for inviting me."

"Thank you for accepting," he answered softly, telling himself he was doing this for Rachael's benefit, because she needed to start getting out more, sharing more of herself with the world. He told himself his motives were good, but he had to admit that some of them were selfish, too. He wanted to be with her and to explore their deepening friendship.

They finalized their plans and hung up, and Jason reminded himself that he was going to have to tread very carefully with Rachael. She was still fragile, still hurting, and despite the fact that he was coming to love her very much, he could do her great harm. He had to be very sure that everything he did was in Rachael's best interests until she was ready to acknowledge his love for her and decide if it was something she could reciprocate.

Belinda had told him a woman would be a fool not to love him. He hoped she was right, because if she wasn't, he was in for a big fall.

CATALINA ISLAND WAS as beautiful and peaceful as Jason had promised. The ferry ride to Avalon took a little over two hours, but since it was Rachael's first time out on the ocean, the time passed very quickly. Once they cleared the busy San Pedro harbor and left the sprawling metropolis of Los Angeles behind, there was nothing to see but miles of ocean in every direction, and the vastness was as awe-inspiring as Rachael had expected it to be.

She and Jason found a bench on the top deck and watched the ocean slip beneath them. Occasionally a sailboat would glide past them in the distance or a huge freighter would appear on the horizon, but for the most part there was little to see and even less to do. They talked when the mood struck them and at other times sat in companionable silence until they reached the horseshoe bay that made up Avalon harbor, Santa Catalina's largest community and only major tourist attraction.

The harbor was like a giant sapphire jewel resting placidly at the base of Catalina's lush green hillsides. Hundreds of pleasure boats of every size, shape and description were anchored in the bay, and even before the ferry docked, Rachael could see the charming little shops and restaurants that dotted the circular shoreline. After they disembarked, Jason purchased tickets to several tours, and they spent the day sight-seeing. A glass-bottomed boat took them along the coast to be entertained by a colony of seals, and a tour bus carried them up into the mountains to investigate the grounds of the Wrigley mansion. Vacation condominiums and magnificent homes dotted the hillsides, and the view looking down into Avalon was spectacular.

They returned to the village for a late lunch and then casually strolled down St. Catherine Way toward the magnificent casino, which sat on a little peninsula at the north end of the bay. Six stories tall, the round, pristine white casino with its red-tiled roof dominated the view of the harbor. They walked through the ornate theater, the casino itself and the grand ballroom, which filled the upper story, and when the guided tour was over, they stepped out onto the terrace that circled the ballroom.

"This is magnificent, Jason," Rachael said, looking down on the boats bobbing in the sparkling clear bay. "It's so peaceful and...*simple* here. I can see why you enjoy it so much."

"I'm glad you like it," Jason said, more interested in watching Rachael than the view. For the first time since he'd met her, she seemed completely at ease. Her smile was easy and natural, her mood was bubbly and buoyant. Even her shyness seemed to have evaporated, which made Jason happier than he could ever have imagined; it meant that she was comfortable with him. She was learning to trust him, to be herself, and that trust was worth its weight in gold.

"How did you know I needed this?" she asked, turning to face him.

"Everyone needs a day of freedom and diversion now and then. I just thought it was your turn."

"But you've seen all this before."

"Not with you."

Rachael smiled up at him, noticing the way the high gingerbread arches of the terrace cast a network of soft shadows across his face. The wind and salt air had caused his hair and beard to frizz, and with his height and broad shoulders, he looked like an adorable, oversized teddy bear. She froze the picture in her mind along with other images of the wonderful day.

"Why are you looking at me like that?" Jason asked, wondering what was going through her head. She looked amused by something, and he had the feeling it was him.

"I was just thinking you looked like a big, overstuffed teddy bear."

"Damn!" He snapped his fingers. "I knew I shouldn't have had that lemon meringue pie for dessert."

"Not that kind of overstuffed," Rachael said, laughing.

"What other kind is there?"

"I meant overstuffed as in cute and cuddly."

"Cute and cuddly?" He eyed her skeptically as he rubbed his jaw. "I'm going to have to do something about my image. This beard is supposed to make me look suave and distinguished. My barber will hear about this."

"Well, don't let him shave the beard, whatever you do."

His eyes lit up with boyish expectancy. "You like the beard?"

"Yes, I do," she said, turning back toward the bay as she remembered the way his soft whiskers had abraded her face when he had kissed her two days earlier.

Jason noted the soft flush of color that crept up her cheeks. "Do beards make you blush?"

"No, of course not!" She faced him again. "I was thinking about . . . last Friday."

Jason could have pretended not to understand and forced her to explain exactly what part of Friday she meant, but he knew very well that she was thinking about their passionate encounter that had almost gotten out of hand. What amazed him was that she brought the subject up at all. It would have been far simpler to have evaded his question. "Has it bothered you, Rachael?"

"If you mean, am I sorry I kissed you, no," she answered quietly. "I'm not sorry. I've tried not to think about it, and when I do, I try to summon a little guilt, but I haven't been able to feel any. Don't you think that's strange?"

"You mean, you want to feel guilty?"

Rachael smiled ruefully. "No. But I feel as though I should. I should feel as though kissing you, *enjoying* kissing you, is a betrayal of Sander."

"So you feel guilty for not feeling guilty. And on top of that, you're feeling even guiltier because you're having a wonderful time today." Jason understood the intricate little nuances of guilt only too well because he'd experienced them himself. He suspected that was the reason Rachael was able to discuss those feelings so openly with him—that and her newfound trust of him.

Could trust be a first, important step toward loving someone? he wondered.

Rachael shook her head in astonishment as she considered his words. "Sometimes I suspect you know what I'm feeling even before I do."

"So you do feel guilty about today?"

She nodded. "A little. I'm actually having fun for the first time in years, and it feels strange."

"I know. But the fact that you can verbalize your guilt means that you know it's irrational. Sander and Micah would want you to be happy. I always believed there were two ways to honor someone you've lost—the right way and the wrong way. The wrong way is to martyr yourself to their memory and bury yourself with them."

"And the right way is to get on with your life and make it something they would have been proud of," Rachael concluded for him, turning to look out over the bay.

"Exactly."

It was a moment before Rachael whispered a soft, "Thank you, Jason."

He couldn't resist slipping one arm around her waist and drawing her into the shelter of his body. "For what?"

She rested her head against his chest and refused to allow herself to feel guilty for loving the feel of his arms around her. "For rescuing me. If you hadn't come along, who knows how long I'd have stayed buried alive."

Jason said nothing, but he brushed his lips lightly against her windblown hair, then rested his cheek against her head. They stood there, lost in their own thoughts as the sun started setting behind the mountains and the bay grew dark with shadows.

CHAPTER FIFTEEN

THE FIRST SIGN went up at Animators on Monday morning. It featured a beautifully executed cartoon depicting a regiment of Western cavalry soldiers playing baseball with a tribe of renegade Indians. The caption read, "Ninth Annual Animators' Picnic and Softball Fiasco this Saturday. Scalpers Welcome."

That afternoon a second sign appeared, and it, too, had a Wild-West theme. A group of ravenous settlers were chasing a terrified cow around a covered wagon, and the caption said something about rounding up the family for an old-fashioned barbecue.

No one would admit to having created either sign, but by the middle of the week, everyone had gotten in on the act. It seemed as though there wasn't a wall, window or desk in the entire complex that didn't have at least one humorously drawn Western-style sign announcing the picnic. By Friday the place looked more like a cartoon factory than an animation house, and Jason was beginning to wonder if anyone but Rachael had done any work on *The Quest* that week. Hers was the only office that was free of picnic-related drawings. He suspected that meant she wasn't planning to attend, and though he understood why she might find the family get-together difficult to handle, he knew he was going to be keenly disappointed if she didn't show up.

Returning from a quick trip to the animation department, he couldn't resist stopping at her office even though he had nothing to discuss with her. He'd already put her to work on all the assignments he could think of, and he didn't even have a bad joke to throw at her. He just felt like seeing her—which wasn't unusual.

He knocked lightly on her door and stuck his head in. "Good afternoon, Rachael. How are things in the salt mines?"

Rachael looked up from her lightboard and smiled happily. "Oh, Jason. I'm glad you're here."

"Then I'm glad I'm here, too," he quipped, closing the door behind him before he crossed to her desk and sat on the edge. "What can I do for you?"

"You can answer a question," she said, growing serious.

"Shoot."

"What would you get if you crossed Davy Crockett with Mrs. Smith and Baskin-Robbins?"

Jason almost choked on his laughter. He'd been ready for a serious question. The last thing he'd expected was a counterattack in their ongoing joke war. "I don't know. What *would* you get if you crossed Davy Crockett with Mrs. Smith and Baskin-Robbins?"

"Pie Alamo," she answered in a deadpan voice.

Jason groaned and grabbed his side as though he'd been mortally wounded. "Oh, that's terrible!" he said. "You've been waiting all afternoon just to ambush me with that, haven't you?"

Rachael grinned. "That's right."

"Don't you know any *good* jokes?"

"As a matter of fact, I do, but considering the quality of the jokes you tell me, I didn't think you'd recognize a good one."

"Ouch!" They laughed together, and Jason marveled at the incredible change in Rachael. Around the rest of the staff she was still shy, but with him she became a different person. Her voice was always soft and her manner demure, but she was allowing some of the delightfully off-center aspects of her personality to shine through, and Jason loved it. In fact, the more natural she became, the more he loved *her*.

"Are you trying to get yourself fired for insubordination, woman?" he said teasingly. "This week I probably wouldn't have any trouble rounding up a lynching party."

Still smiling, she commented, "The Western motif *is* getting a little out of hand, isn't it? This morning Dan came in wearing a ten-gallon Stetson, and he had his son's cap pistol strapped to his hip."

Jason heaved a mystified sigh. "I know. Robb insulted one of his background paintings yesterday, and they're going to shoot it out in the parking lot after work. I don't know if I'm running an animation studio or the O. K. Corral."

"You're enjoying every minute of it, and you know it," Rachael said with an impish twinkle in her eye. "I saw you laughing at that sketch someone did of you dressed as the Lone Ranger being roasted over an open barbecue pit."

"That was a good one, wasn't it?"

"Your picnic is going to be a fabulous success."

"Are you going to be there?" he couldn't keep from asking.

Rachael's smile faded only a little as she regarded him wistfully. "I don't think so, Jason. It's a family thing, and I'm just not sure I'm up to that yet."

"I'll be there to help you get through it," he reminded her gently.

"If that Lone Ranger sketch is any indication, you'll be too busy being roasted to help me with anything," she said lightly.

"I'm serious, Rachael," he told her, refusing to be diverted. "I'm not trying to pressure you into coming, but if you do, I'll be there with all the moral support I can give you."

Rachael glanced out into the courtyard reflectively. "You'll be disappointed in me if I don't come, won't you?"

"Of course not," he said tenderly, reaching out to gently touch her chin and turn her face toward his. "I'll be disappointed if you don't come because your presence would brighten my day considerably. But I would never think less of you if you decide you can't handle it. You have to do what's right for you, not what's right for me."

"I'll think about it," she promised him, feeling as though she was drowning in the warmth of his soft blue eyes. At that moment she would have done anything in the world for Jason Burgess, even attend the company picnic. But he was right. Whatever decision she made, it had to be because it was the best thing for her, not because it was what he wanted. All her life Rachael had done what the men in her life—her father and her husband—had told her to do. She wasn't going to be a puppet anymore, not even for a wonderfully loving friend like Jason. If she did go to the picnic, it would be because she was ready to take another step forward.

She had less than twenty-four hours to decide just how strong she'd grown.

SATURDAY MORNING DAWNED bright and clear; there wasn't a trace of a cloud, or smog in the sky. The western caterers arrived at first light to set up their enormous mobile barbecue pit, and Lorna and Gretchen were right behind them, ready to see that the picnic tables were appropriately placed and the children's tent put up where it was supposed to be.

Weeks of careful planning paid off, and the preparations proceeded without a hitch. Jason spent the morning being bossed around by his daughter and his secretary, and by the time the first employees started arriving, everything was as ready as it was going to get.

Dan Eisenberg, his wife and three children were among the first arrivals, and after a couple of clowns lured his kids to the tent, Dan tried to enlist Jason's help in setting an ambush for Robb Weston. Robb had won their quick-draw contest in the parking lot yesterday, and Dan was out for revenge.

Jason could tell it was going to be an eventful day. Everyone brought their best "Let's party" attitude with them, and he was delighted that his employees were all having fun. In spite of that he felt a little like Ebenezer Scrooge. In the first hour, more than a hundred people showed up, but Rachael wasn't among them. He tried to hide his disappointment and join in the revelry, although his heart wasn't in it.

"What's up, boss?" Robb came up behind Jason and thumped him on the back heartily. He was feeling particularly chipper because he'd thus far managed to escape every one of Dan's attempts to waylay him. "You look a little down in the mouth today."

Jason gave him a reassuring smile. "Not at all."

"But you're usually the life of the party," Robb reminded him.

"I'm saving my strength for the softball game. Speaking of which, are you going to be the umpire again this year?"

"Only if you promise not to let Dan pitch. I don't trust that man with a lethal weapon in his hand today. Come to think of it, you'd better not give him a bat, either."

Jason chuckled. "We'll put him somewhere out in left field and keep him there."

"Good enough." Rob glanced around the crowded lawn. "I haven't seen Rachael around yet. She is comin', isn't she?"

"I don't think so." He tried to keep his voice light so that Robb wouldn't detect his disappointment. "She said yesterday that she wasn't sure if she'd make it or not."

"That's too bad. You know, that girl has really come out of her shell since she went to work for you. I was hoping that being around everyone while they're actin' all wild and crazy would loosen her up even more."

"Or scare her off completely," Jason commented with a grin.

"No, I think she's too happy working with you to be scared off. I'm glad you two hit it off so well."

"It was a little rough there in the beginning, but she's a very special lady. We're lucky to have her with us."

"And speaking of having her with us..." Robb inclined his head toward the house. "I guess she decided to come, after all."

Jason turned, and sure enough there was Rachael, walking across the lawn toward him. She was dressed simply in blue jeans and a bright print shirt, and her smile was a little apprehensive, but Jason didn't think he'd ever seen anyone quite so beautiful. "Well, I guess I'd better go play host, hadn't I?" he asked, then took off like a shot without waiting for his friend's reply.

He covered the ground quickly, so happy, he didn't care if anyone noticed that he was a little too eager to greet his newest guest.

"Hello, Jason. I see you haven't been skewered and basted yet," Rachael said as he joined her. His delighted smile was enough to ease some of the fears she'd had about coming.

"I think they're saving that for the grand finale. I'm so glad you decided to come, Rachael. Everyone's been asking about you." It seemed perfectly natural for him to place one arm around her waist as they continued across the lawn, but what seemed even more natural was her returning the gesture without even thinking about it. Jason wondered if there was a law against being this happy.

He brought her up-to-date on all the excitement she'd missed—which consisted mainly of Dan's attempts to bushwhack Robb, and an impromptu square dance "exhibition" led by the members of the Ink and Paint department. "They tell me the barbecue won't be ready for another hour or so, but there are plenty of munchies to tide you over until then. How about a lemonade? Or would you prefer a beer?"

"Lemonade would be wonderful."

He swerved slightly to the side and led her toward an old-fashioned lemonade stand. "Your wish is my command."

Across the yard, Robb Weston watched them with a sly, discerning smile. He'd suspected for some time now that Jason's interest in Rachael was more than just professional, and now he was sure of it. *As my great-great-grandmother Kitworth would have said,* he thought, *that boy's done gone an' swallowed a love bug.*

"Hi, Uncle Robb. Have you seen Daddy?" Lorna asked, giving her honorary uncle a peck on the cheek before returning her scrutiny to the crowd.

"I think he went that-a-way." Robb pointed in the direction of the lemonade stand.

Lorna shifted her gaze to the east lawn. "Where? I don't—oh, there he is." She started to take a step in her father's direction, then noticed that he wasn't alone. He was with a very pretty woman Lorna didn't remember having met, but who looked familiar just the same. "Uncle Robb, who's that woman with Daddy?"

Uh-oh, Robb thought. *Here comes trouble.* "That's Rachael Hubbard, Jason's new assistant."

"Assistant *what*?" Lorna asked cattily. "If she got any closer to him, she'd be on top of him."

Robb regarded her wearily. "In all fairness, Lorna, Jason doesn't seem to mind."

"Oh, you know Daddy. He's too polite for his own good. I'd better go rescue him. See you later." She took off on a direct course before Robb could tell her he didn't think Jason wanted to be rescued.

"Lorna! Wait up," Cole called, jogging to catch up with his wife. "Where are you headed in such a hurry?" he asked when he finally reached her side.

"I need to talk to Daddy," she told him, never taking her eyes off the woman at Jason's side.

"Honey, I heard someone say that the magic show is just about over. We need to go round up Emmy."

Lorna sighed irritably. "You go ahead and I'll catch up with you in a minute," she suggested, then smiled brightly as she flagged Jason down. "Daddy, hi! I was afraid you'd been kidnapped."

Jason stopped and turned toward his daughter and son-in-law. He felt Rachael tense slightly, as though she was suddenly self-conscious about having her arm around his waist. Reluctantly, he let her ease away from him. "No such luck. Honey, I'd like you to meet my assistant, Rachael Hubbard. Rachael, this is my daughter Lorna, and her husband, Cole Washburn."

Rachael held her hand out to Cole and then to Lorna. The son-in-law's handshake was by far the more cordial of the two. "It's a pleasure to meet you both. Jason talks about you all the time," she said in her always-soft voice.

"He does? That's nice to know," Lorna said, glancing from Jason to Rachael, then back to Jason again. She didn't care at all for the tender emotions she saw in her father's eyes.

"You must be Emily's Princess Rachael," Cole said with a laugh.

Lorna frowned. "Princess Rachael?"

Rachael glanced down nervously. "I met Emily the day you brought her to your father's office and she mistook me for a character in one of the stories Jason drew for her."

"That's right," Cole commented. "All she talked about that night was the beautiful, sad-eyed princess she'd met."

Sad-eyed princess. The phrase ricocheted around in Lorna's head until she finally remembered where she'd seen Rachael. A dozen sketches of her had littered the patio table the day she'd come by to discuss picnic plans with Jason. And apparently he'd created a story for Emily with *Princess* Rachael as the heroine.

This pretty woman with her soft voice; short, sassy haircut; and sad, moppet eyes was more than just her father's new assistant. Lorna had had enough experience with Jason's 'lady friends' to know a threat when she saw one, and the way he was looking at Rachael told her this one could be the biggest threat of all. She hadn't taken her father seriously a few weeks ago when he'd talked about finding someone to love, but now she did.

"You didn't tell me you'd hired a new assistant, Daddy. Whatever happened to that nice Paul Harris?"

"That nice Paul Harris got to be a pain in the—well, let's just say he got to be a pain, and leave it at that."

Lorna turned to Rachael and smiled. "So, where did Daddy find you?"

"I was working in the animation department," Rachael answered, unable to remember ever having been sized up with such hostility. Lorna's tone was pleasant, and her smile carefully constructed, but her eyes were as cold as ice. She felt a tiny shiver run down her spine, and it took considerable effort for her to continue. "Robb Weston recommended me for the job."

"How nice for you." Lorna turned her attention back to Jason. "Daddy, may I talk to you for a minute? We've got a minor crisis on between the western people and the other catering group."

"Sure, honey." Jason smiled down at Rachael. "Don't get lost—I'll be back in a minute."

Rachael nodded. "I think I'll go over and say hi to Deanna."

"And I'm going to go pick up Emily," Cole said, starting off toward the kiddy tent. "It was nice to have met you, Rachael. I know Emily's going to be thrilled when she learns that you're here. She'll want to see you right away."

Lorna had taken hold of Jason's arm and was preparing to drag him off toward the quarreling caterers, but he stopped and looked back at Rachael. He smiled encouragingly at her and noticed that she was taking a deep breath, as though steeling herself for the ordeal of seeing Emily again.

Rachael returned his smile tentatively. "I'm not going to run away, Jason," she promised. "Not yet, anyway."

"I'll be right back."

"What was that all about?" Lorna asked, falling in stride with Jason as they moved across the lawn.

"What was what all about?"

"That intense little exchange about running away."

Jason shrugged. "Rachael's new around here and she's a little shy. I just didn't want her to run away before she got to know everyone."

"I thought she used to work for Uncle Robb in animation."

Oops, Jason thought, realizing his error. "She did."

"Then surely she doesn't need you to introduce her around or play knight in shining armor."

"Have you considered that maybe I want to play knight in shining armor?" he asked, trying to keep his tone light. He didn't like the direction the conversation was taking.

"Oh, Daddy, come on!" Lorna exclaimed, exasperated. "That woman positively screams of pathetic damsel in distress, but I can't believe you'd fall for it. Her I-need-a-big-strong-man-to-watch-over-me act is the oldest trick in the book."

"That's enough, Lorna," Jason said harshly, coming to a dead stop. "You haven't got the faintest idea what you're talking about, and I don't ever want to hear you use that tone about Rachael again. Do you understand me?"

Lorna paled with shock. Jason had never spoken that sharply to her, and she couldn't believe he would do so just because of a transparent little bimbo like Rachael Hubbard. "I'm sorry, Daddy," she said, her eyes pooling with tears.

Normally Lorna's tears were enough to cajole him out of anything, but Jason didn't feel like being a cupcake right now. He softened his tone, but not much. "No, I'm sorry, Lorna. I shouldn't have snapped at you like that, but I meant what I said. Rachael is a sweet, lovely lady who's going through a rough time right now, and we've become good friends."

I'll just bet you have, Lorna thought, swiping at the single tear that had fallen onto her cheek. "Are you in love with her?"

Jason sighed, knowing it would be a mistake to discuss Rachael with his daughter. If the time ever arrived that he felt free to talk about his feelings, Rachael, not Lorna, would be the first to know that he'd fallen in love. "Honey, as I said before, Rachael is going through a very difficult emotional ordeal right now. Believe me, the last thing on her mind is a romantic involvement with me or anyone else, for that matter. We're just good friends. If that changes, I'll let you know."

He patted her on the shoulder, then started toward the barbecue pit again, and Lorna stayed behind a moment, watching him speculatively. It hadn't escaped her notice that

Jason really hadn't answered her question, and that worried her all the more.

Since her mother's death, Lorna had had a secret terror of losing her father, too. Over the years she'd come to understand that death was inevitable, but women were another matter entirely. Her father and mother had had the perfect marriage, and once that ended, Lorna had become the one and only woman in her father's life. She wasn't about to give that up without a fight. No one was ever going to take him away from her.

BY THE TIME Jason reached the caterers, the territorial squabble had already been settled by Gretchen. He promised her a raise effective Monday morning, and she reminded him that she was due for one on the first of the month, anyway.

Since he wasn't needed as a mediator, Jason turned around and retraced his trail to Rachael. The magic show had ended, and children of every age and description were pouring out of the tent. When he finally saw Rachael, his heart leaped into his throat, and he quickened his pace to reach her. Somehow she'd been caught in the path most of the kids were taking to reach their parents, and she was trapped in the middle of the stampede.

Dodging a whooping war party of ten-year-olds, Jason picked his way toward Rachael, who was staring thoughtfully at the children.

"I'm sorry about this, Rachael," he said with a sweep of his hand when he reached her.

She gave him a hesitant smile. "I knew what to expect when I came today, Jason. I'm not falling apart or anything."

"I can see that."

Rachael shifted her gaze toward a picnic table where several children were gathering around Lloyd Pope and his wife. "Do you see that little boy over there—the one with the white-blond hair?"

"Damien Pope? He's Lloyd's youngest."

Rachael nodded. "Micah had hair just like that—as white as snow, and as soft as silk...." There was a long pause, and Jason waited, knowing she was making another comparison, too. "He'd be just about that age. If he had lived."

He took Rachael's hand and she squeezed it hard but didn't look up at him. Instead she glanced around the huge backyard, watching the families, studying the children. Jason stood with her silently, wondering what it must feel like to know you'd lost everything in the world that mattered.

An old-fashioned chuck-wagon bell clattered as one of the western caterers hollered, *"Come and get it!"* and a stampede of another sort was on. This time, children and adults alike began streaming toward the west lawn and lining up at the food-laden tables.

Rachael glanced up at Jason. "Are you ready to eat?" she asked. There was a hitch in her voice and her eyes were shimmering with unshed tears.

"Why don't we take a walk until the crowd thins out a little?" he suggested.

Jason could actually see Rachael's shoulders sag with relief. She needed a few minutes to compose herself, away from everyone. "That would be nice." With her hand still securely in his, they strolled toward the house, onto the deck and into the family room. Jason closed the door behind them, shutting out the raucous noise of the party they'd left behind.

"I'm taking you away from your guests," Rachael said, brushing away a tear that was clinging to the corner of one eye.

"I'm exactly where I want to be," he said, pulling her into his arms, cradling her head on his shoulder. "Do you want to talk about it?"

"You know most of it," she answered, grateful for Jason's understanding and his strength.

"You haven't told me about the accident... how it happened. Can you talk about it yet?"

Rachael swallowed hard and pulled away from him with a little shiver. "There's not a lot to tell.... Sander was driving back from New York, from seeing his sister off for school in Europe. He and Micah were about thirty miles from home when a sudden, unpredicted storm hit—snow, sleet, freezing rain, everything. The State Patrol said that within minutes, the roads were a solid sheet of ice...."

"Rachael, you don't have to tell me—"

She put up a hand to stop him. "No, I need to talk about it. It's one of those things I've been keeping bottled up inside." She gave him a wistful smile. "You always seem to know exactly when I need to let it out."

"The healing doesn't really start until you do," he said gently.

"Oh, I do want to heal, Jason," she told him as tears began forming again.

"I know you do." He wanted to pull her into his arms again, but that wasn't what Rachael needed, so he stood beside her, giving her the distance she needed to be able to tell the story. She described the worsening road conditions and how she'd waited at home that night, still sick with strep throat and worried because her husband and son were long overdue.

"When the State Patrol car came down the lane and pulled into our driveway, I knew. Maybe it was only a natural assumption under the circumstances, but I didn't just know that something was wrong. I knew they were...dead. And then this solemn-faced patrolman came to the door and told me that there had been an accident. They'd been on one of the back roads that led to our house, and as they approached this old covered bridge another car came at them. The driver was going too fast, and when he came out of the bridge he hit a patch of ice. His car skidded sideways on the road, Sander swerved to avoid a head-on collision, and he went into a skid, too...down an embankment...into the river...."

"Oh, Rachael..." Jason whispered. The chilling image was one he knew would stay with him for quite a while.

"I had nightmares for a long time, imagining them in that icy cold water, trapped...drowning, but the coroner promised me that they hadn't suffered too much. The car had rolled several times before it hit the water, and neither of them were wearing seat belts. The coroner thought they were both unconscious by the time the car went into the river."

Tears were running down Rachael's cheeks, but she hadn't collapsed into a fit of agonized sobs as she had feared she might. She looked at Jason. "Well, have I depressed you enough for one day?"

Jason cupped her face and used his thumbs to brush away her tears. "I'm not depressed, and neither are you. You're sad, and I'm sad for you, but you're going to be okay. You proved that just by coming here today. You're a very strong lady, Rachael. I don't think you have any idea just how strong you really are."

She managed a smile. "Keep telling me that and maybe I'll believe it."

Jason shook his head. "That's something you have to discover for yourself."

"I'm trying," she whispered.

"I know you are." Unable to resist her nearness, Jason bent his head to hers and touched her lips lightly. The kiss lingered on for just a moment, then he broke the contact and pulled her to his side. "Come on, I'll show you to a bathroom where you can freshen up before we go out and attack that side of beef."

"All right." She smiled up at him, knowing she could brave anything if Jason was at her side.

They disappeared down the hall, never noticing that Lorna was out on the deck watching them leave, just as she'd watched Rachael lure her father with tears, just as she'd watched them kiss tenderly.

CHAPTER SIXTEEN

IT WASN'T UNTIL about three weeks later that Jason heard the rumor about him and Rachael. Upon walking into one of the sound studios, he had surprised two technicians who'd been speculating on the nature of the relationship between the boss and his pretty assistant. The comments he had overheard weren't crude or derogatory, and he supposed that considering the amount of time he'd spent with Rachael at the picnic, a certain amount of conjecture was to be expected.

He wondered if Rachael had heard the gossip, but decided it was best not to ask her because he wasn't quite sure how she'd feel about it. She'd be embarrassed, he thought. And probably apologetic. He didn't think she was ready to believe that maybe there was some basis for the rumor that the boss had fallen head over heels in love. The friendship they shared seemed to grow stronger every day, but so far that was all it was to Rachael—friendship.

For Jason that wasn't difficult to accept. The year he'd spent in bed with rheumatic fever had taught him the true meaning of patience, and he knew how to wait for what he wanted. Besides, just being Rachael's friend wasn't a bad bargain. He wanted more, of course, but their relationship was anything but one-sided. They worked together beautifully, and after work they occasionally went out for a casual dinner and talked for hours.

Their conversation spanned a multitude of subjects: likes and dislikes in food, movies, books, music, and television—all the trivialities that made for enjoyable chitchat. But they also found it easy to slip into personal discussions. Jason learned about her family, and she about his. With every passing day it became easier for her to talk about Sander, and she had endless questions about Molly and his marriage.

They talked at length about Lorna, too. Jason's concerns for his daughter's happiness were growing stronger as it became apparent that her marriage was about to hit the rocks. She and Cole had left the picnic early after engaging in a bitter, very public quarrel during the softball game, and the next week Lorna had finally admitted to Jason that she and Cole were having problems. She was vague about the source of the difficulties, but she said enough to give him the impression that Cole wasn't happy with the amount of time his wife spent at work and away on buying trips.

Jason had always considered himself a fairly liberated person. He believed in the rights of women to pursue a fulfilling career and receive pay commensurate with men doing the same work, so he could understand his daughter's need to have a life that wasn't entirely defined by her husband and child. But he could also sympathize with Cole, who was undoubtedly worried about how little time Lorna was spending with him and Emily. It was a difficult situation, and Jason had discussed the problem with Rachael a dozen times. Neither of them had come up with a solution, but Rachael had wisely commented that until Lorna was willing to tell him more about it, there wasn't much a father—or anyone else—could do about the problem.

Work on *The Quest* progressed smoothly and Jason began to feel that they were back on schedule. The composer had finally delivered the last bit of music for the film, and most of the dialogue was recorded. The storyboards were filling out, and the rough cut of the first ten minutes of the movie looked better than Jason had expected. The weeks sped by, and he knew he couldn't ask for more.

Rachael felt much the same way. Jason had changed her life in so many wonderful ways that she was beginning to believe she might someday get out from under the dark clouds that hung oppressively over her life. Already there were days when she could see the sun shining through and feel her life being regenerated.

She couldn't imagine what that life would be like without Jason, but she was also cautious. She didn't want to become dependent on him in the same way she'd been dependent on Sander. Relying on someone else for everything, making that person responsible for her happiness, was wrong. She saw that now and was determined never to allow it to happen again. Jason was a friend, and it scared her sometimes to think how much his friendship meant to her, but she refused to allow him to become the center of her life, around which everything she thought, said, or did revolved.

Of course, that was a difficult resolve to hold on to when her life was being almost entirely consumed by her work on *The Quest*. When she'd first taken the job, she'd told Jason she was going to have to find a dream of her own to fulfill, and as the weeks passed, she knew she was coming closer to the time when she'd have to start searching for that dream. Jason trusted and relied on her so much as his assistant, that there was a great temptation for Rachael to commit herself totally to his dream. That was a mistake she kept telling herself she wouldn't make.

"You look lost in thought," Jason told her as he came into her office through the Bull Pen door she'd left open.

Startled, Rachael whirled away from the window where she'd been staring into the courtyard. "You need to remove that jungle out there—it's too much of a temptation to easily distract employees like me."

"Or I could just fire you and leave the jungle," he teased her.

Rachael seemed to consider his idea. "That certainly would be the most cost-effective solution. Should I pack up and never darken your door again?" she asked, moving to the stool by her lightboard.

"Don't you dare. It's taken me over two months to get you broken to the whip." He crossed the floor, sat behind her desk and began leafing through some sketches she had laid out. "So, what were you thinking about so intently before I caught you?"

Rachael slipped her glasses on and went back to work on one of her netherworld drawings. "Independence," she told him.

Jason looked at her with comically lowered eyebrows. "Are you about to start a revolt?"

She smiled. "No, I was thinking more along the lines of personal independence. I think it's time I bought a car. You have to be getting fed up with taking me home on the nights we work late—"

"I enjoy taking you home, Rachael," Jason protested. "I certainly wouldn't feel right about you taking the bus. This is the big bad city, you know."

"Yes, I do know, but when I worked late for Robb, I always took a cab if it got dark before I was ready to leave. I didn't expect the boss to be my own personal chauffeur."

"Consider it one of the perks of your job," he advised her with a grin.

Rachael studied him for a moment. "Don't you think I should have a car, Jason? It's all the rage in Los Angeles."

Jason stiffened as he realized what he'd been doing. He really did enjoy the time they spent together when he took her home, mostly because it made it easy to casually suggest they stop for a bite to eat. If Rachael got a car, she would no longer be dependent on him for occasional transportation, so he'd unconsciously thrown up roadblocks in order to keep that one little hold on her.

"Sorry," he said sheepishly. "If you're ready to brave the L.A. freeways, who am I to discourage such a blatant act of bravery? Have you got a California driver's license?"

"Oh, yes," she assured him, wondering why he'd seemed opposed to the idea of a car in the first place. "You can't cash a check anywhere in the city without one. I couldn't even open a bank account until I transferred my driver's license. I should have gotten a car back then, too, but the idea of all that city traffic terrified me. Buses and cabs seemed a lot tamer."

"What kind of car are you considering?"

Rachael sighed and rolled her eyes. "I haven't the faintest idea what I want. The only thing I know about automobiles is that they use gas and their manufacturers spend a fortune thinking up cute jingles to sell them. Chevrolet's 'Heartbeat of America' tune is kinda catchy, but I don't think that's a valid criterion for making a purchase."

Jason laughed. "Don't let Chevrolet hear you say that." He paused for a moment, wondering what he should do. He'd have been only too happy to offer Rachael his advice—he'd even have offered to accompany her on an expedition to car dealerships—but after the way he'd acted about the car in the first place, he wasn't sure whether he should volunteer or not.

Jason wanted what was best for Rachael, and he had rejoiced at every step she'd taken toward finding herself and discovering all her hidden strengths. But he also knew that he was no saint. Someday he wanted Rachael to see him as more than just a friend, and apparently his subconscious felt threatened by every step she took that didn't include him. Knowing that, Jason had to wonder whether or not he should bow out and let Rachael do this on her own.

He was both relieved and happy when she took that decision out of his hands. "What would you suggest, Jason? I'm at a complete loss."

"How about a Mercedes?"

Rachael's eyebrows went up in surprise. "A Mercedes?"

Why was she reluctant to consider a Mercedes? Jason wondered. Surely money was no problem. "Why not?"

"A Mercedes in *my* neighborhood?" she said skeptically. "It would be stripped or stolen ten minutes after I brought it home from the car lot."

"You have a point," he allowed. "Maybe you should move *and* get a new car."

Rachael smiled at him gently, as though he was an awkward child who needed guidance. "Let's take this one step at a time, Jason."

"All right. No move, no Mercedes."

"I need something small, fuel efficient—"

"Low profile," he supplied, and Rachael agreed. They discussed several makes and models, but they finally agreed that she really wasn't going to be able to make a decision until she actually saw a few cars and took them for a test drive.

As they talked, Jason could see Rachael was bothered by the thought of dealing with high-pressure car salesmen, and finally he couldn't resist offering to accompany her when she went to look.

Rachael smiled at him gratefully. "It may set the women's movement back twenty or thirty years, but I would love to have your help. I've never been good at bargaining with salesmen, and I tend to believe everything they tell me."

"Then it's settled. I'll pick you up early on Saturday, and if we don't find anything, we'll try again another day. There's no law that says you have to buy the first car you look at."

Rachael started to apologize for being such a nuisance and taking up so much of his time, but she stopped herself. Jason was teaching her the meaning of friendship, and one thing she had learned was that friends did things like this for each other. She honestly believed that he enjoyed her company as much as she treasured his, and he wouldn't have offered to help her if he hadn't genuinely wanted to.

Instead of apologizing, she took another step toward self-confidence and accepted the fact that she was worthy of Jason's precious friendship.

"Thank you, Jason. I'll—" The intercom on Rachael's phone buzzed, cutting her off, and she reached toward her desk to answer it. "Rachael Hubbard."

It was Gretchen. "Rachael, is Jason there? His daughter is calling for him."

Rachael looked at Jason. "Lorna's trying to reach you."

"Tell Gretchen to transfer it in here," he said, then reached for the phone once Rachael had relayed the message. "Hi, honey. What's up?"

"Hi, Daddy. I've got a little baby-sitter problem again."

Jason sighed. "You're not bringing Emily to the office again, are you?"

"No, no. Cole and I are thinking about spending the weekend at his parents' condo in Palm Springs—just the two of us—and we thought you might want to keep Emily."

"Oh, honey, I don't know," he said regretfully. Under other circumstances he would have been overjoyed to have his granddaughter for a full weekend, but he'd just made a commitment to Rachael. "I already have plans for Saturday."

"What plans?" Lorna asked.

"Rachael is buying a car, and I'm going along to give her advice and moral support."

"Daddy, you don't know anything about cars," Lorna said disdainfully.

Jason laughed. "Well, don't tell Rachael that. I've got her convinced I'm the next best thing to Lee Iacocca."

Until Saturday had been mentioned in the conversation, Rachael had returned her attention to her lightboard, but when it became apparent that Jason's plans to help her were standing in the way of doing something for his daughter, she stopped and listened. "Jason, what's going on?" she asked in a whisper.

"Hold on a minute, Lorna." Jason put his hand over the mouthpiece and told Rachael, "Lorna and Cole are going away for the weekend and they want me to keep Emily."

"Jason, that's wonderful," Rachael said with a smile. "Maybe some time alone will help them work out their problems."

"That's true, but—"

"And you'd love having Emily for a whole weekend," she continued, cutting him off. "We can go car shopping later. Please don't tell Lorna 'no' on my account."

Jason wanted to inform Rachael that he wasn't considering refusing Lorna on her account, but on his own. He loved his granddaughter and would have enjoyed having her to himself, but all things considered, he'd rather spend the day with Rachael. But he couldn't tell her that without also telling her he was falling head over heels in love with her, and that she was rapidly becoming the most important thing in his life.

Putting aside his selfish streak, he returned to the phone. "Okay, honey, I'd be happy to keep Emily this weekend."

Strangely, Lorna didn't sound quite as relieved as he'd expected her to. "Daddy, you're not thinking of taking Emily car hunting with you and Rachael, are you? You know how Emmy hates shopping."

"Lorna, you can hardly equate the dress department at Gucci's with a car lot," he said, praying for patience. "But no, I won't be taking Emily car hunting."

Her tone brightened considerably. "I think that's wise, Daddy. I'm sure Rachael won't have any trouble buying a car without you."

"Actually," he said tightly, trying not to get angry, "we're just postponing our plans. We'll go the following weekend." Jason regretted giving Lorna that information the moment the words were out of his mouth. Lorna would undoubtedly spend the next ten days thinking up something to occupy his Saturdays with for the next year.

He would have news for her, though, if she took it into her head to interfere with his friendship with Rachael. Daddy's days of catering to his little girl's whims were over—at least as far as the women in his life were concerned. Or, more accurately, as far as one particular, very special woman was concerned.

A somewhat subdued Lorna told Jason she would drop Emily off at his house early Friday evening and pick her up late Sunday night. Jason agreed to the arrangements, and they hung up.

"I hate reneging on plans we'd just made," he told Rachael.

"Don't be silly," Rachael said brightly. "This is much more important. I've managed to get around in L.A. without a car for over two years—I think I can manage a week or two longer. Lorna and Cole need some time together, and you need to spend some quality time with Emily."

"Speaking of spending time with Emily..." Jason paused, wondering how Rachael was going to feel about his suggestion. "You know, Emily's talked about you a lot since the picnic."

"Has she?" Rachael asked quietly, remembering how the little girl had latched on to her while they'd watched the softball game. Since Rachael had seemed ignorant of the story of Princess Rachael and the Magic Eagles, Emily had insisted on recounting the tale.

It hadn't been easy to watch the adorable three-year-old act out all the parts with unbridled enthusiasm, but each minute she had spent with the child had made the next minute a little easier. Rachael had even been a little disappointed when Lorna had whisked Emily away in the aftermath of her quarrel with Cole.

"Yes, she has," Jason confirmed. "She says you promised to draw her a story. Something about—" he thought for a moment "—Mickey Mouse and a dragon?"

Rachael smiled wistfully. "Mickelmoss Monster and the Black Dragon," she corrected him. "It's a story I made up for Micah."

"Do you think you'll be able to tell it to Emily someday?" he asked gently.

"I hope so."

"How about this Sunday? Emily and I could pick you up about noon, take you to her favorite fast-food restaurant, and then go back to my place for an adventure in baby-sitting. Do you think you're up to that yet?"

Rachael sighed heavily, instinctively preparing to tell him no. But she quickly realized that she wanted to go. Being with Jason made her feel freer, and at the same time more secure than she could ever remember feeling. And as she searched her emotions, she realized with some surprise that she had been looking forward to seeing Jason's granddaughter again.

Spending time with Emily would be good for me, but would it be good for Emily? she wondered. What if the little girl said something that reminded her too painfully of Micah? What if she broke down and cried?

"You want to tell me what you're thinking?" Jason asked, fascinated by the emotions that were playing across Rachael's lovely, expressive face.

The idea of refusing to share her thoughts with him never occurred to Rachael. Jason always seemed to understand her even better than she understood herself. "What if I can't handle it? I wouldn't want Emily to think that something she did made me sad."

"If that happens, Rachael, I'll make sure Emily understands that she's not to blame. But I think you *can* handle it."

"Is it fair to use your granddaughter as a guinea pig to test my emotional recovery?"

Jason smiled. "This isn't a test, Rachael. It's a day of watching an old man trying to keep up with an active three-year-old. Actually, if I were you, I'd probably pass—unless you think you'd get a charge out of seeing your boss make a fool of himself."

"Oh, that's an offer I can't possibly refuse! I already know you're a washout as a first-base man," she teased with an impudent grin. "I'd like to see you meet your match with a three-year-old, too. I'll expect you at noon, Sunday."

"It's a date."

Rachael's smile vanished at the use of that particular word, and she grew very still, thinking of their trip to Catalina and all the quiet dinners they'd shared since. "*Are* we dating, Jason?" she asked softly, not sure what she wanted his answer to be.

Jason stood and circled the desk until he was standing over Rachael, smiling down at her tenderly. He placed his hands lightly, reassuringly, on her shoulders. "We're two good friends spending time together until you tell me otherwise."

Rachael stared up into Jason's pale blue eyes that held more emotion than she was prepared to handle. "And then?" she dared to ask.

"And then..." A flippant answer that would dismiss the subject flashed through Jason's mind, but he couldn't let the moment pass. He had to take the risk and pray that he wouldn't lose Rachael because of it. "And then we'll decide if there's a chance for us to become more than just good friends."

"Is that what you want?" Her voice was hardly more than a whisper.

"It's what I hope we can have someday, but I wouldn't trade it for your friendship."

"I don't know if I can ever love again, Jason."

He touched her face gently. "Oh, you'll love again, Rachael. But whether or not it's me you choose to love...that's another question—one I know you're not ready to think about."

When Jason touched her, Rachael felt her pulse quicken as a uniquely feminine ache formed low in her abdomen. Some distant part of her mind, far away from her consciousness, recognized that she was much closer to being ready to think about Jason's suggestion than either of them realized. She was, in fact, very close to realizing that she had fallen in love.

Jason touched her lips lightly with a platonic, reassuring kiss, and they returned to work, both privately wondering what Sunday would bring.

CHAPTER SEVENTEEN

"AND SLOWLY... ever so slowly, Mickelmoss crept toward the deep, dark cave where he knew Li Zard was hiding."

Emily's eyes were as huge and round as silver dollars as she watched Rachael draw Mickelmoss creeping toward the cave. "Was he scared?" she asked, her voice hushed, as though she feared the evil Li Zard might hear her.

"Oh, he was terrified," Rachael said seriously, beginning another sketch that showed Mickelmoss entering the cave.

Across the room, Jason watched Rachael weaving her spell on his granddaughter. Emily was plastered against Rachael's side, tense with the excitement of the story, but only minutes before she'd been shrieking with laughter. Not only was Rachael a wonderful artist, she was a gifted storyteller. And just the few hours she'd spent with Emily were enough to convince him she had been a wonderful mother, too. He'd always known it, but now he had proof.

The day had been hard on her, but she was holding up remarkably well. He would see a flash of sad remembrance in her eyes when something Emily said or did reminded her too much of Micah, and then he would see her store the memory away for safekeeping rather than push it away as she had once done.

Just watching Rachael with Emily reaffirmed his growing love for her, and though she hadn't mentioned the conversation they'd had in her office the other day, Jason was convinced that she was giving what he'd said a great deal of

hought. After all, she knew how he felt about her, yet she adn't changed her mind about spending a quiet Sunday afternoon with him.

Jason wanted desperately to believe that was a good sign. He wanted to believe it meant that she might someday be able to love him. If there was a chance, he knew he would wait for her as long as it took, but the waiting was becoming more difficult. Being close to Rachael, seeing her every day, was making him want her all the more. He had her friendship, he was earning her trust, and every day he discovered a new facet of her wonderfully gentle personality, but he was no saint. He wanted Rachael in every way a man can want the woman he loves—spiritually, emotionally, and physically.

And it was the physical wanting that was starting to get to Jason. Each time he saw her, his hunger increased, and it was becoming difficult to control. He spent too much time imagining what it would be like to make love with her, to touch her intimately and have her touch him. He wanted to unlock the passion he knew she was capable of, and he wanted Rachael to find the key to the door he'd locked when Molly had died—the door that led to the kind of deep completion of the soul that only came from the joining of two people who were meant to be as one.

Over the years Jason had made love with a number of women, but none of them had ever found that key. Or perhaps, Jason reflected, he'd never *given* it to them. No one had ever touched him so deeply that he'd been willing to place his heart in her hand without question, without reserve. Falling in love with Rachael had changed that. He had given her the key without even knowing if she might ever want to use it.

"Look, Grandpa, look!" Emily hollered, racing toward him, waving the sketch pad that now contained the completed story. "Look at Mickelmoss!" She climbed into the

chair beside him and started at page one, telling him her ow
fractured version of the tale, as though he had been abser
during Rachael's narration.

Laughing softly at Emily's enthusiasm, Rachael watche
the charming little girl and tried to ignore the tight fist tha
was squeezing her heart. Just the few hours she'd spent wit
Jason and his granddaughter had made Rachael ache to b
a mother again. She wanted a child. Jason had once told he
that no one could replace Micah in her heart, and now sh
knew what he meant. Her son had died, but her ability t
love—her *need* to love—had not. Someday she would hav
another child.

And so should Jason, she reflected, watching the way h
handled Emily. She couldn't recall ever having seen a ma
who was so gentle with children. He had the patience of
saint, and an instinctive understanding of what a chil
needed. It was a pity that he and Molly had had only on
child; Jason had a wealth of love to give.

But it wasn't too late for Jason to start another famil
Looking at him, it was hard to believe that he was ol
enough to be a grandfather. Emily could easily be mistake
for his own child. Would he ever remarry? Rachael wor
dered. And if he did, would he want children?

For some reason that speculation bothered Rachael, an
she put it out of her mind. The thought of Jason with ar
other woman—loving that woman, giving her his child-
disturbed Rachael deeply, but she was not yet ready to ex
amine why. Jason had already told her in so many word
that he someday wanted to be her lover, and that was mor
than enough for her to handle at the moment.

These past few days since their quiet, intense conversa
tion in her office, Rachael had been plagued by memorie
of the one time she'd been in Jason's arms and had almos
been swept away by the intense longing he'd created in he
Actually, *plagued* wasn't the right word. Each time sh

thought about the way he had touched her, the way he'd kissed her, she felt an anticipation that was almost breathtaking in its intensity.

That day seemed like a lifetime ago, and they had been in each other's arms for all the wrong reasons, but the memory of that brief glimpse of passion was getting to Rachael. She had never considered herself a physical person—certainly not in the sexual sense of the word—and yet lately she was consumed by thoughts of what it would be like to be held by Jason, to be touched and to touch him. She kept trying to convince herself that such feelings were only natural, considering what a handsome, virile man Jason was, and how closely they worked together; but there were other available, attractive men at Animators, men she saw every day, and none of them affected her the way Jason Burgess did. Of course, none of them had become her best friend, and not a single one of them had told her he wanted more from her than just friendship.

"Bravo! Bravo!" Jason cried when Emily finished telling him her version of the Mickelmoss story.

"And he lived happily ever after," Emily decreed, then glanced over at Rachael expectantly. "Didn't he?"

"Of course he did! Until..." Rachael paused, letting the possibility of another Mickelmoss adventure dangle in front of Emily until the suspense became too much for the child.

"Until what? Until what?" she demanded, leaving Jason's lap to rush to Rachael's. "Did Li Zard escape? Did he come back to find Mickelmoss?"

"What do you think?"

"I think he did. He did! How did Mickelmoss get away this time?"

Rachael glanced at Jason, trying to hide a sly grin. "I think...that Mickelmoss is going to need help to defeat Li Zard this time. Why don't you think about it, and then *you* tell *me* what happened. Okay?"

That was too much of a challenge for Emily to resist. "Okay. I think—"

"*I* think," Jason interrupted, "that it's time for Emily and Mickelmoss to take a nap."

"No, Grandpa! Nooooo..."

"Yes, Emily! Yessśss..." He crossed the room and lifted the little girl off Rachael's lap. "You go take a nap, and when you wake up, you can tell Rachael all about how Mickelmoss gets the drop on Li Zard this time."

Emily looked down at Rachael expectantly. "Will you be here when I wake up?"

"Of course."

"Promise?"

"I promise."

That mollified her somewhat, and she allowed Jason to cart her off for a much-needed afternoon nap. When he returned, Rachael was still sitting on the sofa, leafing through the sheath of Mickelmoss sketches, thinking about the night she'd invented the adventure fable for her son.

"That's a wonderful story, Rachael," he said as he sat next to her.

She nodded, but she was a little distracted by a disturbing memory that was running through her head. "Some of the characters are pretty good, aren't they?" She pointed toward Li Zard, the little tree frog who'd earned the title Black Dragon because he knew karate. "I think Li Zard is my favorite. His big round eyes really get to me."

"All the characters are beautifully executed," he told her. "But the story is fantastic, too. It has all the elements needed to keep a child enthralled."

Jason had taken the sketch pad from her to study the pages again, and Rachael rose and moved aimlessly around the room. "I did several Mickelmoss stories for Micah," she told him, then decided she might as well get the rest of it out in the open. "Sander thought they were all silly. He told me they were a waste of time," she said quietly.

That got Jason's full attention, and he had to fight back his instinctive dislike of Rachael's late husband. "I don't know about the rest of the stories, but Sander was wrong about this one. I should know—I earned a very good living for a number of years with children's books."

Rachael stopped behind the high-backed armchair Jason had been sitting in earlier and leaned forward, her elbows resting on the back with her hands tightly clasped. "I'm beginning to wonder if maybe Sander wasn't wrong about a lot of things."

"What do you mean?"

"I mean... Sander made me believe that I wasn't capable of being a good storyteller. He convinced me that I was a fine artist, but that's where my abilities ended." She pointed toward the sketchbook in Jason's hands. "When I told Emily that story just now, I *knew* it was good. I knew it. And it makes me wonder if Sander knew it was good, too. It makes me wonder if he was deliberately trying to hold me back."

Jason could tell this was difficult for her to discuss, but her willingness to talk about it was a very good sign. "That's possible, Rachael. And it's also possible he just didn't understand the children's book market," he commented, feeling the need to give Sander the benefit of the doubt.

"That could be," she allowed, though she didn't sound convinced.

"There's another possibility, too," Jason said. "Maybe he was afraid that if you ever decided to seriously pursue a career in children's books, he'd lose you."

Rachael looked at Jason in surprise. "Lose me?"

He smiled gently. "Do you realize, Rachael, that whenever you talk about your marriage to Sander it's always in terms of the work you did together? *Ravenmede* was the foundation of your relationship—"

"And Sander was afraid that if I explored other avenues I'd abandon *Ravenmede* and our relationship would fall apart. Is that what you're suggesting? That Sander held me back to keep from losing *Ravenmede*?"

"You're doing it again, Rachael," he told her. "You're defining your relationship in terms of the work you shared. I said he might have been afraid of losing *you*, and you automatically translated it to mean losing *Ravenmede*."

Rachael looked down. "Then maybe that's all our marriage was. *Ravenmede* brought us together... maybe that's all that was keeping us together." She felt a cold shiver run down her spine and tears pooled in her eyes. "Oh, Jason...do you know how that makes me feel? It makes me feel panicky inside, as though what I thought was a marriage wasn't really a marriage at all."

Jason rose and moved to her. "You can't let yourself think that way, Rachael. No marriage is perfect, but for the past couple of years, you've needed to believe that yours was. You don't need that illusion anymore." He reached out and lightly stroked her hair. "Did you love Sander?"

She turned to face him and spoke the truth without hesitation. "Yes."

"Then that's all that matters. When you and Sander met, he filled a need in you to belong to someone, to love and be loved. You may never really know what needs of Sander's you fulfilled, but obviously you were the woman he needed, the woman he loved. The reasons don't matter—the love is all that counts."

"In my heart I know you're right, Jason, but... I get so angry when I think that he might have been deliberately holding me back—"

"Rachael," Jason said sharply, "if Sander was holding you back, it was only because *you* allowed it. You have to accept some of the responsibility, too. If you'd tried to publish one of your children's stories and Sander had torn up the manuscript, chained you to a drafting board and refused to allow you to work on anything but the next issue of *Ravenmede*, then you'd have a right to be angry—even hate him—for what he'd done. But that's not the way it happened, is it?"

The image he painted made Rachael laugh. "No, that's not the way it happened. You're right. I let Sander convince me I couldn't succeed on my own because it was easier to do what he told me to do than to strike out on my own and risk failure." That personal revelation wasn't a pretty one, but Rachael managed to smile at Jason in spite of her embarrassment. "Do you know what the real problem is, Jason?"

"No, what?" he asked.

"The real problem is that I keep comparing Sander to you and I feel so guilty because, looking back, Sander doesn't seem like half the man you are. I feel guilty even making that admission, but it's true, and I've got to stop avoiding it."

"I don't want to compete with Sander," Jason told her seriously, reaching out to lovingly capture her face in his hands.

"It's not competition, Jason, it's just a fact. Sander wasn't an open person—not the way you're open and honest about what you think and feel. Because he *seemed* so strong, I never questioned him. I just accepted what I saw on the surface without ever trying to force him to let me see what was beneath his self-assured veneer."

"Would he have allowed you to see it?" Jason asked gently.

Rachael shook her head helplessly. "I don't know. I'll never know."

"Can you accept that?"

"What choice do I have?"

Jason's hands were resting lightly on Rachael's shoulders, and he resisted the overwhelming urge to lower them to her back and pull her tightly against him. "You can spend months, years, living in the past, torturing yourself by trying to correct mistakes you may or may not have made."

"No, Jason." She gave him a tremulous smile. "You led me out of the past.... I'm ready to look toward the future now." She touched his arms lightly and stretched up, seeking his lips. Jason made a sound that wasn't a sigh or a moan, but it contained a wealth of emotion, and he pulled her to him. Their lips met with an intensity and an impatience that startled them both, but neither gave thought to pulling away.

For Jason, months of wanting went into the kiss, and as their mouths mated he felt a primitive need to possess that was almost shattering. What was more, he felt the same need in Rachael. Only this time her need did not spring from a desire to escape the past. This time she wanted the same completion as Jason, and for the same reasons—the right reasons.

They strained toward each other, their bodies touching and inflaming, and it was with incredible reluctance that they both pulled away from the passionate kiss. "Oh, Rachael..." Jason feathered kisses across her jaw and down her throat. "This feels so right—"

"And the timing is so wrong," she finished for him. "Emily—"

"I know." He brushed his lips across hers again and let them linger there just a moment longer than was healthy to the state of his libido.

"Daddy?"

Jason and Rachael broke apart like guilty children who had been caught playing doctor. They'd been so engrossed in each other that neither had heard Lorna arrive, but now they were painfully aware of her standing at the door, staring at them with a mixture of surprise, disbelief and disgust.

Jason was the first to come to his senses. "Lorna? I thought you and Cole weren't coming home until late tonight."

"Obviously," she said crisply.

"How was the trip? Why did you decide to come back early?"

Lorna gave Rachael a withering look that disguised none of her dislike, then turned her attention back to Jason. "The trip was a disaster. Where's Emily? I just want to get my daughter and go home."

Jason moved toward her and placed a comforting arm around her shoulder. "Honey, what happened? Do you want to talk?"

Rachael stepped forward before Lorna could respond. "Jason, I think I should call a cab and go home."

"No, Rachael, please stay." Jason was torn by conflicting emotions. He wanted to talk to Lorna, but he couldn't bear the thought of Rachael leaving just when they'd stepped to the brink of a very important precipice. He looked at his daughter. "Honey, why don't we go outside—"

"Let's not, Daddy," Lorna said sharply. "I've had a miserable weekend, and I just want to go home and get ready for work tomorrow. Where's Emily?"

"She's taking a nap."

"Would you get her, please? We can talk some other time when you're not so... busy."

It was clear that Lorna was unhappy about more than just her disappointing weekend with Cole, but Jason refused to feel guilty about having Rachael there. And he most particularly refused to feel contrite because Lorna had discovered them kissing. It was obvious to Jason that in addition to dealing with her problems with Cole, Lorna was going to have to come to grips with his relationship with Rachael. *And she might as well start now,* he thought.

"All right, honey. I'll go get Emily."

"Thank you."

Jason left the room, but none of the tension in the air went with him. The two women looked at each other, and it was finally Rachael who broke the protracted silence. "I'm very sorry your weekend wasn't what you'd hoped it would be, Lorna."

"How do you know what expectations I had?" the younger woman asked.

Rachael stiffened, refusing to be intimidated by Lorna's obvious dislike of her. "I know that Jason has been concerned about you."

It didn't sit well with Lorna that her father had been discussing such private matters with this interloper. "Well, apparently *your* weekend went better than mine."

"I don't know what you mean."

"I mean, I obviously played right into your hands by leaving my daughter here so that you and Daddy could play house. You've just been one big, happy family, haven't you?"

"No. Lorna—"

"Spare me, all right?" she said sarcastically. "I know you're going after my father—I saw how you acted at the picnic, and I know what I saw today, so there's no need to pretend."

"I'm not pretending anything, Lorna," Rachael said with a frown. "Your father has been a good friend to me—the best friend I've ever had, and I care about him a great deal."

"And why wouldn't you? He's handsome, famous, fabulously wealthy, and he's so tenderhearted that he's very easy to manipulate. But let me tell you something." Lorna advanced a couple of steps toward Rachael. "Daddy's had a lot of women in his life since Momma died, and he's even thought about marrying one or two of them. He never did, though, because he knows and I know that he's never going to love anyone the way he loved my mother. He's never going to settle for second best, so don't get your hopes up."

Rachael drew back as though she'd been slapped, but she didn't retreat. She was seeing a side of Lorna that Jason had never mentioned, and she had to wonder if he even knew that his daughter had this ugly streak of vindictiveness.

Given Lorna's attack on her, it was only natural that Rachael would dislike the younger woman, but she also felt a tremendous amount of pity for her. Lorna was obviously a very unhappy, insecure person.

"I don't think I want to discuss my feelings for Jason with you, Lorna," Rachael said softly. "You obviously dislike me for some reason, and I can't imagine what I've done to earn that dislike."

A stab of fear went through Lorna as she realized she'd said far too much. She and Cole had done nothing but argue over the weekend, and things between them were even worse—if that was possible. She had been off balance and distraught when she'd come into this room, and finding her father and Rachael locked in an intimate embrace had destroyed what little semblance of emotional stability she had left.

She had handled the situation badly, and now she was worried about what would happen if Rachael went running to her father to repeat their conversation. Rachael would undoubtedly like nothing better than to drive a wedge between her and Jason. It had been stupid to give her so much ammunition.

"I'm sorry, Rachael," she apologized contritely. "I don't dislike you—I don't even know you. This has just been such an upsetting weekend, and then to come home and find someone with Daddy like that... I was really only trying to spare you the disappointment of realizing that Daddy is still in love with my mother, and he always will be."

This time it was Rachael who wanted to utter a sarcastic, *Oh, spare me*. Rachael knew that Jason still loved Molly, and always would, but like her own love for Sander, Jason's love for his late wife was frozen in time. It could never be recaptured, nor could it ever grow or diminish. It simply existed. But that didn't mean he could never love again. Rachael had no idea what her own relationship with Jason would grow into, but she did know that he was a man capable of great love.

But for all of Lorna's contrite playacting, which Rachael recognized for what it was, it was also apparent that Jason's daughter really believed that her father would never love again. Or, at least, she *needed* to believe it in order to preserve her mother's memory. Realizing that made Rachael pity the young woman all the more. Jason had undoubtedly been a wonderful father to Lorna, but he hadn't been able to erase the scars and insecurity caused by Molly's death. Any woman who wanted a relationship with Jason was going to have a formidable enemy in Lorna Burgess Washburn.

Jason returned with Emily in his arms, sparing Rachael the necessity of responding to Lorna's insincere apology. Emily was a little cranky, but she went to Lorna without complaint. "Where's Daddy?" she demanded.

"He's in the car, sweetie. Let's go see him." Lorna looked at her father, then at Rachael. "Thanks for keeping her, Daddy. And it was nice to see you again, Rachael."

"Thank you, Lorna," she responded.

"Goodbye, Grandpa." Emily leaned toward Jason for a kiss, but when Lorna started to leave, the little girl protested loudly. "Rachael, too!" She squirmed in her mother's arms until Lorna had no choice but to release her and watch her daughter run across the room.

Rachael knelt and gathered the little girl into her arms for a big hug and a sloppy, smacking kiss. "I have to tell you about Mickelmoss," Emily said conspiratorially.

"Next time, all right?" Rachael suggested hopefully. "You think up your own Mickelmoss adventure and tell me all about it."

"Mickelmoss?" Lorna questioned.

"Rachael drew me a story," Emily informed her mother proudly. "She draws stories as good as Grandpa."

Lorna tensed. Not only was Rachael after her father, she was beguiling his granddaughter, as well. She held out her hand. "That's nice, Emily. Why don't you tell me all about it on the way home?"

"Okay," Emily answered happily, always eager for an audience.

"I'll talk to you sometime this week, honey," Jason said, and Lorna mumbled an affirmative reply, then was gone.

Jason turned to Rachael. "That was . . . uncomfortable, wasn't it?"

"Lorna is very unhappy, Jason," Rachael said sadly.

"I know." He looked at her closely. "Did she say something to upset you while I was out of the room?"

Rachael couldn't lie, but neither could she bring herself to be the cause of trouble between Jason and his daughter. "She wasn't pleased to find us . . ."

"Kissing?" he supplied.

"Yes," she affirmed. "But you knew that."

"It was obvious, wasn't it? What did she say?"

Rachael moistened her lips. "She doesn't think you can ever love again, Jason. And she really believes it."

Jason stepped toward her and placed his hands lightly on her shoulders. "Do you believe that?"

"No," she answered softly. "You have a great deal of love to share, Jason. I know that."

"And do you also know that I want to share that love with you?" he asked, his voice barely a whisper.

"Yes."

"Does it frighten you?"

"Yes."

"Then we'll go very slowly, very carefully, and if there ever comes a time when you think you're ready to share your love with me, you let me know."

Rachael reached up and, with the back of her hand, caressed Jason's face. "I am frightened, Jason, and a little bit confused, but I think I'm ready—to make a start, at least."

Jason didn't think he'd ever heard sweeter words from a sweeter voice. "Then will you start by making love with me, Rachael? Or is that too much, too soon?" He held his breath, aching inside, waiting for her answer. She'd just given him so much, but he wanted more, much more than he had a right to want.

"No, it's not too much. And I don't think it's too soon, either. I want to be with you, Jason," she admitted breathlessly. "I want to make love with you."

Slowly, savoring the gentle light in her eyes, Jason pulled Rachael into the circle of his arms until she was pressed against the length of his body. His lips dipped to hers, and they sealed the beginning of a new relationship with a long, tender, passionate kiss.

CHAPTER EIGHTEEN

"WHAT ARE YOU thinking, Rachael?" The bedroom was dark now, and Jason had no desire to know what time it was. Every thought, every sense was completely filled with Rachael, and suddenly he wished the world would go away and never intrude on them. It was an irrational thought, but it was what he wanted at the moment—to be like this with Rachael forever: pressed close, their bodies touching with nothing between them, sharing a sensual fulfillment that was too awe-inspiring for words.

They had come together slowly, savoring and sampling each other, touching and being touched, removing each other's clothing layer by layer, stripping away shyness and their individual fears of inadequacy, fears that they might somehow disappoint each other. But there had been no disappointment; only a growing sense of excitement, discovery and wonder. They had spent the afternoon coming to know each other, and the evening reveling in that knowledge.

And now it was dark and quiet. Jason's arms were wrapped protectively around Rachael, who lay with her head on his shoulder, one hand resting on his chest and one leg draped across his.

"I'm thinking about beginnings and endings," she told him reflectively.

"Have I made you sad?" he asked quietly.

"No," she said, rising to rest on one elbow so that she could look into his wonderfully handsome face, which was illuminated only faintly by the moonlight streaming in through the window at the head of the bed. Her breasts were pressed lightly against the tantalizingly soft hair on his chest, and just that feathery contact was enough to renew the passion Jason had inspired in her today. "You haven't made me sad, Jason. You've made me happy. Maybe too happy."

"How so?"

She allowed her hand to drift to his face, and she caressed his forehead, his cheek and the soft beard that covered his jaw. "I could fall in love with you," she admitted.

Jason captured her hand and brought it to his lips. "I don't think anything would make me happier, Rachael. If you want to fall in love with me, please be my guest," he said with a teasing smile.

"I'm serious, Jason. I'm not ready to feel...*this much*."

"Then feel only what you *can* feel, what you're comfortable with feeling. I can wait for the rest."

"Will you?"

"As long as it takes," he whispered, cradling Rachael to him as he turned and shifted so that she was beneath him. "I love you. In fact, I have loved you for quite a long time now. If you promise me that you won't run from that love, I promise that I'll wait until you're as sure of your feelings as I am of mine."

He kissed her lengthily and tenderly, moving his hands over her, igniting fires that had only recently been banked. Rachael responded, running her hands down Jason's sides, onto his flanks. He touched her intimately and when she gasped with pleasure, Jason shifted and sheathed himself deeply within her.

"I love you, Rachael," he murmured, holding very still, savoring the intense pleasure of the exquisite moment. "I love you."

Tears pooled in Rachael's eyes and slid down her temples into her hair. Jason deserved to hear her say that she loved him, too, but she couldn't bring the words out. She had loved Sander, but her relationship with him had been built on quicksand. When she committed her love to Jason, she would do so as a whole person, a person strong enough to give him the kind of full, rich, meaningful love he deserved. And if he was willing to wait for her to become that person, Rachael knew that she had no right to ask for anything more wonderful from this world.

Instead of answering him with words, then, Rachael found Jason's lips and kissed him deeply, moving around him and with him in an invitation that was impossible to ignore. They completed the joining that Jason had initiated, moving together until they were both gasping and calling each other's names; until they were one soul that for a moment shared one body and one heart.

RACHAEL SPENT the next week in a lazy fog of contentment. On Monday when she arrived at work she found a dozen red roses in her office along with a paperback book entitled, *One Hundred and One of the World's Worst Elephant Jokes*. She had slipped into Jason's office via the Bull Pen shortcut and tried to admonish him sternly.

"Jason, the roses are beautiful, but everyone will think we're having an affair."

He smiled back at her as only an impudent, extremely pleased-with-himself man could smile and said, "I'm sorry, did you want to keep it a secret? I'll have Gretchen see if she can intercept all those interoffice memos I sent out this morning."

"You're incorrigible," she said accusingly, but laughing.

Jason stood and advanced on her with obviously lustful intent. "That wasn't what you said last night," he reminded her, pulling her into his arms.

"Last night we weren't in the office."

"So you want to keep our relationship a secret?" he asked.

"No, but I don't want to broadcast it, either."

"Does that mean I'm not allowed to chase you around the table in the Bull Pen, intent on seduction?" he asked with a comical leer.

"That's right."

"Then you'll just have to have dinner with me tonight, so I can seduce you over a candlelight supper."

And he had. That night and the next.

At the end of the week, Rachael visited a gynecologist and took care of the birth control issue that had been on her mind even though Jason had been careful to see that she was protected each time they had made love. Being with Jason, being intimate with him, was the most wonderful experience she could imagine, but Rachael knew that accidentally becoming pregnant would confuse an already confused situation.

Jason had made it clear that he wanted a lifetime commitment from Rachael when, and if, she felt she could give it, and she knew instinctively that he would be happy if he discovered she was carrying his child; she knew it because it would make her happy, too. But she still had a lot of growing to do, and a lot of things about herself and her life to come to grips with. Sander was one, and Micah, another. As well, there was a certain knowledge about herself she had to make peace with—the knowledge that she had been a weak woman who had been too dependent on the man she loved. Her entire life had been defined by her husband, and Rachael had to look into herself to find out why she'd let that happen so that it wouldn't happen again.

The answers that came from such soul-searching didn't arrive in a day, or even a week, and Rachael was more than content to allow her relationship with Jason to blossom while she was searching. Jason was content with that, too, which made the time they spent together meaningful and fun, exciting, warm and deliciously tender.

On Saturday, Jason made good his promise to help Rachael buy a car, and they spent the day visiting one automobile dealership after another until she finally fell in love with a small, sporty economy car that seemed perfect for her needs. She filled out the loan papers—a nerve-racking experience since she'd never done it before—and the salesman promised to call her on Monday when the credit check cleared.

"I should have had Martin transfer the funds to my bank out here and just paid cash," Rachael said as she and Jason returned to his car. She held her hands out toward him. "Look at me, I'm actually shaking."

Jason took her hands and pulled her to him for a reassuring hug. "You did fine, and it will be good for you to establish credit here in L.A."

"That's what I thought, but all those papers to fill out, and that grinning salesman..." Rachael shuddered, then put the experience behind her.

Jason chuckled and released her so that he could unlock the door of the Mercedes and seat her. "By Monday evening you'll be the proud owner of a shiny new car, ready to brave the fearsome Los Angeles freeways." He shut her door, circled the car and climbed behind the wheel. "The traffic alone will be enough to make you forget all about that salesman and the loan application."

Rachael laughed. "I think I need my head examined."

"Oh, it looks fine to me," Jason said, leaning toward her to punctuate his compliment with a kiss. "So, where to now, milady?"

Rachael shrugged. "Home, I suppose."

"Your home, or mine? I have a couple of trout in the freezer that would be fabulous baked outside on the grill. Will you join me for supper?"

"I'd love to."

"Done." They pulled out of the car lot and headed for Jason's.

"The weather's starting to get a little cooler," she commented. "Pretty soon your days of backyard barbecues will be over."

"I know. Winters in L.A. aren't frigid, but they do get quite a bit nippier than most people expect. Do you miss the dramatic change of seasons?"

Rachael thought of the Vermont winter that had sent her running for a warmer climate. "I miss the autumn colors, but that's about all. I don't think I'll ever be able to enjoy snow again."

Jason realized what she was thinking and reached over to squeeze her hand gently. "That's something you don't have to worry about here. Speaking of autumn, there's something I need to talk to you about."

"What?"

"It's not a tradition, or anything, but occasionally I host a small masquerade party at my place on Halloween. I have a few friends over, and I usually invite the directorial staff from Animators—about thirty or forty people."

Rachael looked at him skeptically. "You call thirty or forty people a *small* party?"

Jason chuckled. "I guess small is a relative term, isn't it? It's small in comparison to the company picnic. How's that? Anyway, if I have the party this year, would you be my hostess?"

Rachael felt a surge of panic. Attending a party, even as Jason's date, was one thing, but being his hostess was quite another. She would be responsible for the comfort of his guests—a horrifying thought—and, too, the arrangement would leave no doubt as to the nature of their relationship.

"The idea doesn't appeal to you?" he asked when she didn't answer immediately.

"The idea terrifies me. Jason, I've never thrown a party before."

"I'll take care of the arrangements," he assured her. "It's a simple matter of calling a caterer, hiring a bartender and sending out a few invitations. What do you think?"

As always, Rachael's first instinct was to say no. Change frightened her, and this would drastically change their relationship almost before it had had the chance to become firmly established. They would be subtly announcing their involvement to all Jason's friends and their co-workers.

Rachael searched her feelings and was surprised to discover that she really didn't mind who knew that she and Jason had become lovers. In fact, she felt an enormous swell of pride that he would want it known that he had chosen to have a relationship with mousy little Rachael Hubbard.

That was the real problem, she realized. Rachael Hubbard was a mouse. She was timid and shy, afraid of people and the judgments they might make about her. Jason, on the other hand, was vigorous and outgoing. He loved people, and Rachael knew that if she didn't change, if she didn't make the effort to share Jason's life-style, their relationship was doomed.

"If you can handle the caterers and the bartender, I think I can probably manage the invitations," she told him. "Just give me a list of who you want invited, and I'll design something appropriate."

Jason reached for Rachael's hand and brought it to his lips. "That wasn't an easy decision for you to make, was it, love?" he asked, his voice quiet.

"No, Jason, you're wrong. It was one of the easiest decisions I've ever made in my life."

"I love you," he said softly.

"That's what made it easy," she answered.

They finished the ride to Jason's, making party plans as they negotiated the traffic. Rachael had another panic attack when she realized she was going to have to come up with a costume for the occasion, but then she remembered that this was Hollywood—the costume capital of the world—and her fears subsided. She had three weeks to find something suitable, and the more she thought about it, the more she began looking forward to the challenge.

By the time they reached Jason's, she was starting to become enthusiastic about the party, and her excitement was contagious. Jason had given no thought to a costume, either, and they began throwing ideas at each other, laughing like a couple of kids over the limitless possibilities.

"I've got it! I've got it!" Jason said proudly. "I'll come as Smoky the Bear, and you can be a lady forest ranger."

Rachael regarded him dubiously. "That's not very romantic, Jason."

"Oh, you want romance! Well..." He thought for a moment, then remembered that he and Rachael shared a favorite movie. "How about something from *The Three Musketeers*? I'll be the Duke of Buckingham and you come as Anne of Austria, the Queen of France?"

"That has possibilities," she admitted. "Though I can't really see you in a pair of those funny little bloomers and tights. You'd make a wonderful D'Artagnan, though."

"I like it. Why don't—" Jason stopped in mid-thought as he pulled up to the security gate at his house and noticed that there was a car already in the driveway.

"Is that Lorna's car?" Rachael asked.

"Yes, but I wasn't expecting her today." He released the gate and drove up to the garage.

"Jason..." Rachael's buoyant mood evaporated. "Have you talked to Lorna since last Sunday? I mean, does she know about us?"

He shut off the car and sighed deeply. "No. I had intended to talk to her to straighten a few things out, but every time I called her she found an excuse not to talk."

He started to open the door, but Rachael stopped him with a hand on his arm. "I really think I should call a cab and go home so that you and Lorna can talk. She's here, so it would be the perfect time."

Jason nodded, knowing Rachael was right. He and Lorna did need to sit down and thrash through some very important issues, but he hated sending Rachael home in a cab. "Why don't we wait and see why she's here," he suggested finally. "She might just want to borrow something, or ask a favor before she dashes off again."

Rachael agreed to his suggestion, and they went into the house through the front entrance and found Lorna in the family room. One look was all it took to tell both of them that the young woman hadn't come to borrow anything. Her eyes were red and swollen from crying, and it appeared that she'd only barely gotten the weeping under control when Jason came into the room. His entrance sparked another flood of tears, and she rushed into his arms, sobbing pitifully.

"Lorna, honey, what's wrong?" Jason asked, stroking her hair gently as he led her to the sofa.

"I've left Cole," she barely managed to sob out.

"Oh, honey..." He wrapped her securely in his arms, letting the tears run their course.

Rachael stood just inside the doorway, watching them for a moment, but she knew her presence was only an intrusion on a family problem. She started to slip out, but as she turned she noticed Emily outside on the deck. She was sitting at the patio table, her head bent over a piece of paper, and she seemed to be making wild, erratic scribbles with a black crayon. Even from a distance, Rachael could see the tears that were quietly coursing down the little girl's cheeks.

"Jason," she said softly, drawing his attention away from Lorna. She gestured toward Emily, and when Jason saw his granddaughter he thought his heart was going to break.

Rachael moved toward the patio doors. "I'm going to go keep Emily company."

"Thank you."

"Yes, thank you, Rachael," Lorna said brokenly, raising her tearstained face from Jason's shoulder. "She's very upset... but I didn't know how to explain what was going on."

"Don't worry about her, Lorna. I'll stay with her while you and Jason talk." She hurried out the door, leaving the father and daughter alone.

Jason felt utterly useless, but he rubbed Lorna's back comfortingly as she tried to pull herself together. "Honey, please tell me what happened."

"Oh, Daddy, it's such a mess."

"Did you and Cole have another fight?" he asked, starting with the obvious in an attempt to get her to talk.

Lorna shook her head. "It wasn't really *another* fight. It was mostly a continuation of one that's been going on for a long, long time."

"About what? Is Cole objecting to your job?"

"Sort of." She pulled out of Jason's arms and went in search of a box of tissues in Emily's play corner. "You see, Daddy, I'm tired of working for slave wages as an assistant buyer at the boutique."

"You mean you've been offered a promotion, and Cole doesn't approve?" Jason asked, grasping at straws to try and make sense of her fragmented statement.

"No, I want to start my own business, and Cole..." She found the tissues and swiped at her tears. "Cole says I don't have enough experience to run my own dress salon. He says we can't afford it, either, but that's rubbish! I can understand why he wouldn't want to borrow the money from you, and that's why I've never mentioned the idea to you before. But his parents would be more than happy to set us up in business. Most of their money is going to be Cole's one day, anyway. He's just being so pigheaded about it!"

Jason was flabbergasted. He'd had no idea that Lorna wanted to run her own business, and though he applauded her initiative, he couldn't help but feel that Cole was probably right. Lorna was only twenty-two years old, and her sole business experience consisted of two years as an assistant buyer at the boutique. She was good at her job, he was certain of that, but he found it difficult to believe she was ready to start a business of her own.

"Honey. . . are you sure this is what you want? Running a business isn't easy."

"I know that, Daddy!"

"It's demanding, time-consuming, and the potential for failure is tremendous. I don't know a whole lot about the retail trade, but I do know that the competition is fierce."

"I told you, I know all that, but it's what I want!"

"And you're not willing to wait for it?"

Lorna looked at him, aghast. "Why should I wait?"

Jason stood and moved to her. "Because you're very young, Lorna, and you have your whole life ahead of you. There's plenty of time—"

"Did my mother have plenty of time?" she asked sharply as tears formed in her eyes again. "She was only a few years older than me when she died. Did Momma have time to do everything she wanted to do before then?"

Jason felt tears form in his own eyes, as well. He pulled Lorna to him and held her tightly. "No, honey, your mother didn't have all the time she needed. She wanted to watch you grow up. She wanted to have another child. That was all taken away from her, but she died knowing that she was loved and that she'd left a very important mark on this world. You."

Gently he raised Lorna's face to his. "Honey, you could walk out of this house today and be hit by a bus, or you could live to be a hundred. No one knows what's in the future, but you can't live your life thinking that you have to hurry up and squeeze everything into the next few days because you might miss something if you don't."

Lorna squared her shoulders proudly. "I thought you believed in living life to the fullest."

"I do. But that means stopping to appreciate what you have, not ignoring it in favor of grasping for something different."

Lorna nodded and pulled away from her father. "I understand what you're saying, but that doesn't solve my problems with Cole. He's deliberately trying to hold me back. In fact, he's made it perfectly clear that he'd much prefer I didn't work at all. He wants me to stay at home and be a baby factory!"

Jason thought he finally caught a glimpse of the root of Lorna's problem. "You mean Cole wants to have another child, and you don't."

"That's a big part of the problem," she admitted. "Cole is from a big family, so he thinks he has to have one, too. But I don't want that, Daddy. I love Emily with all my heart, but I can't stand the thought of having another child right now."

"So you invented a desire to run your own business as an excuse to keep from having a baby?" Jason suggested tentatively, and he realized he'd made a grave mistake the moment the words were out of his mouth.

"What a horrible thing to say!" Lorna shouted. "How could you accuse me of something like that? My desire to have a salon is not an *invention*, and it has nothing to do with my not wanting another child."

"Lorna, calm down—"

"You know, you're beginning to sound just like Cole!" she accused, stabbing at his chest with one sharp fingernail. "All you men are just alike. A woman is only worth anything if she's at home, barefoot and pregnant!"

"I don't feel that way, and you know it, Lorna."

"I don't know anything except that it was a mistake to try to talk to you about this. I should have known you'd take Cole's side."

"I am not taking Cole's side!" Jason argued.

"Well, it certainly sounds that way," she snapped, then waved her hands in the air as though to ward off any more discussion. "I can't handle this right now, Daddy. I'm going for a drive. I'll be back later."

"Wait just a minute," Jason said sternly, cutting her off as she headed for the door. "You've got a three-year-old daughter out on my patio who's terribly upset."

Lorna heaved a pained sigh. "I know. Daddy, please, will you watch her for me? I can't explain this to her now—I'd only upset her even more."

"Does Cole know where you are?" he asked, sidestepping the issue of Emily.

"Yes. We quarreled this morning and he stormed out. That's when I decided I couldn't take any more of the fighting, and I began packing to leave. When he came back and saw the suitcases, we started fighting again, and I told him I was moving back home with you. I also told him he'd hear from my lawyer on Monday."

Jason was shocked. "You mean you're getting a divorce without even *trying* to work this out?"

"Daddy, Cole and I have been trying for months to work this out, but it's just not going to happen. You said yourself that our arguing wasn't good for Emily. As far as I'm concerned, the only solution is divorce."

"Then you don't love Cole anymore?"

That took some of the wind out of Lorna's sails, and she seemed to deflate right before Jason's eyes. "I don't know if I do or not."

Jason touched her shoulders lightly. "Then don't you think you'd better take some time to find out before you make a mistake you might regret for the rest of your life?"

"I don't know.... I'm just so tired of all the fighting."

"Don't do anything rash, baby. That's all I'm saying. You and Emily can stay here with me while you think things through."

"Thank you, Daddy." She gave him a hug, and they held on to each other for a long moment. Lorna finally broke away and looked out the windows at her daughter. Jason turned, too, and saw Rachael seated in one of the deck chairs with Emily curled up on her lap, sound asleep.

"Emily likes Rachael very much," Lorna said quietly, trying to decide how she felt about seeing her little girl in another woman's arms.

"Rachael's a wonderful person, Lorna. A kind, gentle, loving person." He paused for a moment. "Honey, I was going to tell you this anyway, but since you're going to be staying here for a while I'm sure you'd figure it out for yourself. Rachael and I are dating now. She has some things she needs to work through before we talk about making a serious commitment to each other, but I have a lot of reasons to hope that day will come."

"I don't want to hear about this now, Daddy," Lorna said, her voice shaking as tears welled in her eyes.

"You're going to have to face it someday, honey."

"Just not today, all right?" She whirled and nearly ran from the room, stopping at the door only long enough to ask, "Will you put Emily down for a nap?"

"Of course."

"I'll be back later."

"All right, honey." Jason watched her go, and was torn by conflicting emotions. Like any father, he only wanted the best for his child, but in a situation like this, who knew what the "best" really was? Would it be better for Lorna to divorce her husband and start a new life, or should she stick it out and try to make the marriage work? She and Cole wanted different things, and even though Jason didn't completely agree that what Lorna wanted was right, he wasn't sure that meant Cole was right, either.

The only thing he was sure of was that even under the best of circumstances, Lorna would have a very difficult time accepting his relationship with Rachael. Given her emotional state at the moment, it might very well be impossible. For just a second Jason toyed with the idea of seeing less of Rachael to minimize the stress it would put on his daughter, but he dismissed the notion almost the moment it was born. Pretending that he wasn't in love wouldn't help Lorna, and he'd already promised himself that he was through with catering to his daughter's every whim where his relationships were concerned. One way or another, Lorna was going to have to cope, because nothing was going to stand in the way of his love for Rachael.

Of course, Jason didn't really understand that his daughter could be just as determined as he was, and what they each wanted with respect to Rachael were two entirely different things. Jason wanted marriage, and Lorna would do anything she could to prevent it.

CHAPTER NINETEEN

DESPITE THE UPHEAVAL in his life and his household, Jason insisted on continuing with preparations for a Halloween party. Rachael designed the invitations, Jason supplied the guest list, and they both visited Western Costume Co., to hunt for appropriate disguises for the event. Rachael finally found a magnificent silver ball gown that had actually been worn in the movie *The Three Musketeers*, but because of his size, Jason ended up having his D'Artagnan costume made.

As the weeks sped by, Lorna and Cole seemed unable to make any headway in solving their problems, though Jason told Rachael several times that Cole, at least, did seem to want a reconciliation. The young man called Lorna frequently and came by several times a week to see his little girl. Emily was delighted to be staying with her grandpa, but Jason knew she was terribly confused because her daddy wasn't staying there, too.

And Lorna...Jason couldn't quite figure Lorna out. Though she made no more mention of seeing a lawyer about a divorce, she seemed remarkably uninterested in spending time with Cole to thrash out their problem. She went to work every day, and many times came home so late that it fell to Jason to pick up Emily at the day-care center, take her home, feed her supper and put her to bed. After two weeks of having his life turned upside down, Jason began to see why Cole might have a problem accepting his wife's work schedule.

Rachael was remarkably understanding about the dates he made with her and then had to break because he had to baby-sit with Emily. Several times when Lorna had to work late, Rachael and Jason rearranged their plans and took Emily out with them or stayed at Jason's, where it was easier to entertain the little girl. Those evenings were delightful until Lorna came in from work and suddenly everything became tense and uncomfortable. Jason had tried to talk to his daughter on several occasions, hoping to convince Lorna to make friends with Rachael, but though she always promised to try, she never seemed to make the effort.

The only place Jason's life ran smoothly was at the office. *The Quest* was progressing at a snail's pace—just as it should have—and everything was right on schedule.

"Okay, folks, if there are no questions, I guess that's it," Jason said at the conclusion of another productive staff meeting. "Deanna, I'd like to have those revised model sheets for scene twenty by Thursday's meeting."

Rachael glanced down the table at her and smiled. "If you need a hand meeting the deadline, just give me a buzz, Dee."

"You're on," Deanna answered, throwing the other woman a thankful smile as she gathered a stack of costume designs Jason had just rejected.

The meeting was adjourned, and Rachael moved to the storyboard to number and remove some of her sketches that needed more work. Across the room Jason was conferring with Deanna again, and as everyone filed out, Robb Weston sauntered casually toward Rachael.

"Good work you been doin', Rachael." He complimented her loudly enough for anyone listening to hear, then he dropped his voice conspiratorially. "I need to see you in your office for a quick confab."

"What's wrong?"

"Shhh. It's a secret. Just tell Jason you got a phone call to make or something, and meet me next door."

"All right," Rachael agreed, though she couldn't imagine what the big secret could possibly be. Robb strolled out with a wave at Jason, leaving Rachael behind to think up a lie. Normally she and Jason spent a few minutes reviewing the decisions that had been made at the meeting.

"Excuse me for interrupting, Jason," she said as she came up beside him. "I have to make a phone call about my costume for the party. I'll be back in just a minute."

"Sure, go ahead. This is going to take a while." He turned his attention back to Deanna's sketches, and Rachael realized that she probably could have slipped out without saying a word; Jason never would have missed her.

She stepped into her office and found Robb there, waiting. "What's going on?" she asked, closing the door behind her.

Robb sighed heavily. "I've got this problem, Rachael, and I'm hoping you can help me out."

"Of course. I'll do anything I can."

"Well, you know Jason's birthday is coming up—"

"No, I didn't know," Rachael said with surprise. "When is it?"

"This comin' Saturday."

"Halloween?"

"That's right."

Rachael laughed. "Do you mean to tell me that Jason Burgess is throwing *himself* a birthday party?"

Robb nodded, chuckling. "That's right. He usually does, every year. He says he's afraid folks would forget, otherwise."

"They can't forget if they don't know," Rachael muttered, wondering why Jason hadn't passed on that important bit of information.

"Well, now you know," Robb said with a grin. "Anyway, most of the employees chip in for a present and a cake. Gretchen's taking care of all the arrangements, and we'll have a little party in the cafeteria Friday afternoon."

"So what's your big problem?"

"This year the directorial staff decided to take up their own collection to get him something special, and I got put in charge of collecting the money and buying the gift, only I don't have even the slightest idea what to get him." He put on a pitiful, hangdog expression for Rachael's benefit. "I thought you might help me out."

"Robb, I'll be delighted to contribute to the birthday fund, but I don't think that's all you have in mind, is it?"

"Actually I was hoping you'd go buy the gift. I know you and Jason have become good friends," he said tactfully, "and I thought you might have some idea what he'd like."

"I don't have the slightest idea, Robb. But I will give it some thought."

Robb perked up considerably, as though the weight of the world had been lifted from his shoulders. "Good. I'll bring the money by before I leave work today, and you can present the gift to him at the party Saturday night. I know whatever you choose will be fine with the rest of the gang."

"Now, wait a minute—" Rachael started to protest, but Robb was already out the door.

Feeling as though she'd been hit by a whirlwind, Rachael sank into the chair behind her desk. *A gift for Jason.* Not only did she have to think of a present to give him from his creative staff, she had to think of something special just from her.

Again, Rachael wondered why Jason hadn't told her about his birthday. Apparently he'd assumed that she'd hear about it at work, or maybe he'd thought Lorna might enlighten her.

Now that's a laugh, Rachael thought. The idea of Lorna telling Rachael anything would have been funny if it wasn't so pathetic. If Rachael knew Lorna—and she was coming to believe she did—it was more likely that Lorna was hoping she wouldn't find out. It would give Jason's daughter a great deal of pleasure to see Rachael embarrassed in front of Jason's friends and colleagues.

Except for their first confrontation the day Lorna had found Rachael and Jason kissing, the girl had been unfailingly polite, but beneath the attempt at good manners lurked an unmistakable coldness. Had Lorna not already made her feelings clear, Rachael would have assumed that her aloof attitude was just a symptom of the emotional confusion she was suffering because of her marital problems. But Rachael knew that was not the case. Lorna detested her. She saw Rachael as a threat, and though she had not said so outright, Rachael knew that Lorna was looking for ammunition she could use to destroy her relationship with Jason.

Rachael was determined not to allow that to happen, but neither did she want to cause trouble between Jason and his daughter. She realized that if push came to shove and Jason had to make a decision between the two women in his life, he would choose Lorna over Rachael. Having lost her own child, Rachael couldn't bring herself to blame Jason for that; she merely accepted it as a fact.

That meant that Rachael was going to have to do something about making peace with Lorna. She'd known for weeks that she needed to sit down and talk with her, but confrontations weren't easy for Rachael, so she'd been putting it off. Although it didn't really have to be a confrontation, she tried to tell herself. In all fairness, Rachael had to admit that she hadn't made much of an effort to forge a friendship with Jason's daughter. Being outgoing, taking the first step, just wasn't in Rachael's nature, so she'd been sitting back, waiting for the situation to improve. That wasn't going to happen without some effort on her part, and perhaps the problem Robb Weston had tossed into her lap would be just the thing to break the ice.

Acting quickly, before she had time to chicken out, Rachael buzzed Gretchen and asked for Lorna's phone number at work. She dialed the number, praying that she wasn't making a mistake.

"Lyon's Boutique."

"May I speak with Lorna Washburn?" Rachael asked, then paused to clear a lump of anxiety from her throat. "This is Rachael Hubbard calling."

"Just a moment, please." Rachael was placed on hold, and it was a moment before Lorna came on the line sounding surprised and a little concerned. "Rachael? Is something wrong with Daddy?"

"No, Lorna, it's nothing like that," Rachael hastened to assure her. "I'm sorry to bother you at work, but I have a problem I was hoping you could help me with."

"Problem? What kind of problem?" She didn't sound encouraging, but Rachael forged ahead.

"The directorial staff here has just put me in charge of buying a birthday present for your father, and I'm at a complete loss."

"And you want me to suggest something?"

"No, actually what I was hoping was that you might go shopping with me," Rachael said in a rush. "I don't know when your day off is this week, but I'm sure I can get away from the office for a couple of hours and meet you."

The request seemed to fluster Lorna. "My day off is Friday, but . . . well, I do have things to do . . ."

"I know your free time is limited, Lorna, but I want to get Jason something special from the staff. And, too, it would give us a chance to get to know each other better." Rachael held her breath, realizing she'd probably killed any hope of getting together with Lorna. Becoming friends with her father's lover wasn't high on Lorna's list of priorities.

A lengthy silence followed the suggestion, but when Lorna finally did answer, Rachael was pleasantly surprised. "Sure, Rachael, why not? I've already got Daddy's present, but I'd be happy to help you find something for him from the staff."

"Thank you, Lorna." They finalized plans to meet Friday afternoon, and Rachael hung up breathing a sigh of relief.

Am I crazy? she wondered. Just one brief conversation with Jason's daughter had left her trembling. Several hours with the hostile young woman might be more than she could handle. Jason wouldn't be around to act as a buffer between them, and without her father's presence, Lorna would have no reason to don her mask of politeness.

I must be insane, Rachael told herself, and a little voice in the back of her head replied, *No, honey, you're just in love.*

"It's the same thing," she muttered as she returned to the Bull Pen to complete her meeting with Jason, wondering what excuse she was going to come up with to get some time off Friday.

RACHAEL WASN'T a very convincing liar, but when she told Jason she wanted to take Friday afternoon off so that she could pick up her Halloween costume and take care of some errands, he didn't question her. In fact he told her to feel free to take the entire day, since she'd put in so many overtime hours, but Rachael declined his offer. She was already worried enough about spending the afternoon with Lorna; she didn't need free time to worry about all the things that could go wrong. Work would keep her preoccupied.

But it didn't keep her from becoming nervous. By the time she arrived at the appointed meeting place on Friday, Rachael felt like a long-tailed cat in a room full of rocking chairs. And to make matters even worse, Lorna arrived late, leaving Rachael standing just inside the entrance to Neiman Marcus under the intimidating scrutiny of a suspicious security guard.

"Rachael!" Lorna finally swept into the department store like a gust of arctic air. "I'm so sorry I'm late. Have I kept you waiting long?"

Rachael glanced at her watch. *Thirty-four minutes and an odd number of seconds.* "Not too long," she answered with a smile, feeling like a general directing troops into battle. She could tell from Lorna's attitude that the girl had arrived late deliberately, just to irritate her. But two could play Lorna's game, and Rachael was determined to hold her own until they reached a point where game playing was no longer necessary.

"Did the staff give you any idea what they'd like to get Daddy?" Lorna asked, getting right to the point.

"No, they left it up to Robb Weston, and he left it up to me."

Rachael gave her a general price range that included the money Robb had collected plus her own contribution, and Lorna began moving past the cosmetic counters toward the men's department. "Cologne is always a nice, safe gift, but if you want to give him a shirt or anything like that I have his size written down right here." She produced an engagement calendar from her purse and consulted the special gift section in the back.

When Rachael didn't jump at either of those ideas, Lorna made several other unimaginative suggestions—ones that Rachael could easily have come up with on her own. They floated through the men's department, and Rachael was appalled when Lorna began pointing out gift possibilities that were completely inappropriate. The last straw was a garish print silk shirt she held up, proclaiming that Jason would love it. Rachael knew better. The style and color were "in," yes, but Jason wouldn't have been caught dead in it.

"I've never seen Jason wear anything even remotely similar to that, Lorna," she pointed out tactfully.

"Granted, it's not the sort of thing he'd wear to work, but I'm sure Daddy would love it."

"I hate to disagree with you, but I don't think it's quite what the staff would want to give him."

Lorna put the shirt back on the rack and looked at Rachael coldly. "Are you trying to say I don't know my own father's taste?"

Rachael wanted desperately to escape Lorna's frigid stare, but she refused to run. She'd expected a confrontation at some point during the day, and this was obviously meant to be it. "No, Lorna, I think you know Jason's tastes very well, and you also know that he'd hate that shirt. What you really want is to prod me into buying him a tasteless gift so that I'll be embarrassed in front of Jason and all his friends tomorrow night."

Lorna stiffened, realizing she'd underestimated the enemy. Rachael had always projected such an air of fragility that Lorna had thought getting rid of her would be a piece of cake once she set her mind to it. But though there was still a certain vulnerability about Rachael, there was very little of the weakness Lorna had expected. "I didn't come here today to be insulted or picked on, Rachael. I came because you're my father's friend and I wanted to be nice for Daddy's sake."

"Then help me pick out a *nice* gift," Rachael said softly, although a gentle warning in her voice told Lorna she wasn't dealing with a fool.

The younger woman took heed of the warning. She started making more sensible suggestions, and finally she led Rachael upstairs to a specialty shop on the second floor where they found a beautiful sweater that they both agreed Jason would love.

Rachael paid for the sweater, and while they were waiting for it to be gift wrapped, a display just across the floor caught Rachael's eye. She still hadn't decided on a personal gift for Jason, and when the clerk returned with the sweater, Rachael asked Lorna if she'd mind giving her an opinion on one more item. Together they headed toward the fantasyland of whimsical, one-of-a-kind gift items. There were music boxes of every description, carousel horses and fantasy figurines crafted in every imaginable medium from ceramic to pewter to gold. But the castles were what captured Rachael's full attention. There were dozens of them in every size and shape imaginable. The one that caught Rachael's eye sat in the center of a lighted display cabinet. It was almost an exact replica of the majestic castle that Jason had created for the story of Princess Rachael and the brave young man who had climbed the forbidden mountain to capture one of the enchanted eagles.

Emily had insisted on showing her Jason's drawings, and though Jason had not yet come up with an ending to the tale, Rachael knew that the blacksmith was destined to save the princess from a life of loneliness. The correlation between the princess's story and her own life had not been lost on Rachael, and she had been deeply touched. Giving Jason this castle would let him know just how much.

"I'd like this one, please," Rachael said without hesitation to the eager clerk who'd followed them to the display case.

"Rachael, you can't be serious," Lorna said, astonished not by the gift, which she knew Jason would love, but by the price. "That's a handmade, signed sculpture by Turillo. It's worth a small fortune. The sweater—"

"The sweater is from the staff," Rachael told her gently. "This is from me."

Lorna shook her head, aghast. No mere animation assistant could afford to buy a twenty-five-hundred-dollar gift for her boss, or her boyfriend, without batting an eyelash. The horrible idea that Jason might be giving Rachael more money than just a salary occurred to Lorna, and every unkind thought she'd ever had about her father's mistress suddenly seemed completely justified.

She waited impatiently while this gift, too, was wrapped, but when they moved away from the counter, she couldn't keep silent any longer. "How can you afford a gift like that, Rachael? Did you convince Daddy he should be paying some of your bills because he stays at your house so much?"

Strangely this attack didn't faze Rachael. Just the opposite, in fact. It gave her the entree she needed to begin the discussion that had been her real purpose in seeing Lorna today. Friendships began with understanding, and in order to become closer to Lorna, Rachael knew she was going to have to disclose a few things about her personal life. It might well be a waste of time, and it would not be easy, but for Jason's sake Rachael had to give it a try.

"Lorna, your father has only spent one night at my house, so please don't try to make it sound as though we're living together. That's not the case, and you know it."

"But you are sleeping with him," she said accusingly.

"You're a grown-up, Lorna. That shouldn't shock you."

"Of course it doesn't," she answered, stopping in an out-of-the-way corner of the lobby. "What shocks me—but shouldn't—is that you're accepting money from my father in exchange for certain *favors*."

Rachael sighed and prayed for patience, but remarkably she didn't become upset by Lorna's accusation. For all her twenty-two years, and the fact that she had a child of her own, Lorna was little more than a child herself. She was selfish, vindictive and immature, and Rachael found it impossible to be intimidated by a girl who was this troubled and confused. She was Jason's daughter—and Molly's—which meant that somewhere deep inside Lorna there had to be a person who'd learned about kindness and love. There had to be a gentler soul who had become frightened and confused and was now striking out at the world—in this case, the woman she saw as a threat to her relationship with her father.

Feeling far more pity than anger, Rachael kept her voice mild. "That's an ugly accusation, Lorna. And it's not true."

"Then how can you afford a gift like that?" She stabbed a finger at the Neiman Marcus shopping bag.

"I have a great deal of money."

"You mean you *expect* to have a great deal of money once you marry my father!"

"Jason and I haven't discussed marriage, Lorna. But maybe you and I should." Rachael glanced around. "There's a coffee shop in here, isn't there? Why don't we find it so that we can discuss this a little more privately."

"It's a bistro," Lorna corrected her smugly. "This way." She led Rachael to the brightly decorated café that served espresso, rather than ordinary coffee, so that it could justify the pretentious label for people who cared about such things. To Lorna it was a bistro in a swank Beverly Hills emporium; to Rachael it was just a coffee shop in a department store.

They found a corner table that offered a little privacy, and once the waiter had taken their orders, Lorna got down to business. "You said you wanted to discuss marriage," she began. "Well, that's fine. Only let's agree to be honest, why don't we?"

"I hadn't planned to be anything but honest."

"Yes, but if I say something you don't like, you can always go running to Daddy and try to use it against me."

Rachael shook her head sadly. "Lorna, the last thing I want is to cause problems between you and Jason. I couldn't come between you, even if I tried. Don't you realize that?"

"*I* know it, but I wasn't sure you did."

"Meaning that I should stand forewarned, because you'll do anything you can to keep me away from Jason?"

"That's exactly what I mean," Lorna said.

"Your father means a great deal to me—more than I could ever hope to make you understand."

"Oh, I understand. Daddy's a very famous, powerful, wealthy man. There are a lot of women who find that attractive."

"And you think that's all he has to offer a woman? His wealth and influence? You don't think that his kindness, his warmth, his incredible gentleness and compassion could be attractive?"

"I think money means a lot more to some people."

"No, Lorna, you use that as a convenient excuse to dislike the women your father dates. Jason hasn't told me very much about his past relationships, but he's said enough to let me know that you've opposed every single one of them. Doesn't he have a right to find happiness?"

"Daddy's never going to love anyone the way he loved my mother," Lorna answered tightly, falling back on an old refrain. "Do you really think you can take her place?"

"I wouldn't even try."

"Then what makes you think he's going to marry you?"

Rachael paused as the waiter arrived with their coffee. When he left, she answered quietly, "Jason and I haven't discussed marriage, Lorna. I told you that. I have some very personal... feelings to work through before I can make a commitment to your father."

"Such as?" Lorna asked, remembering that Jason had told her much the same thing.

Rachael looked down, toying with the handle of her coffee cup. "My husband and three-year-old son were killed in a car accident several years ago. It's taken me a long time to put my life back together, and I don't think I could have done it without Jason." She looked at Lorna, unsure how this revelation was affecting her. "I have to be very sure that I can be the kind of woman Jason needs and deserves before I commit to the sort of relationship he wants."

Lorna felt an automatic surge of sympathy for Rachael's terrible loss, but she couldn't let it weaken her dislike for her. Lorna had spent too many years being terrified that someone was going to take her father away from her, and Rachael's sad story made her even more of a threat. Jason was so kind and softhearted that he would instinctively feel protective of Rachael. He might even mistake pity for love—in fact, he apparently already had.

Lorna knew Rachael's admission had to be handled with extreme caution. "I'm very sorry for your loss, Rachael. I had no idea."

"You couldn't have had," Rachael answered, feeling a glimmer of hope that she'd finally reached Lorna on some level.

"I said some very cruel things—about the money and all that. I'm sorry." She paused thoughtfully, then asked, "I suppose your husband left you well provided for?"

Rachael had come this far by opening up to Lorna, perhaps they could go even farther if the girl knew the whole truth. "Yes, he did, Lorna. Are you familiar with the art comic *Ravenmede*?"

That took her by surprise. "Of course."

"Working under a pseudonym, my husband and I created that comic, and I still retain the rights to it even though I'm no longer one of its principal artists. I don't need your father's money, Lorna. I have more of my own than I could ever possibly spend."

"But if you created *Ravenmede*, why on earth would you be working as my father's *assistant*? That doesn't make sense."

"*Ravenmede* was something I created with my late husband, and I would never feel right working on it without him. But I needed a job—something to keep me busy, so I applied for a position as a breakdowner at Animators."

Lorna knew enough about the fantasy art world to know that she was addressing someone who was respected, even important. This still wasn't making sense. "And they hired someone with your background as a breakdowner?"

Rachael shook her head. "Except for Jason, no one at Animators knows that I was associated with *Ravenmede*." She explained how Jason had discovered her secret after Robb had set her up for an interview, and she made a point of telling Lorna that Jason had respected her desire to keep her past private.

"Why would you not want anyone to know?" Lorna asked.

"As I said before, I still have a lot of things to work through, Lorna, and the work I did on *Ravenmede* is one of them. If everyone knew that I was a part of the Garrett Mallory team, I'd become an instant celebrity. People would ask the same kind of questions you're asking, there would be more pressure placed on me, and I'd have to suffer through endless 'Oh, you poor thing' speeches...." She shrugged. "It would complicate my life at a time when I'm not sure I could handle any more complications."

Lorna smiled, despite her memory of the oh, so touching tableau she'd witnessed the day of the picnic when she'd seen her father kissing away Rachael's tears. "You mean complications like a daughter who'd rather not see you involved with her father?"

Rachael smiled, too. She had reached Lorna, after all. "Among other things."

Lorna leaned across the table and took Rachael's hand. "Don't worry about me," she said with a reassuring smile. "All I want is what's best for Daddy."

Rachael should have realized that there was something drastically wrong with Lorna's sudden altruism, but she didn't. Not right away, at least.

CHAPTER TWENTY

"YOU ARE THE most beautiful thing I have ever seen in my life," Jason whispered with more than a touch of awe when Rachael came out of the guest bedroom in her costume for the masquerade party.

She looked down at the low-cut, shimmering silver dress with its wide pannier that flared out dramatically at her hips. "Thank goodness you have a large home, or there wouldn't be room for the guests. This dress alone will fill up most of the family room—" she looked at him and grinned "—and your hat will take up the rest."

"I beg your pardon," Jason said with a laugh as he flourished the wide-brimmed, extravagantly plumed hat in the air. He struck a pose that beautifully displayed the cut of his lace-laden shirt, his long-skirted *justaucorps* coat, and his high-topped, supple leather boots. "I will have you know that my hat shows a certain amount of *panache*."

"You have the right historical period, D'Artagnan, but the wrong work of literature. We're decked out for *The Three Musketeers*, not *Cyrano de Bergerac*."

"Methinks thou art a most impudent wench, milady," he said, advancing on her with lascivious intent. "You had best beware! A king's musketeer takes what he wants when he wants it, and right now methinks what I want is thou."

Rachael squealed with delight when Jason grabbed her, pulled her to him forcefully, then bent her over his arm and buried his face in her bosom. "Ooh, suh, I do believe I'm goin' to swoon," she drawled.

"Now who's mixing their metaphors, Scarlett?" he teased, bringing her upright, but not allowing her to escape. The movement brought them close, and all playfulness left Jason's voice. "You are truly beautiful."

"It's the wig and the dress," Rachael said softly, more than willing to be caught up in the sensuous mood Jason had created with just one look.

"No, it's not just what's on the outside that's lovely. It's what you have inside that makes me love you."

"Oh, Jason..." Rachael sighed, wanting very much to tell him that she loved him, too, but she wasn't ready. The love was there and she'd known it for weeks, but there were things she had to accomplish for herself before she could give Jason the words he wanted to hear. She had made a decision about the direction her life was going to take, and she had to implement that decision or she would never be a whole person.

In her heart she knew that Jason would approve of what she was going to do, but she wasn't ready to tell him yet—not until she'd done this one important thing on her own, independent of Jason and whatever life they might hope to have together. It would mean leaving Animators, embarking on the pursuit of her own dream, and she had to take the first step alone. Once she had done that, she would tell Jason that she loved him.

If he accepted her decision, they had a chance for a life together; if not, she would lose him. Rachael knew she was taking a risk, but she was trying to find herself, and if she didn't take the chance, it would mean she had nothing to give Jason.

"If you think I'm expecting you to say you love me, you're wrong," Jason told her tenderly. "I'm not trying to push you."

"I know that," she answered, wondering if he could see his love reflected in her eyes.

"When you're ready to say the words, I'll be listening. Until then, I can wait."

"Patience is one of your better virtues, Jason."

"And dost thou think, milady, that some day my patience might be rewarded?"

"Oh, my dear sir," she murmured lovingly, "you may most assuredly count on it." She offered him her lips, and Jason accepted the invitation with great tenderness and more than a little ardor. When they finally broke apart, they were both a little breathless, and Jason tugged self-consciously at the skirt of his coat.

"Obviously my costumer did not take your effect on me into consideration when he made these trousers."

Rachael blushed scarlet and excused herself with a curtsy, telling Jason she needed to retrieve her feathered owl mask from the bedroom. By the time she returned, Lorna had joined Jason in the family room.

Emily was with Cole for the weekend, and Lorna had gone all out for the party. She was dressed as Cleopatra, and her gown and headdress were opulent, beautiful, and—Rachael thought—just a little too revealing for her father's taste.

Jason was eyeing his daughter's generous cleavage with a look that was far removed from the manner in which he had regarded Rachael's. He waved one hand ineffectually in front of Lorna's torso. "Don't you have a scarf, a handkerchief, or something you could put over that?" he asked awkwardly.

"Oh, Daddy, really!"

"Honey, you look absolutely beautiful, but it's just a little too—too—" He couldn't find the right word, but an idea did come to him, and he snatched his hat off his head. "Here, take one of my feathers—"

"I will not!" Lorna exclaimed, laughing. "Rachael, will you please tell my father that I'm not going to be arrested for indecent exposure."

Pleased to be included in their playful father-daughter tug-of-war, Rachael was only too happy to take Lorna's side. "Jason, Lorna looks magnificent, and there's absolutely nothing wrong with her gown."

"Thank you, Rachael. You look stunning, by the way."

Jason looked at the two women with some surprise. Lorna was actually being pleasant to Rachael. It was a far cry from her usual aloof attitude, and he began to feel a glimmer of hope that his daughter had finally accepted the relationship.

Lorna slipped on a gold demi-mask. "Now that my attire has passed approval, shall we go greet our guests, Daddy?"

Oops, Jason thought as his faint glimmer of hope died. Lorna had been the hostess at every party he'd given in the past twelve years, and he hadn't thought about how his daughter would feel when she realized that her place had been usurped by Rachael. "Actually, honey—"

Rachael saw the same storm brewing as Jason and she tried to salvage what could be a very uncomfortable situation for all of them. "That's an excellent idea. You two greet everyone at the door, and I'll stay in here to direct them to the bar."

Lorna looked from Jason to Rachael. "Oh, I'm so sorry. I didn't even think. Of course you would be Daddy's hostess for the evening." She put her hand on Rachael's arm and gently nudged her toward Jason. "You two do your thing in the foyer, and *I'll* see that everyone is comfortable in here until all the guests have arrived." The doorbell chimed, and she shooed the stunned couple out of the family room. "Go on, now."

Numb with shock, Jason took Rachael's arm and led her to the front of the house. "Who was that masked woman?" he asked.

Rachael laughed. "I think it was your daughter."

"Naa. Couldn't be. What's going on?"

"Lorna and I had a little talk yesterday, and I think it might have done some good."

"Yesterday? When?"

"I asked her if she'd help me choose a birthday present for you, and we went shopping together."

"She helped you pick out the castle?" Jason asked, pleased that Rachael had made such an effort to befriend his daughter.

"She approved of my choice, yes," Rachael replied. The castle had been a private gift, and she'd made the decision to give it to him this afternoon, rather than have him open it in front of an audience tonight. And she was glad that she had. Presenting him with such an expensive gift in front of his friends and colleagues would have raised a lot of questions like the ones Lorna had asked yesterday about how Rachael could afford such an extravagant gift. But more than that, it had given her the chance to savor the moment with Jason. He had known instantly that the castle was meant as an unspoken symbol of love, and he had been deeply moved.

"Do you think Lorna realized what the castle represents?" he asked.

"No, I don't think so, Jason. She didn't seem too familiar with the story of Princess Rachael."

The doorbell rang again, but Jason stopped in the foyer, turning Rachael toward him. "It does look like the castle I created for Emily, but your gift means more than that, doesn't it?"

Rachael looked up into his hopeful eyes. "Is your story more than just a simple fairy tale?" she asked, turning the tables on him.

"You know it is."

She smiled gently. "Then you know that the castle is more than just a pretty sculpture. It's a symbol of the hope you've given me, Jason—hope and all the other wonderful things you've brought into my life."

He pulled her into his arms. "I needed to hear you say that." He pressed his lips to hers, but the doorbell chimed a third time, and Jason reluctantly released her and admitted the first arrivals.

Of the thirty-three guests that showed up, there were only eight that Jason absolutely could not identify. All the costumes were elaborate and creative, but there was almost always something—the person's voice or a distinctive mannerism—that gave them away.

Some, like Robb Weston and his wife, who came as Rhett Butler and Scarlett O'Hara, were a little too easy to recognize, but others, such as the man dressed as Blackbeard the pirate, Jason was certain he'd never met before. And he would have sworn that the scantily dressed serving wench with Blackbeard was Belinda Matheson, except for the fact that he hadn't put her name on the guest list. He wanted Rachael and Belinda to meet someday because he was certain they would like each other, but this party hadn't seemed like the proper place to introduce an old lover to the woman he hoped to marry.

As an icebreaker, Jason had invented a clever mystery game, and the first hour of the party was spent with the guests grilling each other to discover the identity of the ruthless international spy Jason had planted among them. Once Lloyd Pope had been "unmasked" as the villain in question, Jason suggested that everyone reveal their true identities, and he was more than a little surprised to discover that the serving wench he'd thought was Belinda actually *was* Belinda.

She removed her mask, as did her date, Blackbeard, and approached Jason, laughing. "You really didn't know who I was, did you, Jason?"

"You had me completely fooled," he answered, giving her a kiss on the cheek.

Belinda gestured to her date. "Jason, this is Mike Aravelli."

Jason offered his hand. "Pleased to meet you, Mike. And this—" he put his hand on Rachael's waist "—is Rachael Hubbard. Belinda is an old and very dear friend, Rachael," he explained.

The two women were exchanging greetings when Lorna swept up and took charge. "Belinda! How nice to see you again!"

Lorna embraced the lovely brunette as though she was a long-lost relative, but Rachael noted that Belinda was far less enthusiastic, not to mention surprised, by Lorna's effusive greeting. Rachael was certain that neither Mike nor Belinda had been on the original guest list Jason had given her, so she assumed that Jason had decided to issue his friend a personal invitation.

Jason, on the other hand, smelled a rat—a rat with red hair and Cleopatra cleavage. Rachael couldn't possibly have invited Belinda, he knew *he* hadn't, and Belinda would never have considered crashing a party without an invitation. That left only Lorna, and since his daughter claimed to detest Jason's former girlfriend, the only possible reason she could have done it was that she hoped to create an uncomfortable scene to embarrass Rachael.

The idea that his daughter could stoop to such a childish, malicious trick sickened and infuriated Jason.

"Rachael, have you met Belinda?" Lorna asked when she'd finished fawning over Belinda's costume. "She and

Daddy...dated a few years back. In fact, I thought for a while she might become my step-mother."

"Lorna..." Jason said with a stern warning in his voice.

Rachael felt sick, not because she was in the presence of someone Jason had obviously cared deeply about at one time, but because Lorna had so successfully deceived her. Their conversation the previous day had meant nothing to the girl; it had merely made her a little more crafty in her approach.

"Yes, Lorna, Belinda and I have already met," she said evenly, then turned to Belinda and smiled graciously. "I hope we'll have the opportunity to get to know each other."

"I hope so, too," Belinda answered as she caught on to the little game in which she'd become an unwitting pawn. Obviously the reason Jason hadn't recognized her was because he hadn't invited her. "In fact, why don't we start now? This confounded mask has destroyed my makeup—would you mind showing me where I can take a moment to repair it?" She turned to her date. "Mike, would you be a dear and get me a drink? I'll be right back."

Oblivious to what was transpiring, Mike happily trotted off to fetch Belinda's drink, and Rachael gestured toward the hall that led to the sleeping wing of the house. "Right this way, Belinda."

"Oh, Belinda knows the house—" Lorna began as the two women moved off together, but Jason silenced her.

"That's enough, Lorna," he said quietly. "Your juvenile little prank has failed miserably, and you're the only one with egg on your face."

She looked up at him with wide, innocent eyes. "I don't know what you mean, Daddy."

"Are you telling me you didn't invite Belinda?"

"Well, of course I did. I saw a copy of the guest list you gave Rachael, and when I couldn't find Belinda's name on it I just naturally assumed it was an oversight."

"You really expect me to believe that?" he asked incredulously.

"It's the truth."

Jason shook his head sadly. "Lorna, the two women who just walked out of this room together are wonderful people, and more than that, they both personify the meaning of the word *class*. It must be a trait that they were born with, because I tried to teach it to you, but apparently it can't be taught."

He stepped closer, keeping his voice low. "I let you destroy my relationship with Belinda in the misguided belief that you needed special handling because of your mother's death, but I'm beginning to realize that the only special handling you needed was my hand firmly applied to your backside!"

"Daddy!" Lorna gasped, unable to believe that her father would say such horrible things to her.

"Don't *Daddy* me," Jason snapped. "You're my daughter, Lorna, and I love you, but right at this moment I don't think I *like* you one little bit." He sighed irritably as tears began forming in Lorna's eyes. "And don't turn on the juice, honey, 'cause it's not gonna work tonight."

Turning sharply on his heel, Jason stalked away, leaving Lorna seething in his wake. She'd known he would be a little piqued at her for inviting Belinda, but she hadn't expected anything like this. He would get over it, though, Lorna reasoned. Once Rachael Hubbard was out of his life, everything would get back to normal.

Plan One hadn't caused Rachael quite as much discomfort as Lorna had expected, but that was all right. Embarrassment hadn't been her main goal. There were a lot of good things that could come from throwing her together with Belinda. Even now, Lorna could imagine the two women comparing notes. With only the best intentions, Belinda Matheson would tell Rachael the sad story of how

Jason had come close to proposing marriage, then backed away. Since Lorna hadn't been able to convince Rachael that Jason was never going to marry her, maybe Belinda could.

Yes, a lot of good could come from their meeting, Lorna thought smugly. Plan One was working quite well, and Plan Two, she was convinced, would work even better. Her father would probably be angry with her at first, but his anger would pass once Rachael was out of their lives forever.

RACHAEL ESCORTED BELINDA to the guest bedroom where she'd gotten ready for the party, but once they arrived, Jason's former girlfriend gave her makeup only a cursory glance in the vanity mirror. "Is what just happened what I *think* just happened?" she asked as she sat on the stool at the vanity.

"Yes," Rachael confirmed, arranging her skirts so that she could sit on the bed. "Lorna was trying to make a point, I believe."

Belinda rolled her eyes. "Lorna was trying to make a scene! The little witch. I could strangle her, and no jury in the world would ever convict me."

Rachael laughed lightly. Belinda was so refreshingly open that she was impossible to dislike, but then Rachael had no reason not to like her. The fact that this woman had had a relationship with Jason and still remained his friend only proved that she was a very special person. "Lorna isn't always subtle, is she?"

Belinda grew serious. Intuition told her that this demure, lovely woman was the same one Jason had spoken to her about months ago, and she saw no reason to beat around the bush. "Has Lorna been giving you much trouble?"

"No, this is her first overt act of war," Rachael replied, appreciating Belinda's candor. "Actually I'm a little surprised. Since Jason and I started dating, she's been very cool toward me, but we've had only one real confrontation. I had thought we were making progress—until this happened."

"Don't let her fool you," Belinda advised her. "She may not be subtle, but she is dangerous."

Rachael studied the other woman closely. "Was she telling the truth—did you and Jason consider getting married?" she asked, then hastily retracted the question. "I'm sorry, I have no right to ask you that."

"Don't be silly. My relationship with Jason is water under the bridge."

"Thanks to Lorna?"

Belinda shook her head. "No, thanks to Jason. I love him, and he's a dear, dear friend, but he has a blind spot a mile wide where his daughter is concerned. Lorna was still in high school when Jason and I were dating, and she used every manipulative trick in the book against me."

"Stunts like the one she pulled tonight?"

"Oh, no, nothing so elaborate, but twice as effective. She kept chipping away at my confidence by telling me Jason was still in love with Molly. Her best weapons, though, were her tears, which she used with devastating effect on Jason. I never witnessed one of her special routines, but from what Jason told me, she would start crying pitifully, and then she'd invoke her mother's memory and remind Jason that poor little Lorna had only one parent and she couldn't bear to lose him, too. It was Jason's misplaced, totally unearned guilt that finally broke us up."

"I'm sorry," Rachael said softly.

"No, I'm the one who's sorry—for you," Belinda replied. "I've watched you and Jason tonight, and it's obvious that he's very much in love with you. Tread carefully with Lorna, but don't let her destroy what you and Jason have."

"From what you tell me, I may not have any choice in the matter," she said, feeling a terrible emptiness in the pit of her stomach.

"Oh, Rachael, I'm sorry." Belinda rose and moved to the bed to sit next to her. "I didn't mean to discourage or upset you, truly. And I certainly didn't mean to imply that a relationship with Jason is hopeless. Maybe he just didn't love me enough, or maybe he's learned his lesson. Whatever the case, I can see that he treasures you, and that's going to be hard for Lorna to fight. Just hang in there and don't do something stupid like bowing out graciously because you don't want to come between Jason and his daughter."

"But I *don't* want to do that," Rachael replied. "I couldn't bear it."

"Let Jason make that decision, Rachael," Belinda said firmly. "He's a big boy now. This is a problem between him and his daughter. Let them solve it."

Rachael thanked Belinda for her wise counsel, but she was still thinking some dark, disturbing thoughts when they returned to the party. She tried to shove them aside and enjoy herself, but it wasn't easy.

And when Lorna launched Plan Two, it became impossible.

CHAPTER TWENTY-ONE

"ARE YOU ALL RIGHT?" Jason asked when Rachael returned to the party. He guided her to a quiet corner away from the other guests and studied her with concern.

She wanted to set his mind at rest, but the smile she gave him was hesitant, at best. "I'm fine."

"I'm so sorry about what Lorna did," he said apologetically. "I can't believe she could be so childish."

Rachael took his hand. "No harm was done, Jason. Just forget about it. I'm glad I got to meet Belinda. She's wonderful."

"Yes, she is. And so are you," Jason replied, placing one arm around Rachael's waist. "I wanted the two of you to meet someday, but not under these circumstances."

Rachael managed a rueful chuckle. "At least I know where I stand with Lorna, now."

Jason frowned, remembering something she'd said earlier. "What did you two talk about yesterday? What made you think she'd changed her mind about us?"

"She as much as said so," Rachael replied, shrugging her shoulders helplessly. "We had a long, very honest conversation—or so I thought. I told her about Sander and Micah, thinking that if she was ever going to stop disliking me I needed to let her get to know me."

"And she seemed to respond to you?" he asked, trying to think through Lorna's puzzling, contradictory behavior.

"Yes. She took my hand and told me she wanted only what was best for you. I thought that meant she would accept our relationship, but apparently I was wrong."

"Maybe not," Jason said, wanting to give his daughter the benefit of the doubt. "After all, Lorna had to have sent Belinda that invitation weeks ago—long before the two of you had your conversation. Even if she'd changed her mind, she couldn't very well have *un*invited her, could she?"

She could have warned us, Rachael wanted to say, but didn't. If Lorna had had a change of heart, she would never have made such a point of letting Rachael know that Belinda and Jason had once been close. No, Lorna had wanted to create an uncomfortable situation. Rachael was convinced of that. But if Jason needed to believe that Lorna wasn't a shrew, so be it. No matter what, Rachael was determined not to cause problems between the man she loved and his daughter.

"I suppose that's possible," she answered, keeping her reservations to herself. She gave him a bright smile and changed the subject. "That's enough serious talk for one night. We still have some very important business to take care of."

"What business?" he asked, responding instantly to her lovely smile.

"Surely it didn't escape your notice that most of your guests arrived with birthday presents for you."

He frowned. "Presents? Oh, you mean all those boxes that are piled on the table in the foyer. I did wonder what all that was about," he told her with a smug grin. "Do I get to open them now?"

"There's no time like the present."

Jason groaned at the pun. "Just for that I might not offer to help you bring them in here."

"I wouldn't let you, anyway. You're the birthday boy, remember. You just hang around and play host. I'll take care of the gifts.'' She rose on tiptoe to kiss his cheek, then headed toward the kitchen to tell the caterer it was time to bring in the cake she'd ordered earlier in the week without Jason's knowledge. While that was being prepared, she had one of the waiters help her carry in the gifts, and presently, everyone was singing ''Happy Birthday,'' while Jason cracked them up with his comical impression of a man acting surprised.

''For me? Oh, you shouldn't have!'' he exclaimed as the presents were piled in front of him. ''But since you did...''

Everyone laughed and formed a circle around him, some sitting, some standing, as Jason dug into the gifts with gusto. There was the usual assortment of gag items, all of which Jason treated as priceless treasures, but there were some lavish gifts, as well.

Standing beside Jason's chair, Rachael took charge of handing him the brightly wrapped packages and then making sure that all cards were kept with the corresponding gifts so that he could send the appropriate thank-you notes after the party. She handed him the package wrapped in Neiman Marcus's distinctive paper, and Jason announced with some surprise, ''From the directorial staff at Animators.''

''You'd better check to see if it's ticking, Jason!'' someone called out.

''Don't be silly,'' he scoffed. ''The people I work with love me, don't you, guys?''

A general chorus of good-natured disagreement rumbled through the room, but all that stopped when Jason finally got the present open and showed them the sweater. ''I love it,'' he said with a broad smile.

''Well, if you don't, you can blame Rachael,'' Robb told him from across the room. ''She picked it out.''

''With Lorna's help,'' Rachael added.

Jason looked up at her, and if the room hadn't been full of people, he would have pulled her to him for a kiss. In lieu of such a public display, he merely thanked her, but the way he said it left Rachael no doubt that he was also expressing his gratitude for the effort she'd made to become friends with Lorna by including her in the shopping expedition. In fact the look they exchanged said a lot of things, many of which were easily translated by those who were watching. Jason wasn't making any secret of his feelings for the woman at his side.

Rachael handed him another gift and watched as he began laughing and joking with his friends once more. She admired his gregarious personality and even envied it a little. It was taking all the courage she could muster to smile and converse with the guests, trying to make them feel at home, yet Jason did it with an ease he took for granted. She desperately hoped that one day it would be easy for her, too, because Jason's friends were an important part of his life. She couldn't allow her own feelings of inadequacy to ever hold Jason back.

Like Rachael, Lorna had presented her gift to Jason earlier in the day. She'd taken off work early to get ready for the party, and while Rachael had been in the guest room dressing, Jason's daughter had presented him with a handsome leather bomber jacket, complete with long silk scarf. He'd proudly shown the jacket to Rachael, which was why they were both a little surprised when the last present to be opened that evening had a card that read, "Something special for you, Daddy. From Lorna, with love."

Lorna was seated on the sofa, and when he came to her gift she leaned forward, smiling.

"I hope you like it, Daddy. I saw it today and just couldn't resist."

"I'm sure I'll love it, honey, but you shouldn't have," Jason replied as he tore through the wrapping paper. The box was large, but weighed only a few ounces, so Jason suspected that whatever was inside was merely camouflaged by a big box; and he was right. When he took off the lid, he had to leaf through a ream of tissue paper to reach the bottom.

"What is this?" he asked with a grin, pulling out what at first appeared to be a magazine sheathed in a plastic cover. The thin book had been resting facedown in the box, and when he turned it over, his happy smile faded.

"It's a copy of the very first volume of *Ravenmede*," Lorna explained pleasantly. "They're collector's items now, you know. And if Rachael will agree to sign it for you, it'll be even more valuable. Garrett Mallory's signature will make it virtually priceless."

A confused murmur went through the room, and Rachael felt as though she'd been kicked in the stomach by a mule. It was unthinkable that *anyone* could deliberately perpetrate such a cruel trick, but knowing that Jason's daughter was capable of it made her physically ill. Yesterday she'd made a point of telling Lorna that she didn't want anyone to know about her former life, and this had been Lorna's response. It was without a doubt the most vicious thing anyone had ever done to Rachael, and as far as she was concerned, it was unforgivable.

"Garrett Mallory?" someone on the other side of the room said. "I thought he was dead."

"Yeah, didn't he die in a car wreck a couple of years ago?" Lloyd Pope asked.

"He had a partner, though, didn't he?" Deanna remembered, just as confused by Lorna's statement as everyone else. "Wasn't his wife..." Her voice trailed off as she finally put the pieces together. "Oh, Rachael...were you—"

"Yes," she answered quietly, unwilling to give Lorna the satisfaction of seeing her crumble. The truth would have come out sooner or later, and Rachael decided to handle the situation with all the dignity she could muster. "My husband and I were the creators of *Ravenmede*."

She looked at Lloyd. "You're right, Lloyd, he and my son were both killed in a car accident several years ago."

A sympathetic murmur went through the crowd, and several of Rachael's co-workers asked more questions, understandably confused about why she had kept her past such a secret.

"Did you know you had a legend working for you, Jason?" someone asked.

Jason looked from Lorna to Rachael, wondering what was going on. This had obviously taken Rachael by complete surprise, and though she was pale and drawn, she was handling the furor better than he might have expected. "I knew that Rachael had been part of the Garrett Mallory team," he confirmed. "I just didn't know that my daughter knew it," he finished softly.

"Oh, Rachael told me all about it yesterday, Daddy," Lorna replied innocently. "We had a wonderful time together."

Rachael had had all she could possibly take. "If you'll excuse me, Jason, everyone, I think I need to repair my makeup." She turned and hurried out of the room, and behind her, speculative conversation began buzzing like crazy. She tried to shut out the knowledge that they were all talking about her, hoping that she could reach the guest room before she collapsed in angry tears.

She had almost reached the door when Jason caught up with her. "What was that all about, Rachael?" he asked, turning her toward him. "Did you really tell Lorna?"

Rachael dug her fingernails into the palm of her hand. "Of course I did. How else would she have found out? And I also made the mistake of telling her that you were the only one who knew, and I wanted to keep it that way!"

Jason shook his head in astonishment. "I can't believe she would do something like this," he muttered.

"Oh, I can, Jason," she snapped, too angry to censor herself. "Your daughter is a spoiled, vicious, vindictive bitch."

"Now, wait a minute, Rachael—"

"No, you wait a minute! For your sake, I tried to make friends with her, and this is what it got me. That stunt with Belinda was nothing compared to this! Giving you that copy of *Ravenmede* and telling everyone I should autograph it was an act of cruelty, pure and simple. She wanted to hurt me, Jason. That's all. If I had burst into tears or made a scene, it would have been a bonus, but all she really cared about was stabbing a knife into my back—the knife *I* gave her!"

Jason took a deep, wavering breath. "Rachael, that's my daughter you're talking about. She's spoiled, thoughtless, and willful, but I can't believe that she would *deliberately* set out to hurt anyone."

"Then how do you explain her last-minute gift?" Rachael demanded.

Jason shrugged, feeling more confused and helpless than he could ever remember. "I don't know. Maybe she didn't realize that you hadn't told everyone—"

"*She knew*, Jason! I made it clear that what I was telling her was to be kept just between us. And *she* made it clear to me tonight that she is *never* going to accept our relationship. This is only the beginning of one long, hellish nightmare, and I don't think I want to stick around to see what she comes up with next."

Tears threatened to spill down her cheeks, and she whirled away, hurrying into the bedroom. Jason followed, but Rachael blocked his entrance. "Rachael, nothing like this will ever happen again, I promise. I'll talk to Lorna."

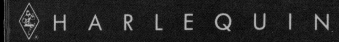

SWEET PROMISE

Erica was starved for love. Daughter of a Texas millionaire who had time only for business, she'd thought up a desperate scheme to get her father's attention.

Unfortunately her plan backfired and she found herself seriously involved with Rafael de la Torres, a man she believed to be a worthless fortune hunter.

That had been a year ago; the affair had almost ruined her life. Now she was in love with a wonderful man. But she wasn't free to marry him. First of all she must find Rafael . . .!

Printed in U.S.A.

"Fine, you do that, but I can't discuss it any further. Not right now. I'm too angry—I'll say things that we'll both regret later. Please, just leave me alone for a while."

"Rachael—" Jason reached out and lightly cupped her face in his hands "—I love you. Nothing is ever going to change that."

"I'm not the one you have to convince, Jason," Rachael said in a hushed voice. She pulled away from him gently. "Look, I wasn't going to tell you this until Monday, but I think this is as good a time as any. I have some vacation time coming, and I want to take it at the end of next week."

"All right." He looked at her closely, and for the first time he had absolutely no clue as to what was going through her mind. The idea that she was somehow shutting him out left him feeling lonely and not a little frightened. "I could get a few days off, too, you know. We could drive up the coast to Big Sur—"

Rachael could see that Jason was hurting, not only because of his conflicting emotions about Lorna, but because of her own behavior, as well. There was nothing she could do about it, though, not while she was still too angry to even think straight. "I'm sorry, Jason," she interrupted, trying to keep her voice calm. "I already have plans. I'll be in New York for several days, and I have some personal business to take care of in Vermont."

New York meant Lamplight Comics, and Vermont was her home. For one sickening moment, Jason thought he might be losing Rachael for good, but he refused to allow himself to believe that. He had to believe that her days of running away were over; she wouldn't leave L.A., leave *him* without warning or explanation. "Is it anything you can talk about?"

"No," she answered as her tears finally started to flow. "You've helped me come this far, Jason. Now, there are some things I have to do on my own."

"This is serious, isn't it?" he asked, fearing her answer.

Rachael nodded. "Yes."

"I'm here for you if you need me."

"I know that. It gives me strength," she told him tenderly. "But I'm not strong enough to fight a war with Lorna, Jason. What's more, I won't even try, because eventually it will come down to you having to decide between us. That's not fair to you, to me, or to Lorna."

"That's not going to happen."

Rachael reached out and touched his face. "Open your eyes, Jason. It's already started."

She backed away and closed the door quietly before finally giving in to the anguish Lorna had caused.

THE NEXT WEEK was, without a doubt, the worst week of Lorna Burgess Washburn's adult life. The night of the party, after Rachael and all the other guests had left, Jason had been brief, angry, and to the point with his daughter. He told her in no uncertain terms that he loved Rachael, he planned to marry her, and that there was nothing Lorna could do to prevent it. He also told her flatly that it was time she started looking for another place to live.

"This is your home, Lorna, and it always will be," he had told her. "But you can't live here forever. Go back to your husband or find your own apartment—whichever you think is best—but I want you out as soon as you can find something suitable. Is that clear?"

Jason's edict had only strengthened Lorna's hatred of Rachael, but though she remained convinced that her father would eventually calm down, her confidence had been badly shaken. She and Jason had spent Sunday avoiding each other, and the chilly silence that pervaded the household had been palpable and deeply disturbing.

Returning to work Monday morning had been a blessed relief, but once there, she discovered that her problems had only just begun. Two orders that she had placed on her buying trip two weeks earlier arrived at the store, and for the first time, Lorna found herself on the wrong side of Odette Lyon, the owner of the boutique. Not only was Odette unhappy with Lorna's selections from the prestigious Herve Ratton collection, she was positively furious because Lorna had mistakenly ordered ten identical evening gowns, but only one set of Ratton's sportswear series.

As far as Odette was concerned, it was an error of monumental proportions, and she had been quick to let Lorna know it. After that, things had gone from bad to worse. Every customer who entered the boutique was surly and demanding, which tried Lorna's already-thin patience to the limit. And because she was in trouble with Odette, the other employees began avoiding her like the plague.

Lorna returned home every day close to tears, but her father was no comfort whatsoever. He was rarely home, and when he did come in, he showed no sign of having forgiven Lorna for what she had done to Rachael. Lorna's only consolation was that Jason's absences were due to late hours at the office, not dates with Rachael Hubbard. And what was even more encouraging, Lorna had learned that her nemesis had gone to New York for a few days. Knowing this, Lorna had redoubled her efforts to make peace with her father in the hopes of repairing the damage Rachael had done, but Jason had not been too receptive.

As the days passed, Lorna noticed that his anger seemed to evolve into a kind of depression that disturbed her. He was quiet, almost sad, even. Not since her mother's death had Lorna seen her father so subdued. Only with Emily did he make an effort to be cheerful, but even Lorna's daughter had noticed that there was something wrong with Grandpa.

The change in Jason seemed to be more than the little girl could take, and Lorna's bad week became even worse when she received a call from Emily's sitter informing her that Emily was becoming a real problem at the day-care center. Unhealthy personality changes they had noted over the course of the past few weeks had suddenly grown in proportion, and Mrs. Davina was concerned. Emily was constantly fighting with the other children. She had become territorial and uncooperative; she threw tantrums and destroyed things.... Mrs. Davina had given Lorna a long list of the child's problems and had capped off their conversation by suggesting that the child needed counseling.

By Friday Lorna had had all she could take. Her father was barely speaking to her, her daughter was becoming unmanageable at home as well as at the sitter's and her job had turned into a nightmare....

And it was all Rachael Hubbard's fault.

CHAPTER TWENTY-TWO

RACHAEL LOOKED DOWN at the contract she and her business manager had spent two days negotiating. It was Friday, and though it was cold and dreary in New York, Rachael had never felt more like celebrating. She had done it, and what was more important, she had done it on her own. Ambergris Books had just purchased the rights to publish four Mickelmoss stories, and had eagerly assured her that they would welcome any other children's tales she cared to submit.

For the first time in her life, Rachael felt free and independent. She felt like a whole person. If Jason had been there to share this triumphant moment, it would have been perfect.

"Are you sure you won't reconsider and come back to *Ravenmede*?" Roger Lampasat asked, though he knew it was pointless. When Rachael had called him several weeks ago to ask if he would arrange for her to meet with his friend, Damon Jacobi, publisher of Ambergris Books, Roger had known he had lost Rachael for good. For two days now, through her negotiations with Damon and meetings with her business manager, Roger had tried to change her mind, but to no avail. He was treating her to a celebratory lunch, and though he was happy for Rachael, Roger didn't feel much like celebrating.

Rachael smiled at him as she held up the contract. "It's too late. The deal with Ambergris is signed, sealed and delivered."

"And it doesn't bother you that *Ravenmede* is going down the tubes?"

She put the contract aside and grew thoughtful. The waiter had already taken their order, and they had plenty of time to talk. "Yes, Roger, it does. I hadn't looked at a copy of *Ravenmede* since Sander died, until you sent that stack of recent issues to my hotel room yesterday. I looked through them, and you're right. *Ravenmede* is in serious trouble. Artistically it's a grave disappointment."

"You could change all that," he told her for what seemed like the hundredth time, but Rachael held her ground.

"No, Roger, I couldn't. If I tried to produce *Ravenmede* I'd be going backward, not forward." She touched the contract. "This is mine, *all* mine, and no one can take it away from me."

"Then what the hell am I going to do about your comic? You know, dear, you have a stake in its future, too. You still own sixty percent. I've been hanging on, these last couple of years, in the hopes that you'd be coming back as soon as you got your life together. But if you don't resume production..."

He left the threat hanging, but Rachael knew he was insinuating that he might halt publication. She also knew that he was bluffing. Martin Chomsky had informed her that though her royalties from the sale of *Ravenmede* had been on a decline, the comic was still making a handsome profit.

"Roger, please don't insult my intelligence," she said with a grin. He was only trying to salvage the reputation of Sander's comic, so she couldn't be irritated by his blatant manipulations. "You're still making a profit on *Ravenmede*, and as long as that continues, you wouldn't dare cancel it."

Roger sat back in his chair and laughed. "I can't get over the changes in you. It's hard to believe that the lovely, decisive, self-assured woman sitting across this table from me is the same Rachael Hubbard who used to hide out in a loft in Vermont, afraid that someone was going to notice her."

"Sander is dead, and I had to grow up."

"I'm proud of you, Rachael. You've come a long way down a very long and difficult road." He threw up his hands in surrender. "And if you can live with what's happening to *Ravenmede*, I guess I'll have to live with it, too."

"Oh, but I don't think I can live with it, Roger," she told him. "Sander would hate what his pride and joy has become."

"Then what do you suggest we do?"

"We have to find another artist. Maybe someone young and fresh who was once inspired by what *Ravenmede* used to be."

He looked at her as though she was from Mars. "And where do you suggest we find this genius?"

Rachael shrugged. "I don't know, but I'll help you look. If it's all right with you, I'll conduct some interviews in Los Angeles, and if I find any likely candidates, you can fly out to meet them."

Roger looked at her with a sly smile. "And what if that's not all right with me?"

Rachael leaned back in her chair. "I still own sixty percent, remember? And you might also recall that our contract is due to be renegotiated in January. If we can't improve the quality of *Ravenmede*, I won't renew our agreement."

Roger threw back his head and laughed with pure delight. "Rachael, I hope this won't hurt or offend you, because I mean it strictly as a compliment, but if I didn't know better, I'd swear I was negotiating with Sander Hubbard. Even before *Ravenmede* became a success, he was one of the few people in this world who had the nerve to stand up to me."

"I will take that as a compliment, Roger. Sander was a brilliant businessman. Maybe some of his light rubbed off on me without my even realizing it."

"Or maybe your own light was hidden by Sander's shadow," he suggested mildly.

Rachael smiled gently. "I may never know which, but it really doesn't matter. I've made peace with the past, and I'm ready for the future now."

Roger held up his water goblet. "To the future."

"To the future."

JASON SAT in his office, drumming his fingers tunelessly against his desktop as he stared off into space. Since Rachael had announced that she was going to New York, he had felt as though his world was caving in. His rational self told him that she wasn't going to leave him, she wasn't moving back east, and she hadn't given up on their relationship.

But rationality had no influence over fear, and Jason was desperately afraid. He kept remembering the uncompromising, furious look on Rachael's face when she'd told him flatly that she wasn't going to stick around to see what dirty trick Lorna might come up with next. He was going to lose Rachael—if he hadn't already—and there didn't seem to be anything he could do about it. If Lorna refused to accept Rachael, Jason would be forced to make a choice between his daughter and the woman he loved, and no man should ever have to make that kind of a decision. Either way the end result would tear his heart out.

Rachael was his future. She made him happier than he'd ever thought he could be again. When he was with her, the lonely corners of his life were suddenly filled with love, and he could see himself growing old with a gentle, loving woman beside him. He could see the children they might raise together, and he could picture a life filled with love and endless possibilities. A man was lucky if he found real love only once in his life, but to find it twice was a gift too precious to be taken for granted. He loved Rachael, and losing her would destroy something he wasn't sure he could afford to lose.

But Lorna was all he had left of Molly. She was his flesh and blood—the only reason he'd had for living after his wife had died. No matter how confused and treacherous she had become, she was still his daughter, and he loved her. He wanted to help her; he wanted her to be happy. He couldn't just banish her from his life forever.

Did anyone really expect him to throw twenty-two years of love and nurturing out the window? If he said to his daughter, *Make peace with Rachael, become her friend, or never set foot in my house again,* could he live with the consequences if she chose to leave and never return?

No, he couldn't. Jason knew that. He had accepted the reality that Lorna was not the person he wanted her to be, the person he'd believed she was, but he couldn't stop loving her just because she'd disappointed him.

Would Rachael understand that? he wondered. Did he mean enough to her that she would bear with him until he could turn Lorna around? She'd given him reason to believe that she loved him, but was the love strong enough to withstand whatever Lorna might throw at them?

The uncertainty of the situation was driving Jason crazy, yet there was nothing he could do about it until Rachael returned from New York—if she returned.

His intercom buzzed, and he reached for the phone. "Yes, Gretchen, what is it?"

"I've got a call for Rachael on line one, and I'm not sure how to handle it," she told him. "Some guy from Johnson Moving and Storage in Vermont needs to get a message to her. He says there's been a mistake made, and if he doesn't get hold of her, she'll go to the wrong warehouse tomorrow when she comes to get her stuff. Whatever that means. Do you know how to reach her in New York?"

Jason felt a wave of panic wash through him. Rachael had said that she would be going to Vermont, and he knew that she had put virtually everything she owned in storage before she came to California. There was no reason for him to believe that there was anything ominous about this phone call, but as he gave Gretchen the number where Rachael could be reached in New York, he couldn't escape the feeling that the shaky foundation of his life had just collapsed.

Without a second thought for the work that needed to be done that afternoon, Jason left his office early and went home.

"YOU WANTED TO see me, Odette?" Lorna asked as she stepped into her employer's office.

"Yes. Please have a seat. This isn't going to be easy for either of us."

Lorna felt a stab of fear that she was about to be fired, but she brushed the notion aside. "What's wrong?"

Odette Lyon was a former fashion model who'd managed her career so perfectly that she'd been able to open the exclusive Lyon's Boutique on Rodeo Drive after her modeling career had ended. At forty-eight she was still as strikingly beautiful as she'd been at twenty-eight, and just as shrewd.

"Lorna, dear, I know that you and your husband separated a month or so ago, and even before that catastrophic event I realized that you were having some sort of personal problem. I've tried to be patient and sympathetic, but I do have to draw the line somewhere." She spread her graceful hands wide. "I'm a businesswoman, darling, and what you see here at Lyon's has taken me a lifetime to build."

"I realize that, Odette. I have nothing but the highest respect for all that you've accomplished."

"Thank you, dear, but that's not my point. This week alone, I've had to deal with *four* irate customers who complained that you were impossibly rude and uncooperative." Lorna started to speak up in her own defense, but Odette hurried on. "I'm receiving the same kind of complaints from the rest of my staff, and I don't even want to talk about the Ratton fiasco. It's taken me the better part of this week to correct what was an absurd error on your part."

"Odette, I'm sorry, but—"

"No, Lorna, I'm not listening to any 'buts.' I know you're sorry. I've always thought you were a bright girl with a tremendous amount of initiative and business sense. I made you an assistant buyer so that I could utilize your assets and minimize your weakness, which has always been in the area of customer contact. Unfortunately you have given me reason to doubt your usefulness in either capacity."

Lorna felt the blood rush from her face. "Am I being fired?" she asked in a small voice.

"No, Lorna, not yet. I'm not a heartless monster, but quite frankly, dear . . . you're a mess. You're irritable, irrational and undependable. Right now, Lyon's is *the* in place to shop, but if I leave you in the salon waiting on customers, I'll be out of business in a matter of weeks. And since I can't trust you to deal with the major fashion houses on my behalf, I don't seem to have anything for you to do at the moment."

Lorna was close to tears, but her pride managed to hold them back. "I don't know what to tell you, Odette. These past few weeks have been absolute hell."

"I know, dear. That's why I'm going to suggest that you take some time off. You have a week's paid vacation coming, but I think you should take more than that. Take a month or two and pull yourself together. Take stock of what's happening to you. Reconcile with your husband, divorce him, get into therapy, spend a month at Club

Med...do *anything*," Odette said dramatically, "but get your act together, Lorna, because otherwise, you can kiss this business goodbye!"

Odette pulled a check out of her desk and handed it to Lorna. "This is your salary up to and including today, plus the vacation pay you have coming. I'd rather you didn't come back until after the first of the year. Your job will be waiting for you, and if you've managed to straighten your life out, I expect that we'll continue as before. If not—" she shrugged helplessly "—I think you understand my position."

"Of course I do, Odette."

Vacillating between the need to cry and the urge to tell Odette Lyon exactly what she could do with her job, Lorna stood and left the office. By the time she reached home, she was still dreadfully shaken, but she was determined to weather this storm. In fact, she told herself, this might even be the perfect opportunity to strike out on her own. It would serve the patronizing Odette Lyon right if Lorna Washburn started her own Beverly Hills boutique in direct competition. That would show her who needed to get her act together—that would show them all!

Somehow, though, the realization that she could be on the brink of starting her own salon didn't seem quite as attractive to Lorna as it once had. If she worked very hard on Jason, she was certain she could convince him to finance the venture. They were barely on speaking terms at the moment, but that would soon change, and he would give her anything she wanted, just as he always had. She could do it. She could start her own boutique.

But surprisingly, the idea of making her dream a reality scared the living daylights out of her, and Lorna realized that all her ranting to Cole about wanting her own business had actually been nothing but talk.

That personal revelation was a little too much for Lorna to handle. A feeling of inadequacy closed in on her, and as she pulled into the driveway she came once again to the brink of tears.

Though it was only the middle of the afternoon, Jason's car was in the garage, and Lorna was so relieved he was home that she didn't stop to question why he'd left work early. All her life he'd been there for her when she needed him, so it only seemed right that he should be here now.

"Daddy? Daddy?" She hurried through the house, searching for him, and finally found him on the deck, sitting in a chair by the pool. There was a stillness about him that Lorna found disturbing, and she stopped just outside the patio doors. "Daddy? Are you all right?"

Jason turned his head a little, but didn't look at her. "What are you doing here, Lorna?"

She approached him slowly. "I lost my job," she told him tearfully. "Odette said I could come back in a couple of months, but I think she'd be happier if I didn't. She said some really terrible things about me, Daddy."

Jason looked out over the lawn. "Well, Lorna, look at it this way. You win a few, and you lose a few."

"What does that mean?" she asked, frightened by the incredible deadness of her father's voice.

"You may have lost a job, but it appears that you've won your war with Rachael. I should think that would have you dancing in the streets."

Lorna sank into the chair opposite her father, cutting off his view of the lawn. "What does Rachael have to do with anything?" Jason looked at her then, and the bleak, empty expression in his eyes truly terrified her. It was the same look he'd had for months after her mother had died. "Daddy, what's happened?"

"Rachael is gone, maybe for good. She's taking her things out of storage in Vermont, and for all I know she's moving back east to resume production of *Ravenmede*. You've won, Lorna. Congratulations."

The sense of triumph Lorna had expected to feel—knew she should feel—didn't come. Even through her own despair, Lorna could see that her father was hurting. "Maybe it's for the best, Daddy. I mean, if Rachael was so unstable that she would leave without even saying goodbye to you—"

"For the best?" Jason said incredulously. "How the hell would you know what was best for anyone but yourself? You don't give a damn about me, your husband, or your own daughter. All you care about is Lorna! What Lorna wants! What Lorna *thinks* she wants!"

"Daddy, please, don't," she begged as tears of genuine anguish began flooding down her cheeks. "I'm sorry."

"For what? Destroying the only chance for happiness I've had since your mother died?" Jason came to his feet, planted his hands on the table between them and glared down at his daughter with a fury she'd never seen before. "Last week you deliberately set out to hurt one of the kindest, gentlest, most loving women I've ever known. She reached out to you for *my* sake, and you maliciously—hatefully—used everything she told you in a way you knew would do the most damage."

"I'm sorry!"

"No, you're not," Jason said with disgust. "You're incapable of feeling remorse. The only thing you're sorry about is that I refuse to believe that you made an innocent mistake in judgment."

"Daddy, that woman is trying to turn you against me!"

"No, Lorna, you're managing that quite well on your own. Since you left Cole and returned home, I've seen things in you that make me ill." Jason paused a moment, trying to control his anger and disgust, but the effort failed. "I love Rachael. Do you understand? Do you even know what the word means anymore? I love her more than I ever thought it was possible to love again."

"But look what she's doing to us," Lorna choked out, sobbing.

"Damn it, Lorna, stop blaming everyone else for what happens in your life! *You're* the one who's tearing us apart, not Rachael! My God, didn't you listen to anything Rachael told you? Didn't any of it sink in? Two and a half years ago, she lost her only child, a beautiful little boy who was exactly Emily's age. The car her husband was driving went off an embankment into an icy river, and for the rest of her life she's got to live with a kind of emptiness so vast and so deep that it's nearly incomprehensible.

"If Rachael is truly gone, if I've lost her, it's not because she didn't care enough about me, it's because she cared too much! She knows what it feels like to lose a child, and she didn't want to be responsible for coming between you and me. That's the kind of unselfishness you couldn't even begin to understand."

Lorna covered her face with her hands and wept, unable to believe her father could think such horrible things about her. But what he said had a ring of truth she found hard to ignore. She had hurt Rachael deliberately, spitefully. And her reason for doing so didn't seem as justified as it had at the time.

Jason looked at his daughter and realized that her anguish was real, not a ploy for sympathy, but he refused to be moved by her tears. He'd started his diatribe in uncontrollable anger because he was so afraid he'd lost Rachael, but he suddenly realized that what he'd said to Lorna was what he should have said long ago. She needed to be brought low, lower than she'd ever been, and Jason knew he had the ammunition to take her there. He sat and steeled his heart against her tears.

"I had a long talk with Cole last night, Lorna. Though God only knows why, he still loves you and wants a reconciliation if you'll agree to go with him to see a marriage counselor. If you don't agree, he's going to start divorce proceedings. And he's also going to sue for custody of Emily."

That brought Lorna's head up, and she gasped with astonishment. "He can't do that! No court would give him custody!"

"Under normal circumstances, no," Jason agreed coldly. "But Emily is in serious trouble, and you don't seem to be able to give her the kind of emotional support and stability she needs. Right at this moment I don't think you're fit to raise my granddaughter, and I'm willing to go to court and testify that in my opinion Emily would be better off with her father."

"You wouldn't... do that to me," Lorna sobbed, horrified.

"No, I wouldn't," Jason replied. "I'd do it *for* Emily. I love you, Lorna, but obviously I made some terrible mistakes in raising you. I coddled and pampered you, gave you everything you ever asked for, but it wasn't enough. Or maybe it was too much. I was trying to compensate for Molly's death—trying to be both mother and father. All I succeeded in doing was raising a selfish, neurotic child in a woman's body."

Lorna dashed at her tears and tried to pull herself together. "I'll take Emily and go away," she threatened.

"No, you won't. You've never once stood on your own two feet, Lorna, and you're in no shape to start now. For crying out loud, think about someone other than yourself for once in your life. Think about Emily and what's best for her."

"I'm her mother!"

"Since when do you care about that?" he asked in a low voice that was as effective as a slap in Lorna's face.

"You really hate me, don't you?" It wasn't an accusation, it was a statement that contained equal amounts of despair and fear.

Jason stood and looked down at her. "No, Lorna. I'm your father. I love you. There's a bond between us that can never be broken. You've stretched it to the limit, and I don't know if I can ever forgive you for pushing Rachael out of my life, but God help me, I still love you and always will."

"I love you, too, Daddy."

"I don't think you know what love is, Lorna. Look at your daughter sometime—*really* look at her, see her as a human being and not just as a dress-up doll to play house with—and maybe you'll figure out what love is all about. *Then* tell me you love me, and maybe I'll be able to believe you." He turned and started for the house. "I'm going to the club for a few days. I'll leave a message on my answering machine for Rachael in case she tries to get in touch with me. Can I trust you not to erase it?"

It was the knowledge that she deserved her father's distrust that was the last straw for Lorna. With a pained sob, she ran past him into the house, into her room, slammed the door and cried because her heart was breaking, and she couldn't find anyone to blame but herself.

CHAPTER TWENTY-THREE

WHEN HER PLANE arrived Sunday afternoon, Rachael went from the airport straight to Jason's. The unsettled way things had been left between them bothered her, and she needed to set that right. She needed to explain her decision to him, share her accomplishment, and most of all she needed to tell him that she loved him. It was time; she was ready.

Lorna was the only shadow that clouded Rachael's horizon, and she had no idea how to deal with the girl. She was praying that somehow she and Jason together could make Lorna understand that their love was no threat to her relationship with her father.

At times during the past few days, Rachael had felt that the situation was hopeless, but at other times she'd been convinced that her love for Jason was strong enough to withstand anything, even his spiteful daughter. As she drew nearer to his house, she wished she knew which of those two outlooks for the future was correct. She also wished she could shake the feeling that Lorna was the only one who had the answer.

Rachael pulled up to the security gate and buzzed for admittance. Her heart sank when Lorna, not Jason, answered the summons. She identified herself and the gate swung open. By the time she pulled up the driveway, Emily was already out the front door, running across the lawn toward her.

"Rachael! Rachael!" she squealed happily as she threw herself into Rachael's waiting arms. "I missed you so much."

"I missed you too, princess." She hugged the little girl tightly, then looked at her as she moved toward the house. Emily's eyes were ringed with ugly dark circles, and her skin was as pale and thin as parchment. "Have you been sick?"

Emily shook her head, then laid it on Rachael's shoulder. "I been sad. I miss Daddy, and Mommy made Grandpa go away. Did she make you go away, too?"

Rachael rubbed the child's back reassuringly, wondering what on earth she was talking about. "No, darling, your mommy didn't make me go away. I had some very special business to take care of, but I'm back now."

"For good?"

"Oh, I hope so, darling." She stepped onto the front porch and saw Lorna standing in the doorway, watching them. She was dressed in jeans and a sloppy sweatshirt—a far cry from her usual fashionable attire—and a pair of dark sunglasses shielded her eyes. Rachael suspected that the glasses were meant to camouflage the fact that she'd been crying, but the redhead's splotchy, uneven complexion was a dead giveaway. "Hello, Lorna."

"Rachael." She stepped back to allow her to enter. "Daddy's not here right now. He's spending a few days at his club in Marina del Rey."

"Mommy made him go away," Emily repeated unhappily.

"I'm sure that's not true, Emily," Rachael said, wishing she could read Lorna's strange mood. Her voice was flat and lifeless.

"I'm afraid it is true, Rachael. Daddy and I had an argument, and I guess he felt a little time apart was called for." She looked at her daughter. "But that doesn't mean he'll be gone forever, baby. Grandpa will be back soon." She held her arms out to Emily. "Come here, honey."

"No!" Emily shouted, grabbing on to Rachael's neck for dear life. "You made Grandpa and Daddy go away, and I hate you!"

"Emily, that's enough!" Rachael said firmly. Lorna's arms dropped to her sides, and behind her glasses tears began streaming down her face. Though she hadn't thought it was possible, Rachael actually felt sorry for Jason's daughter. It was clear that Lorna had been devastated by something she had absolutely no idea how to cope with.

Emily's harsh rejection was apparently more than Lorna could handle, and she turned and fled down the hall. Rachael watched her go as she rocked the little girl comfortingly. "Honey, you don't hate your Mommy. You can be mad at her, and that's okay, but you don't really hate her, do you?"

The little girl thought it over, then shook her head.

"That's what I thought. Don't you think you'd better tell her you're sorry?"

Emily nodded, and Rachael didn't let go of the child as she took off in search of Lorna. "Why does Mommy cry all the time?" Emily asked presently.

"She's sad about something, I guess. Would you like me to see if I can make her feel better?"

"Can you make Grandpa come home, too?"

"I can try."

"I love you, Rachael."

Rachael fought back the tears that stung her eyes. "I love you, too, princess. And your mommy and daddy and grandpa all love you. You're a very lucky little girl."

"Don't feel lucky," Emily said grumpily.

"Some days are like that, sweetheart."

They found Lorna in the family room, and when Rachael lowered Emily to her feet, the little girl moved cautiously to her mother and apologized. Lorna gathered her daughter to her, and they held on to each other for a long moment. "Baby, will you go to your room and play while I talk to Rachael? Can you do that for me, please?"

Emily looked from Rachael to her mother and finally agreed. She gathered up several dolls from her play corner and toddled off to her room.

"Are you all right, Lorna?" Rachael asked.

Lorna slipped off her glasses. "Do I look all right?" she asked without rancor. "No, don't answer that. You have every right to dump on me, too, but I don't think I could handle it at the moment."

Rachael considered that admission alone a major accomplishment, but she knew better than to accept a contrite attitude from Lorna at face value. She'd learned her lesson the hard way. "Did you and Jason quarrel about me?"

Lorna wanted to say yes, but she'd spent two days in hell with no company but her own, and she'd forced herself to face a few cold, hard facts. "No, we fought about me, Rachael. It seems that my father thinks I'm a selfish, hateful, childish neurotic."

"Are you?" Rachael asked bluntly.

Lorna laughed mirthlessly. "Apparently so."

"What do you plan to do about it?"

"I'm not certain. Cole was here earlier and we talked about seeing a marriage counselor. That seems like a pretty good place to start."

"Then you're going to get back together?"

"I'm not sure. Frankly I'm not sure of anything anymore." A silent stream of tears began flowing again, but she didn't hide behind her glasses. "Why did you decide to come back, Rachael? Daddy said he thought you'd left for good. I haven't seen him that . . . empty since Momma died."

"He thought I wasn't coming back?" Rachael was stunned, unable to imagine how he had gotten that idea, or how he could believe she would ever be able to leave him. "Why would he think that?"

Lorna shrugged. "He said you were going to Vermont to get some stuff you left there and he was afraid you meant to stay back east."

Rachael wanted to kick herself around the block. She never should have kept her motives for going to New York a secret. Knowing that she had hurt Jason was almost more than she could stand. "No, Lorna, I'm not leaving L.A. This is my home now, no matter what happens between me and your father."

"And that's up to me, isn't it?" she asked quietly.

Rachael sat next to Lorna on the sofa. "I love your father more than I ever thought it was possible to love someone."

Lorna glanced away from her. "He said the same thing about you."

"Can you accept that?"

"I don't want to lose him," she answered tearfully.

"That's entirely in your hands, Lorna, don't you realize that? I'm not threatened by Jason's love for you, I have no reason to try and separate the two of you." She reached out to touch Lorna's shoulder lightly. "If you continue to fight me, eventually you'll create more problems than Jason and I can handle. You'll force Jason to decide between us, and it will tear him apart. We'll all lose—even you—because no matter what he decides, he'll never forgive you. He'll always resent you, and nothing will ever be the same again."

Lorna swiped at the moisture on her cheeks. "I know that. I'm just so scared and confused." She looked at Rachael. "And I am truly sorry for what I did to you at the party."

"You have no idea how much I want to believe you're sincere, Lorna."

"Believe it, Rachael. Daddy said something that made me realize how cruel I'd been. You see, I wasn't thinking about your feelings or how much it must have hurt to lose your husband and son. You weren't even a real person to me. You were just a threat, like all the other women in Daddy's life. I was playing a childish game, and I hurt you."

"Yes, you did," Rachael said quietly.

"You know, I don't think my momma ever hurt anyone in her whole life," Lorna said with a sob. "She was so kind and funny. That's how I want to be with Emily—the way you are with her—but I don't know how." She turned to Rachael, afraid to reach out for the comfort she so desperately needed. "Can you teach me?"

"Oh, of course I'll help you, Lorna," Rachael promised, barely holding back her own tears. She gathered the girl into her arms, and this time the bonds of friendship Rachael felt forming were genuine.

JASON TOSSED his duffel bag onto the chair next to the door, then went back through the room one last time to be certain he hadn't forgotten anything. One of the advantages of belonging to the trendy Del Rey Health Spa was that members were guaranteed a room at only a moment's notice. This was the first time Jason had ever exercised that privilege, but he was glad he had. A few days away from Lorna, away from everything, had worked wonders on his state of mind.

The peace and quiet at Del Rey had given him the chance to realize that his fears that Rachael had left for good were groundless. They had problems, yes, but Rachael would never run away without a word. He felt foolish for even having suspected she was capable of something so heartless.

Lorna was another matter altogether. He hadn't altered his opinion about his daughter in the least. He had said some terribly harsh things to her on Friday, but she had deserved them all. He was going home now, praying that at least some of what he'd told her had sunk in and done some good.

Finished with his last-minute check of the room, Jason went to the phone to call the front desk and request that they prepare his bill. A knock at the door stopped him, though, and he returned the receiver to its cradle.

"Rachael?" he questioned, hardly able to believe his eyes when he opened the door and found her standing there.

She gave him the soft, wistful smile he loved so much. "Aren't you a little too old to run away from home?"

Laughing with relief, Jason pulled her into the room, into his arms, and gave the door a push to close it. "I've missed you," he told her, then captured her lips for a long, branding kiss.

"I missed you, too," she murmured when they finally came apart for air.

"Apparently you got the message I left on my answering machine." It felt wonderful to have her in his arms, but there were still things that had to be settled between them, and he reluctantly released her.

"No," Rachael told him, wandering a little farther into the room. "I went to your place straight from the airport. Lorna told me where I could find you."

"Willingly? Or did you have to torture her?"

"Willingly. She seemed tortured enough already by the argument you two had on Friday. From what she told me, you said some things that forced her to take stock of her life."

"I said some very cruel things to her, Rachael, but they were things she needed to hear. The question is, have they had a positive effect on her?"

Rachael nodded, remembering the way Lorna had cried in her arms, and the way they had talked honestly and openly afterward. "I think so. She's agreed to see a marriage counselor with Cole, and she even asked me if I would help her learn how to be the kind of mother she should be to Emily."

Jason felt a ray of hope. "Do you think she was sincere?"

"I'm positive of it, Jason. More than anything in the world, Lorna wants to be like her mother. But she's finally realized that not only is she completely *un*like Molly, she's not even a person her mother would be proud of. I think she really wants to change. And she also wants to give me a chance—give us a chance."

"Do we have a chance, Rachael?" Jason asked, praying that Lorna's change of heart meant that Rachael might be ready to give him the answer he needed to hear.

"I don't know, Jason. I really thought so until Lorna told me that you were convinced I had skipped town and wasn't planning to come back. Do you really believe I would do something like that?"

"A man who's afraid of losing the most precious thing in the world to him isn't always rational. Gretchen got a strange phone call from a storage company in Vermont, and I didn't know what to make of it."

So that was it, Rachael thought. "I'm having some personal items shipped out here, Jason. That's all. I went through the warehouse yesterday with an auctioneer and consigned my furniture to him for sale and instructed the moving company to ship the rest to me. There are some things in those boxes I'm ready to have with me now—photo albums, keepsakes, some stories I wrote for Micah—and there are some things that need to be disposed of because I want to trade in an old life for a new one."

She touched his face gently. "I never meant for you to think that I was running away from you. I couldn't do that. I love you too much."

"Oh, Rachael." Jason gathered her into his arms and buried his face in her hair. "I love you, too. So very much."

"I know," she murmured lovingly, then pulled away. The urge to stay in Jason's arms forever was strong, but the need to meet him on equal terms was just as powerful. "I have something I need you to see. It's the reason I went to New York." She reached into her purse and extracted the contract.

"Have you decided to resume production on *Ravenmede*?" he asked, taking the papers from her.

"No, that would be going backward, and I only want to move forward now, with you."

Rachael's words were all Jason could ever have hoped for, and more. Yet there was a restraint in her, as though something was holding her back—as though, despite her avowal of love, there was a wall between them. He unfolded the papers, saw the contract, and realized what that wall was.

She had sold her Mickelmoss stories. She had declared her love for Jason, and now she was also declaring her independence. Sander would never have accepted her quest for the fulfillment of her own dream, and Rachael knew it. It was that tiny remnant of fear that was holding her back.

But Jason wasn't Sander, and he had never been prouder or happier than he was at this moment.

"You sold them," he said with a broad, joyful smile that crumbled the pitiful little wall Rachael had hidden her fears behind.

"I sold them," she answered, returning his smile. "I'll stay at Animators until the storyboards are complete, but then I'll be leaving."

"Out east?" he questioned, though he knew very well what her answer was going to be. He just needed to hear all the words and savor the moment.

"No. I'm here to stay, Jason. You're going to have a devil of a time getting rid of me."

"What if I don't want to get rid of you?" he asked, opening his arms and his heart as Rachael walked into both without hesitation. "What if I want to marry you? What if I want to be part of everything you are, and make you a part of me?"

Rachael touched his kind, loving, handsome face. "You've already done that, Jason, just by being you. Now you're going to have to live with the consequences."

"Gladly, my love. Gladly." He lowered his lips to hers, and in her sweet, giving response, he felt Rachael entrusting him with her heart.

It was the most beautiful gift he had ever received; one he happily returned in kind.

Harlequin Superromance.

COMING NEXT MONTH

#374 SILKEN THREADS • Connie Rinehold

At age thirty-two, fashion designer Sabrina Haddon finally met the daughter she'd given up sixteen years earlier—and the girl's irate adoptive father. The sparks between Sabrina and Ramsey Jordan were instant, but a relationship was impossible. Sabrina could only hope that in time the delicate threads of their individual lives could be woven together....

#375 HANDLE WITH CARE • Jane Silverwood

Dr. Jim Gordon barely made it back alive to Maryland after being held hostage overseas. Wounded in spirit, he felt rejuvenated when he met Dory Barker and her teenage daughter. But he failed to realize that the pretty pottery instructor was also one of the walking wounded....

#376 REMEMBER ME • Bobby Hutchinson

While researching a children's book, Annie Pendleton met ambitious pediatrician David Roswell, and before she knew it Annie was as hard-pressed to balance the duties of single parenthood as her lover was to balance his work load. Perhaps this stress explained Annie's chronic physical pain, but maybe it was David's opposition to decisions she'd made—decisions that dramatically affected them both.

#377 WORDS OF WISDOM • Megan Alexander

He'd broken their engagement, and he hadn't said why. All Jenny Valentine knew for sure was that men like Luke Beaumont ought to come with warnings tattooed on their foreheads. Luke thought he'd done the noble thing by breaking their engagement. Well, he'd had enough of being noble. Only now it seemed that Jenny had had enough of *him*....

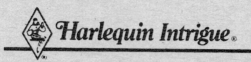

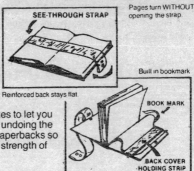

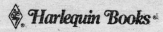